MANY ARE COLD: FEW ARE FROZEN

Sondra lowered her internal suit pressure and switched to pure oxygen. She hyperventilated for a couple of minutes, until she felt her head swimming.

Now. Before she had a chance to change her mind or think more about the implications of what she was doing. Suit off.

Forty seconds.

Into the tank harness.

One minute twenty seconds.

Connections—fourteen of them. Can't afford to rush. Can't afford to make a mistake.

Two minutes twenty seconds.

Sondra's lungs were empty. She felt them collapsing within her rib cage. Five more connections, just five. Not much to ask. Her head was swimming again.

Three minutes and thirty seconds.

Two more attachments. Tank turning dark, have to work by feel.

Four minutes something.

Last one. Was that right? Can't tell. No more feeling in fingertips. Spears of ice, down throat and into chest.

Five . . .

Total darkness. *Personal* darkness. Strange way to go. But when it came to the final moment, maybe every way seemed like a strange way to go. And go *where*? No one had ever managed to answer that question. Maybe she would do it, be the first.

Sondra turned to solid ice, wondering if her personal darkness would ever end.

Baen Books by Charles Sheffield

Proteus Combined
Proteus in the Underworld
Brother to Dragons
Between the Strokes of Night
The Mind Pool
Dancing with Myself

CHARLES SHEFFIELD

PROTEUS IN THE UNDERWORLD

PROTEUS IN THE UNDERWORLD

This is a work of fiction. All the characters and events portrayed in this book are fictional, and any resemblance to real people or incidents is purely coincidental.

A Baen Books Original

Baen Publishing Enterprises
P.O. Box 1403
Riverdale, NY 10471

ISBN: 0-671-87659-7

Cover art by Gary Ruddell

First printing, May 1995

Distributed by Simon & Schuster
1230 Avenue of the Americas
New York, NY 10020

Printed in the United States of America

PROTEUS IN THE UNDERWORLD

Dedication

To
Elizabeth Rose
and
Victoria Jane

CHAPTER 1

How do you capture a legend?

Sondra Dearborn had rehearsed and varied her opening speech over and over as the skimmer flew across the open expanse of the southern Indian Ocean.

I have a question . . . I have a difficult problem . . . I would like to show you something . . .

She was arriving unannounced, without invitation. From everything that she had heard the first minute would be crucial. Excite his interest and curiosity, and there was no end to his time and patience. Fail that first minute and there would be no second chance.

The water below the speeding skimmer was glassy calm, dark and gleaming in the April sunlight like oiled fabric. At a height of ten meters and a speed of three hundred knots, Sondra felt no sense of motion. Her destination lay in the most remote part of the emptiest ocean on Earth. The nearest sea-city was five hundred kilometers to the north. All she saw, ahead or behind, was the unvarying horizon. The operation and navigation of the solo skimmer was wholly automatic. Sondra was left with nothing to do but brood on her options.

Show him. That had to be the answer. Words could fail, they could be badly delivered or misunderstood. But once he had *seen* it . . .

Sondra looked behind her and down to the fine-meshed cage in the bottom of the hold. She could see movement within, a slow twisting of metal chains. When she listened hard she fancied a rustling of rough skin against the grille. It could not escape. All the same, she was constantly aware of its presence just a few feet behind her.

"We will be arriving in two minutes." The skimmer was merely providing its regular status update, but it was almost as though it had sensed Sondra's desire for the journey to end. "Wolf Island now lies directly ahead."

Less than twenty kilometers. But the island was small, a low one-kilometer circular pinprick in the waste of open ocean. Sondra found herself seeking it anyway, at the same time as she told herself that it was too soon.

Wolf Island. It had seemed a self-indulgent and even arrogant name when she first heard it. Only later did she discover that Behrooz Wolf had not named the island after himself. Rather, in a quixotic gesture he had upon his retirement sought out an uninhabited island that had carried his name for four hundred years, since it was first discovered by the mad explorer—deemed mad in an age of madness—Captain Guido Wolf. No relation to Behrooz Wolf, so far as Sondra could tell; or indeed to her, Sondra Wolf Dearborn.

But there at last the island was visible, a flattened lop-sided pyramid of green and black appearing against the metallic blue of sky and sea. As they came closer and descended to surface travel mode the skimmer changed course, circling the green shoreline to make its final approach to a narrow spit of black rock that formed Wolf Island's southern tip. The only dock was there, with inland from it a small beach of white sand. A set of steps in the rock led upward from the beach, ascending to a house whose brown rooftop was just visible from sea level.

Sondra took a deep breath as the skimmer completed

its arrival and halted at the jetty. The moment of truth was almost here. She stepped down into the hold and lifted the cage by its metal handles. It was heavy, at least twenty kilos, but she tried to hold it away from her body, wrinkling her nose at the musky smell that came from inside. She heard a hiss, of surprise or anger. She struggled across the beach and up the stairs with eyes averted, sand and bare rock hot beneath her sandaled feet.

The house she came to was a mixture of solid strength and openness. It could take advantage of balmy days of summer breezes, or close itself tight against the gales that scoured land and sea at latitude thirty degrees south. Sondra approached the front of the house and set down her burden. The sliding door was slightly open. She went to it, pushed the tinted glass wide enough to put her head through, and found she was looking into an empty room. It was sparsely furnished; by someone, Sondra decided, who valued possessions for their utility and worried not at all about appearances.

"Hello. Mr. Wolf? Is anyone home?"

The room's high wooden ceiling echoed her voice. There was no other reply. Sondra paused at the threshold, then went inside. This was something she had never anticipated. Behrooz Wolf had returned to the island three months ago. There was no evidence that he had left since then. But if he had, and she had come eight thousand miles for nothing, she was the biggest fool on Earth.

"Mr. Wolf!"

Nothing. Sondra went on through the empty house until she found herself at another door in the rear. That too was ajar. It led outside to a garden, surprising in the planned luxuriance of its growth. To the far left stood an odd row of brown conical boxes, each about two feet tall, while a paved path curved away to the right. Tall flowering shrubs bordered the stones of the path and made its turning course invisible after the first thirty meters.

Sondra followed the twisting trail between the line of bushes. It was almost flat but it curved steadily. She realized that it was leading her around the rocky outcrop that formed the center of Wolf Island. She was ready to turn back, convinced that there was nothing to be found in that direction, when suddenly she emerged from the shrubs and found herself standing at the edge of another narrow beach of white sand. Before she could take another step forward two mastiff hounds appeared from nowhere. They raced across to Sondra and crouched at her feet, fangs bared. Their growl was a unison rumble of menace.

Sondra froze. She was usually not afraid of dogs, but the two huge specimens only a few inches from her exposed toes were too big to take chances with.

"Janus! Siegfried! We can do without that noise." The quiet voice came from Sondra's left. A moment later a man came strolling her way along the pebbled margin of the beach.

She recognized him at once from his pictures at the Office of Form Control. He was of medium height, dark-haired, thin-faced and thin-lipped. His eyelids drooped, half hiding dark eyes. He was barefoot, dressed in a simple outfit of uniform grey, and he looked about thirty years old. Thanks were due there to the biofeedback machines of the Biological Equipment Corporation, because Sondra knew that he was in fact seventy-eight, almost seventy-nine.

It was Behrooz Wolf: Bey Wolf, the legend. The former Head of the Office of Form Control; the man who had solved the mystery of Robert Capman's disappearance; the man who had pursued Black Ransome into the Halo, and vanquished him there in his own dark stronghold; the only man whose messages to the Logian forms on

Saturn were guaranteed a reply; the sole inventor and developer of the multiform; the ultimate human authority and undisputed master of practical form-change.

The man who refused to work with anyone.

Sondra had left the heavy metal cage behind her at the front door. Every prepared word vanished from her head. What she *felt* like saying would certainly do nothing to help her case: *But you look so ordinary, not at all like anyone special.*

In any case, Wolf beat her to it. "You don't look like my mental image of Friday," he said. "Or Crusoe, either. Don't worry about the hounds, they're just being playful." And, as the dogs moved away from her feet in response to his snapped fingers he went on, "The last shipwreck in this ocean was a hundred years ago. No one comes here by accident. I own the island, and I'm sure you know that this is all private property."

"I'm Sondra Dearborn. Sondra *Wolf* Dearborn. We're actually related to each other." And when that near-platitude produced nothing, not even a raised eyebrow, she had to keep going even though she was convinced that she had already blown any chance she ever had. "I'm with the Office of Form Control, I joined them a couple of years ago. I really need your help."

"Do you now. I wish you knew how many people have told me that in the past three years." He didn't sound interested, he didn't sound angry—he didn't sound *anything*. He just turned to walk down the beach toward the placid water with its rippling two-inch wavelets. "Before you go any further, let me mention that I told all of them the same thing: *No*. Your form-change problems are yours, not mine. I'm retired."

"I came a long way to see you." Sondra slipped off her sandals and hurried after him across the soft sand.

"I know. Eight thousand miles." He pointed off to the left along the beach, almost directly at the sun. "West-north-west, the Office of Form Control Headquarters lies right in that direction. I didn't hear your flier. More to the point, nor did they." He pointed to where the two dogs were running in and out of the water and scratching for something in the wet sand.

"I came the final fifteen hundred kilometers by skimmer."

At last there was a hint of interest, a puzzled expression. "Why? Why didn't you fly?"

It occurred to Sondra that this was his first direct question. And her opportunity.

"The pilot who was supposed to fly me here took one look at my luggage and refused to carry it."

But Wolf didn't take the bait. He simply whistled to the dogs and turned back toward the house. "The skimmer trip must take at least three hours," he said over his shoulder. "I was going indoors anyway, for a cold drink and a bite to eat. If you like you can join me before you start back."

"That would be nice." Sondra, walking along the path to the house right behind Wolf, resisted the urge to jump up and down in triumph. "Can I at least show you what I brought with me?"

"Why not."

Hardly an enthusiastic reaction. But at least part of Wolf's frozen old-man attitude was contrived. He could move quickly enough if he wanted to. When the two hounds, Janus and Siegfried, came close and shook themselves to spray both Wolf and Sondra with cold sea-water, she saw his agile leap away from them. She was hugely pleased. She hadn't lost yet. He would change his mind as soon as he saw what was in the cage.

When he went through to order food in the kitchen she hurried to the front door and carried the cage through to the middle of the living-room. She peered in through the heavy mesh to make sure that the chains were still secure. Gritting her teeth, she unlocked the cage's top and slid it open. There was an immediate silent rush of movement within, followed by the snap of taut links and a hiss of rage. Sondra took a deep breath, wishing that she could somehow close her nose. Bey Wolf was going to change his mind about eating or drinking when that smell hit him.

And then she realized that he was already present. He had come up silently behind her, to lean over and peer right down into the cage.

"Mm. Yes, odd enough." He was casually straightening up again. "I ordered hot food, and it will take a few minutes for the house to prepare it. But here's your drink."

He was holding a glass full of dark-brown liquid out to Sondra while he sipped his own.

"Don't you want to . . ." Sondra gestured at the cage. "I mean, I'm sorry about bringing this in just before we eat. I know it's disgusting. But if you want to take a closer look . . ."

"I hardly think that will be necessary." Wolf settled down onto a rocking-chair that faced the garden beyond. He had the look of a man who spent a lot of time sitting there.

". . . for you to really see what it's like . . ."

"I already know what it's like." Wolf leaned back and closed his eyes. The wet dogs padded forward to slump at his feet. "Physically: male, about eleven or twelve kilos. Hypertrophied mandible and upper jaw, with enlarged incisors and sharpened super-prominent canines. General body structure shows some achondroplasia—typical dwarfism. Ichthyotic skin in an extreme form, fully scaled on arms and legs and back. Enhanced reactions, about three times as fast as a normal human. Behavior is clearly feral, and the present form represents a purposive but regressive change. I judge that the chance of a successful form-change correction is close to zero. That enough?"

"But you hardly even looked!"

"You are wrong." Wolf sighed and leaned back in the rocking-chair. "I have looked and looked and looked, more than you are able to imagine. I have been studying the results of purposive form-change for over fifty years. I have seen the avian forms, the cephalopod and serpentine variations, the ectoskeletal forms, the wheeled forms, the Capman lost variations, all the mistakes and mishaps and blind alleys of half a century." Wolf sipped again at his drink, eyes still closed. "What you have there is well within the envelope of familiar alternatives. Illegal, of course, but not even close to an extreme form. Why don't you close the cage now? I can tell that you are uncomfortable with it open."

"I am. I'm afraid it might break the chains and get out."

Sondra slid the cover back into position. She had played a high card, and Bey Wolf had not even opened his eyes. But she still had her trump card to play. "While you're in the analysis mode, I'd like your opinion on two other things. How long do you think that this form has been like this? And how old do you think it is?"

"I have no way to judge how long the form has been this way. But it would take about four months in a form-change tank to achieve that shape. As for the age" —Wolf shrugged— "for that I would need a longer observation period, to watch movement and reaction to stimuli. It could be anything between nineteen and ninety years old."

Gotcha.

"It could be." Sondra waited, holding the moment. "But it isn't. It's four months old. And it's not an illegal form. It was *born* this shape, and it's growing fast."

Wolf's eyes blinked fully open and he offered Sondra her first direct look. "It failed the humanity test? Then it should have been destroyed two months ago."

"No. That's the problem. It was given the humanity test two months ago. And it *passed.*"

"Then it should have been placed in a form-change tank at once for a remedial medical program."

"That's exactly what was done when it was shipped to us. But the programs didn't work at all. No useful change took place during two whole months in the tank. That's why I came to you." Sondra gestured again to the cage, where scaled skin was rasping horribly against metal links. "The humanity test determines what's human, because only humans can perform purposive form-change. We have something here that *passed* the humanity test. That means it can't be destroyed and must be protected. But it clearly *isn't* human, and it's immune to form-change. It's my job to find out what's going on."

Wolf had been sitting up straighter in the chair. For a moment, Sondra thought she saw a real light of curiosity in his eyes. Then he was leaning back again, nodding his head.

"Very true. As you stated, it is *your* job to find out what is going on with a form-change failure. If you were hoping that by coming here you might also make it *my* job, I have to disappoint you. I told you once, I tell you twice. I'm retired."

CHAPTER 2

Sondra had lost. Bey Wolf would not help her. And because she had lost, she could at last relax for a little while.

Ownership of a private island was proof of wealth, but a far more impressive proof came to Sondra when she saw the quality of the house's food service. As Wolf led her through to a dining room that faced out over the ocean toward the setting sun, she saw the settings for the chef. The "bite to eat" that he had offered would be a banquet.

She sat opposite Wolf at a long table of polished ebony and watched him in puzzled silence as a succession of elaborate dishes appeared. He had been gone from the Office of Form Control for three years, but Behrooz Wolf anecdotes were told there all the time. Sondra had built up a distinct mental image of the man who now sat facing her. He was supposed to be cool, nerveless, and ironic, a man of immense mental energy who loved the challenge of tough form-change problems better than anything in the world (except possibly for his known obsession with the fusty and obscure works of long-dead poets and playwrights). He was also an ascetic, as little interested in elaborate food as in clothes or form-change fashions or social fads.

So how did a man whose energy had been legendary turn into a remote idler untouched by a unique new twist on purposive form-change? How did the ascetic fit with the array of epicurean courses that were appearing before them?

Sondra had no answers, but she noticed something during the seventh course. Wolf had described every dish to her in detail and made sure that both of them were served generous portions, but he hardly touched anything on his own plate. Instead he distracted Sondra with easy, fluent talk about the island and its history—and he watched her.

She finally pushed away her plate, the latest course untasted. "I didn't travel eight thousand miles for you to study me while I eat. And I have no more interest in fancy food than you do. I came here to talk to Behrooz Wolf."

"You can learn more about a person by watching them eat one meal than by listening to them speak for a whole day."

"And?"

"You like food well enough, but you don't worship your stomach. That's good." Wolf pushed his plate away from him but he kept his eyes turned down toward it. "You say you came to talk to me, Sondra *Wolf* Dearborn." Her middle name was slightly emphasized. "So, talk to me. Then it will be time for you to go home."

Since she had already lost, Sondra had nothing more to lose.

"I'm terribly disappointed—in you." She blurted it out. "I'd heard about you from my family ever since I was a small child. I've read about all your most famous cases, here on Earth, out in the Horus Cluster, off in Cloudland and the Kernel Ring. You're the reason I joined the Office of Form Control. And you're still a *legend* in that office" —there, she had used the word she had sworn never to use—"as a man who can solve any form-change mystery, no matter how strange."

"I am not to be held responsible for office gossip, nor for your own preconceptions. If that's all you have to say to me, you should go."

"I don't believe that it is gossip. I believe it's true. Three years ago you'd have had that poor creature out of its cage and been examining it in two seconds. You've changed. I want to know why you changed. You can hide away here on your island, but there's still a real world out there with real problems to be solved."

"There is indeed." Wolf was smiling. She had hoped to break through to him, but he remained as cool and unemotional as ever. "As there has always been. I have had" —he paused, and gave her another careful inspection— "fifty-one years more than you to work on such problems."

Evidence of humanity from Wolf at last, in the form of a touch of wounded ego. Like most people, Sondra held her physical appearance at age twenty-two. She was actually twenty-seven and a half, and somehow Wolf had read that. With his last statement he was just pointing out to her that his mistake about the age of the caged form-change failure was an exception.

But he was continuing: "You say I hid away. I say, I need solitude. It is also time for me to move out of the way and allow the next generation—yours—to spread its wings. *Crabbed age and youth cannot live together*."

It was one of his damnable old quotations, she was sure of it. Sondra didn't know who had said it—and she certainly didn't care. "That's rubbish. We *need* your experience. You talk about being old, but unless you have an accident you'll be around for another fifty good years. You developed the multiforms just four years ago, and that was your best work ever."

"In whose opinion? Yours?"

"Mine and everyone's. The multiforms add a whole new dimension to form-change. You are still at your peak and it was criminal of you to retire. Do you think you are going to sit loafing in your rocking-chair and staring at the ocean for another half century? Next thing you know you'll dodder around in your garden, growing vegetables and keeping bees."

She realized that she was pushing hard, still trying to goad him to a response that was more emotional than rational. And finally he was frowning. But it was in wry amusement, not anger.

"You need my experience?" he said. "Very well, you will have it. And then you must go. You said that the creature in the cage was *shipped* to you. From where?"

"From the Carcon Colony. Out on the edge of the Kuiper Belt."

"I know the region. Strange territory. Strange people. Have you been there?"

"No. It's a long journey and an expensive one. My cheapskate boss—or rather, my boss's boss—is hoping I can find the answer here, without making the trip out."

"Who is your boss's boss?"

"Denzel Morrone."

"I know him. He smiles pleasantly, but don't turn your back on him." Wolf was standing up. "Morrone knows me, too. Go back and tell him that you talked to Behrooz Wolf. Say that Wolf told you the chances of solving your problem without visiting the Carcon Colony are close to zero."

"Suppose he asks me why?"

"Just tell him that if it were my problem—which it isn't—I'd be on the next ship out. You don't need to tell Morrone this, but chances are it's a software problem in the form-change equipment used for the original humanity test. You need to check the routines first-hand and in person. Until you do that you are lacking basic information. *It is a capital mistake to theorize before one has data.*" Wolf led Sondra toward the back door, where he had placed the cage with its feral contents. Twilight was well advanced and the creature inside was quiet, perhaps cowed less by coming darkness than by the presence of the two mastiff hounds. They lay stretched out on opposite sides, guarding it.

Wolf picked up the cage without giving the creature inside a second look. As he led the way around the house toward the jetty where the skimmer was moored, he jerked his head to the row of brown conical boxes that Sondra had noticed when she arrived.

"Know what those are?"

"Not really. They look like bird houses, but I don't see any way in to them."

"There is a way in—if you're small enough." And, when Sondra stared, first at him and then back at the nearest cone, "You had it right earlier. Those are beehives. I keep honey bees. And I do grow my own vegetables—or at least, the garden servos do it for me."

"You live here alone? No regular visitors?" It was absolutely none of Sondra's business, and she was not sure why she was asking.

"Alone. No regular visitors." They were approaching the jetty, its black rock almost invisible against the dark water. "No irregular visitors, either, until you came." Wolf stepped into the skimmer and lowered the cage carefully to the deck. "Go to the Carcon Colony, Sondra Dearborn. That is my only advice."

"Sondra Wolf Dearborn. I'll ask Denzel Morrone if I can go. If I do, can I come back here and tell you what I find?"

He remained silently crouched over the cage for so long that Sondra wondered if he had seen something new inside. But at last he straightened and shrugged.

"Why not? If you wish to return, and if you believe

that what you have will interest me. And with one other condition: next time, give me advance notice of any possible visit. The hounds are not dangerous, you know that." Wolf started the skimmer's engine, then quickly stepped ashore. "But it could be fatal to assume that nothing on this island is dangerous to an unexpected visitor."

Startled, Sondra glanced up at him. His face was no more than an inscrutable pale oval in the near-darkness. She turned to gaze at the hulking deformed pyramid of rock that formed the center of Wolf Island. It seemed larger than before, the island's dark heart looming black against the evening sky.

The skimmer moved silently away from the jetty and began the long journey north; but the brooding obsidian hill remained in Sondra's memory, long after the island itself had vanished into the night.

Wolf watched the little vessel as it disappeared into the fading line between sea and sky. As the day ended, his work could begin. The bees in one of the hives had swarmed that morning. He had followed them up the rocky central hill of Wolf Island and carefully noted the location of the tight swarmed cluster. Now with the temperature dropping and the bees somnolent it was time for the next step.

Bey retraced his path up the hill with an empty container and a monofilament cutter. When he returned he was carrying the swarm, undisturbed and in the precise order in which it had been created. He had learned on his previous tries that it was not enough to follow the normal beekeeping practice of shaking the bees of the swarm into the container. For his plans, order seemed to be vitally important.

He went back into the house and descended two levels from the main floor. The lab that he came to had been cut from the solid basement rock of Wolf Island. Bey had not lied to Sondra. He *did* need solitude—for the freedom from vibration and noise that it provided, and for the absence of inquisitive neighbors which remoteness guaranteed. What he was doing was not illegal, but it was certainly the sort of thing that might raise eyebrows.

Bey suspended the swarm of bees above a table, from which it could be moved directly into any one of the waiting form-change tanks. Once the swarm was in position he paused. Even with the aid of his miniaturized servos, what came next was going to be infinitely tricky and tedious. He was not going to enjoy the next twelve to fourteen hours. He had to attach tiny optical fibers for biofeedback control to every bee in the swarm, then network the result into the computer so that responses were possible on both the individual and the composite level.

No point in waiting. The work could not be split into shifts, it had to be done in one long session. The sooner he began, the sooner he would be able to rest. Bey sighed, adjusted the microscope, and settled to his task. It called for great care but little brain work. He had plenty of time to think, and to wonder again if he really knew what he was doing.

The idea behind his new work derived from the multiform theory that Bey himself had invented four years earlier, for the creation of human composites. Now he wanted to take it far beyond the point that anyone else—Sondra Dearborn, or even the workers at the Biological Equipment Corporation—would believe possible. The use of biological form-change for humans was two hundred years old, widespread, and almost universally accepted. The corollary, that humans and humans alone could achieve such interactive form-change, was embedded so deeply in society that it had become the definition of humanity itself.

Sondra, like Bey himself, was too young to remember the great humanity debates. She accepted their final outcome as a necessary and inevitable truth.

What is a human? The answer, slowly evolved and at last articulated clearly, was simple: an entity is human *if and only if* it can accomplish purposive form-change using bio-feedback systems. That definition had prevailed over the anguished weeping of billions of protesting parents. The age of humanity testing had been pushed back, to one year, to six months, to three months. Failure in the test carried a high price—euthanasia—but resistance had slowly faded in the face of remorseless population pressure. Resources to feed babies who could never live a normal human life were not available.

And in time the unthinkable had become the unquestionable. The validity of the humanity test had been established beyond doubt over the years, by attempts to induce form-change in everything from gnats to whales to daffodils. Every one had been unsuccessful.

Now Bey was questioning the unquestionable. The development of the multiforms had made him re-evaluate his own deepest assumptions about form-change—things that everyone "knew must be true," commonsense things like the earth being flat, or the sun going round the earth, or atoms being indivisible, or nothing being able to travel faster than light.

Humans could operate as a multiform ensemble in a form-change environment, but not if more than six people were involved. Therefore, composites behaved differently in form-change than their individual units. Nothing surprising there. An individual cell from a human being did not respond to form-change feedback stimuli at all.

But a colony of social insects, bees or ants or termites, was a single, functioning entity. A hive possessed a complex structure and a survival capability that far transcended those of individual—and expendable—bees.

Three years ago, Bey had examined the long history and literature of form-change and found it wanting. The data he was looking for on social insects did not exist. He would have to create it. What he had not expected was that it would take so long.

Bey straightened his aching back, leaned away from the microscope, and glanced up at the wall clock. Sondra's skimmer journey should be over, and she would now be flying back to Form Control headquarters. She didn't know it but she had been given a tough job, one too hard for someone of her experience. The Carcon Colony was likely to eat her alive. While he, of course, sat loafing around in his rocking-chair.

Bey smiled to himself. Sondra's energy and directness pleased him in a way that he found hard to define. He began to examine the tendriled tangle of fibers, sprouting like white hair from one side of the swarm's dark mass. The night's work was just beginning. By dawn, if he were industrious and lucky, he would be finished with the connections. And then he would be ready for the more difficult next stage.

Bey was industrious, but not lucky. Minor movements within the swarm forced him to re-define part of the network. By the time that he placed the final assembly into a form-change tank, adjusted the settings, and emerged from the basement lab, the sun was high in the sky.

He peered out at a day that promised high wind and rain. He closed the house, helped himself to a hot drink, and collapsed into bed. Before he closed his eyes he set the skull contacts into position and programed four hours of deep sleep. He would be awakened early only if there were a disastrous failure in the lab, or a high-priority call was received at Wolf Island.

Bey was forced back to consciousness by a house signal buzzing urgently at his ear. Even before he sat up he knew that he had slept no more than two hours. His eyes did not want to focus, his mouth was dry, and his whole brain felt grainy.

He removed the contacts from his temples and turned at once to the status monitors. If the swarm was disintegrating so soon, after all his work . . .

Everything in the lab reported as normal. There had been no change of status in the tank, which was as it should be so early in the experiment.

It meant that the house had chosen to waken him based on some urgent external signal, a call at a level high enough to override Bey's own demand for rest. He keyed the communications system. An image popped into view instantly, projected into the viewing area beyond the bed.

"Mr. Wolf!" The man wore one of the standard forms of BEC management. He was handsome, impeccably dressed in a style new to Bey, and grinning broadly. "I have good news."

Bey scowled back at him. "How did you get in?"

"Top priority interrupt circuit. My name is Jarvis Dommer. I'm with BEC."

"I can see that. What do you want?"

"To make you an offer you can't refuse." Dommer seemed to have more teeth than a normal person, and now his grin widened even farther. "Mr. Wolf—may I call you Bey?"

"No."

"Fine." The smile remained intact. "Mr. Wolf, you may have heard that BEC has a whole new line of commercial forms on the drawing-board, planned for release two years from now."

"The marine and free-space forms. Sure. I've seen the advertisements."

"Good. But what you haven't seen—because we've kept quiet about it—is the plans for multiform versions of the new releases. We'll be using your own ideas, the ones that you sold to BEC three and a half years ago. And we said to ourselves, who better than Bey Wolf to be our exclusive consultant on this? No one knows as much as he does about the promise and potential of the multiforms—"

"No. I retired three years ago. I'm not interested."

"That's because you haven't heard what we can offer you."

"I said no. I have enough money. Forget it."

"I'm not talking just a high consulting rate, the way you are thinking. You'd certainly get that, the most we've ever paid. But I'm authorized to offer you a *royalty* as well, one percent of everything that BEC makes when one of these new forms is licensed. Nobody in history has *ever* been offered that by BEC. You may think you're well off now, but compared with what you can be you're a pauper. You won't just be a millionaire, you'll be a billionaire, a trillionaire, a jillionaire. You'll be so wealthy that you'll be able to—"

Bey hit the disconnect. The image of Jarvis Dommer, still talking a mile a minute, faded slowly away. Bey reset the house interrupt levels so that for the next three hours all messages, no matter their priority level, would be recorded for his later review.

He lay down again and reset the controls to continue programed sleep. In the two minutes that the skull contacts needed to adjust his brain wave patterns, he thought about the BEC proposal. Jarvis Dommer was absolutely right about one thing: the offer to pay royalties for use of a form-change program to an individual was absolutely unprecedented. And since BEC was the biggest business enterprise in the whole solar system, Bey would surely become obscenely wealthy. He should feel flattered and overwhelmed by their offer.

He didn't. He was too cynical for that. Instead he wondered what horrible problems BEC were having with the new forms. To promise so much, someone must be completely desperate.

CHAPTER 3

Bey Wolf understood form-change theory and practice better than any human alive. Sondra admitted that, without reservations. What he didn't understand so well, maybe not at all, was *people*.

Back on Wolf Island he had made it sound logical and easy. Go to Denzel Morrone, head of the Office of Form Control. Explain that a visit was needed to the Carcon Colony. If necessary, cite Behrooz Wolf's own assertion that the journey was essential if Sondra was to find out why a clearly non-human caged form had somehow passed the humanity test.

In the real world it wasn't so simple. Sondra had waited in the ante-room to Denzel Morrone's office for more than two hours while a succession of senior officials from the Planetary Coordinators swept in and out. The whole Form Control department had recently moved to an expensive new building, all airy columns of carbon composite and transparent outer walls. Sondra, perched above a thousand feet of open space, could see all the way across an ocean of smaller buildings to the dull grey bulk of Old City. The Office of Form Control had come a long way—physically as well as financially—since Denzel Morrone took over two years ago.

It had also changed in other, more subtle ways. Sondra,

finally admitted to Morrone's presence, told him at once that she would like to travel out to the Carcon Colony. Morrone, dressed in the smart new uniform that he had designed for members of the Form Control office, listened carefully as she explained her reasons: she must make a direct on-site inspection of the biofeedback equipment used in performing the humanity test. The tests that she had performed on Earth had all shown the caged form unable to interact with form-change equipment. It should never have passed the humanity test. Therefore a problem, hardware or software, existed within the colony's form-change tanks.

As she concluded with a repeat of her request to visit the Carcon Colony, Morrone slowly shook his head.

"I understand your position, Sondra. But I don't think you understand mine. What you have described sounds like a purely technical problem. It isn't. It's also politics. Solar system politics."

"I wouldn't be doing anything political in the Carcon Colony."

"Nothing *overtly* political. But the colony is in the Kuiper Belt, and that lies in the transition zone between the Inner and Outer Systems. *Anything* involving the Outer System is politics. If I request that you make a visit there it's another way of saying that we don't think they are competent to evaluate the performance of their own equipment."

To a political mind, everything is politics. Bey Wolf would probably have said just that. Sondra was shrewd enough to keep the thought to herself.

Morrone was continuing, a soothing smile on his big, pleasant face. "I'm not saying I won't grant your request. I may. What I am saying is that I need to think about it further. Keep this whole thing in perspective, Sondra. The humanity test is given to every baby. That's nearly three hundred thousand tests every day. And here, after centuries of use, we have one isolated failure. On a statistical basis we don't have a problem at all."

And on a statistical basis there was no need for an Office of Form Control. By definition, the office was concerned only with the anomalous: the form-change failures, the illegal forms, the investigation and labeling of borderline cases.

It wouldn't help to say that either. Sondra changed tack. "I spoke to Behrooz Wolf about this. He feels that I ought to go out to the Carcon Colony as soon as possible."

Morrone's face froze. "Why did you talk to Wolf?"

Sondra, ready to mention that Bey was a distant relative of hers, decided that a statement of kinship would be a bad idea.

"I met him. Socially."

Not quite a lie. She had stayed to dinner.

But Denzel Morrone was shaking his head. "The discussion of our problems with someone outside the office shows very poor judgment. I expect discretion on the part of my staff. Wolf's opinions on this subject are not relevant. He is no longer part of the Office of Form Control."

"But he ran it for almost half a century!"

"He did." Morrone snapped out the words. "And what happened? Under his guidance it remained an obscure component of a small and insignificant department. It should hardly be necessary to point out to you that the growth of influence of this office—and with it your own opportunity for employment and advancement—came *after* Behrooz Wolf had retired."

Sondra wanted to snap back, that when it came to solving form-change problems everyone said one Bey Wolf was worth a hundred Denzel Morrones. She bit her tongue. Morrone obviously knew office opinion. He had his own inferiority complex, otherwise he would not have reacted so violently when she quoted Wolf's suggestion. And everything that Morrone said was also true. The office had seen a spectacular growth in funding and influence since he took over.

"I'm sorry." Sondra did her best to sound contrite and truly apologetic. "My job is very important to me. I really want to understand what caused this form-change problem, even if it turns out to be no more than an isolated case."

"We all want to understand what happened." Morrone's self-control had returned and he was smiling again. "As I said, I'm not *refusing* your request. I merely want time to think it over." He touched the surface of his desk and the door of the office slid open. Sondra's meeting was ending. "But let me offer you a piece of advice. According to your record you have traveled little beyond the Inner System. In particular you have never been to the Carcon Colony. That is not a place for casual visits. I suggest that you learn more about it and confirm that you actually wish to go there. And if you change your mind, I won't be surprised."

As Sondra left Morrone's office and began the eighty-floor dropchute descent toward ground level she reviewed the meeting. Using Wolf's name had been a disaster. Bey obviously had no idea how much his successor resented his fame. But in spite of that, Sondra had not been given an actual refusal. She would certainly do what Morrone suggested and find out more about the Carcon Colony. She had been assuming that it was just another of the thousand small groups who populated the Kuiper Belt and the Halo. Apparently there was something more to the colony than she had realized.

"Strange territory, strange people," Bey Wolf had said. How strange? And strange how?

As she reached the ground floor, Sondra noticed something else. More and more of the staff she passed looked like male and female versions of Denzel Morrone. Apparently his internal campaign for an Office of Form Control identity that went well beyond clothing was succeeding.

Sondra had been born on Earth. She had been given a rather standard planetary education, which meant that she knew a great deal about the Inner System out to Pluto, and less and less about the rest of Sol's retinue as the distance from the Sun increased.

She had spent tourist time on Mars and Ceres and cruised the Europan deep ocean. She had flown past the off-limits planet of Saturn, with its Logian forms busy on projects beyond the comprehension of any human. She had visited the moons of Uranus, and in derived reality aboard a deep submersible she had watched the Ergatandromorphs, constructed synthetic forms, as they worked on the Uranian Link deep within their mother planet.

And there her first-hand experience ended. Beyond the Inner System, in order, came the Kuiper Belt, the Kernel Ring, and the vast extended region of the Oort Cloud. Cloudland, diffuse and underpopulated (by Inner System standards, not by its own) reached out to a full third of a lightyear from the Sun. Beyond that, and last of all, came the Dry Tortugas. Those arid, volatile-free shards of rock marked the edge of Sol's domain and shared their gravitational allegiance with other stars.

Sondra knew that the regions were all different, with their own inhabitants and customs and life-styles. The Kuiper Belt almost qualified as part of the Inner System. It was a collection of planetoids and cometary fragments, orbiting from the distance of Persephone, only fifty times Earth's distance from the Sun, to about six times that far. The inhabitants of its numerous colonies preferred to wear the forms of the Inner

System, rather than the skeletal and elongated shapes of the Cloudlanders.

Or at least, most of them did. Sondra, connected to the Form Control general data bank, watched in astonishment as numerical, descriptive, and pictorial information flowed in about the Carcon Colony.

> *The Carcon Colony (employ directed hyper-trail reference OP/M), a contraction of* Carbon-silicon Colony, *was established in 2112. Its founders rejected the philosophical dualism that separates carbon-based intelligences (e.g. humans, Logians) from silicon intelligences (e.g. computers, Ergas; employ directed hyper-trail reference HI/AI). They argued that the path of evolution dictates a direct synthesis of the two forms, and they set out to create that synthesis within their own persons and progeny. The assignment of functions, both physical and mental, was to be made on the basis of efficiency, not prior prejudice or historical roles. The resulting organisms are true* Cyborgs, *although the residents of the Carcon Colony reject this designation, preferring to use the term* Optimorphs.

Sondra followed the trail keys and found before her the Optimorph image bank. The displayed entities were not, as she had expected, a bizarre mixture of elements—human trunks, maybe, with mechanical arms and legs and glittering inorganic eyes. They were superficially human. But the torsos and heads bulged in strange places. The skulls had foreheads that came far out over the eyes. Limbs possessed what looked like second joints between shoulder and elbow, and between hip and knee.

It would take a long time to study the contents of the hyper-bank in the detail that they deserved. Sondra began to down-load the descriptive and pictorial data for later analysis.

It was a task that could be done without much concentration. As she worked another thought came drifting into her head. The Carcon Colony used form-change equipment, but its needs were likely to be very different from the standard applications on Earth. Different how? That knowledge was surely vital to anyone trying to solve the problem of the feral form.

So why hadn't anyone before Bey Wolf mentioned to Sondra the importance of knowing just what went on in the Carcon Colony?

She was beginning to worry about that question when the display that she was using suddenly went blank. An interrupt appeared in place of the Carcon Colony index and grabbed her attention.

TO: OFFICE OF FORM CONTROL, EARTH HQ.
(ADDED INTERNAL OFFICE ROUTING: SONDRA DEARBORN)
FROM: FUGATE COLONY.
SUBJECT: ANOMALOUS FORM.
REPORT TO OFFICE OF FORM CONTROL: NEWBORN 06:21, USF STANDARD DATE. HUMANITY TEST APPLIED, 8:23. TEST PASSED, 8:24. CONTROLS FAILED SAME DATE 8:24 UPON EMERGENCE FROM TESTING TANK. MAXIMUM GEE TRANSFER HAS BEEN MADE TO EARTH, SHIPMENT TO HQ OFFICE OF FORM CONTROL, ON 8:25. ARRIVAL EARTH ORBIT 8:27. WARNING: THIS FORM CANNOT BE TAKEN TO THE SURFACE OF EARTH. IN ADDITION, FORM MUST BE HANDLED AT HIGHEST LEVEL OF SECURITY. IT IS *DANGEROUS*. FOUR COLONY MEMBERS WERE ATTACKED, TWO WERE INJURED.

Sondra hardly read the rest of the message. She was receiving it through a high-level override of her standard communication channel. That, along with the office's internal routing, implied something else: responsibility for sorting out the problem with this form, like the feral one that she had shown to Bey Wolf, would be hers.

The new form was being dumped right into her lap. She cringed at that particular mental image, even as another thought rushed in: now not even Denzel Morrone could point to the wild form as an isolated, unique, never-to-be-repeated incident.

Sondra felt out of her depth. Just when she was hoping to understand the Carcon Colony, a new form and a new place had been thrown at her.

At least she had *heard* of the Carcon Colony—vaguely—before the first form appeared; but what and where was the Fugate Colony?

Sondra resisted the urge to dash off to Transportation and seek the most rapid way of getting to space. The new form would not arrive at Earth orbit for another twenty-four hours. And this time she intended to know a lot more about its origin before she was forced to confront it.

Fugate Colony. History, location, size, inhabitants.

Sondra remained at her terminal and set the data trail. While the key words were being pursued and the information collected, she had time to wonder again about the value of her training. Two years ago her doctorate in form-change theory, with its dissertation on the Capman C-forms and the Wolf multiforms, had seemed the perfect preparation for a career in the Office of Form Control. Now it appeared useless. Particularly in view of the information that was flashing onto her display.

The Fugate Colony was established by the followers of the psychologist and physician Reuben Mikhlin. Mikhlin argued that (1) the size of the human brain at birth produces a head that is almost too wide for the birth canal; (2) there is a tendency for babies to be born prematurely to reduce this problem; (3) thus the actual size of a baby's brain is less than it should be; (4) the human brain would continue to increase in size if it were not constrained by the birth process and by the rigid bone structure of the skull; (5) an increased mature body size would be required to support the larger brain size (employ directed hyper-trail for GIANTISM); (6) large body sizes can be supported only in a low-gravity or water environment.

The development of form-change techniques, simultaneously with easy space travel, permitted the followers of Reuben Mikhlin to proceed beyond theory to practice. The Fugate Colony was established in 2131 in the Transition Zone, close to the outer boundary of the Kuiper Belt . . .

The information went scrolling on, but Sondra didn't even see it—because the image viewing area had become active. The original images had been taken in free-fall, without scale, but some careful archivist had added in a reference image of an Earth human. Sondra saw a huge body, sixty feet long and broad in proportion, floating whale-like in the field of view. The hairless skull was full-sized with respect to the body, but oddly soft and amorphous in appearance, as though bone had been replaced by soft and flexible cartilage.

Sondra stared at it for a long time. And then, almost against her will, she saw her fingers move to the communications palette. She found herself dialing Behrooz Wolf.

Sondra got at least one thing right. She had not expected Wolf to be pleased to hear from her. And he was not.

"You can't possibly have been there and back." His voice was accusing. "Not even on the fastest ship in the fleet."

"I haven't. I'm still on Earth."

"So why are you bothering me?" Wolf was standing in a large white-painted room, part of the house that Sondra had never seen before. "I told you, the answer to your problem lies in the Carcon Colony."

"It used to. Not any more." Sondra waved her hand at the screen, although she knew it was invisible to him. "There's been another one. Out in the Fugate Colony."

"The what?"

"Fugate Colony." Sondra felt better. She wasn't the only one who didn't know everything. "It's out in the Kuiper Belt, same as the Carcon Colony. This form passed the humanity test, just like the other one. Then they lost control of it."

"How?"

"I don't know. The form is on the way to Earth orbit—but it can't land on the surface. Will you come and look?"

"No, I won't. Why aren't you on the way to the Carcon Colony?"

"Denzel Morrone didn't approve my request."

"What?" Wolf was frowning. "I told you to tell him I said it was essential."

"I did. But that made it worse. He hates your guts." There, she had said it.

"Nonsense! Why, I got him that job. They consulted me before they made him head of the office."

"Then that explains just why he hates you. Look, never mind all that"—Bey was scowling horribly at her— "there are more important things to worry about. Can I come to Wolf Island and see you again? I'll bring everything I can get about the new form, and about the Fugate Colony."

"No. I told you, it's *your* problem." Wolf reached out to cut the connection, then hesitated. A thoughtful look came into his eyes. "Has this new wild form been assigned to you, too?"

"Yes. Deciding what's happening is going to be my responsibility."

"And you say that the form can't land on Earth. Why not?"

"I don't know." *Her first direct lie to Behrooz Wolf.*

"But I promise you this: if you let me come and see you, I'll find out before I arrive."

Wolf was nodding slowly. "You can come and see me. On one condition: you come here unofficially, and you do not tell anyone in your office you are doing it."

He cut off communication without another word. Sondra found herself staring at a blank screen.

She had won. She could visit Bey Wolf again. It was the reason that she had called him. It was exactly what she wanted.

So why didn't it feel like success? Why did she feel as though Behrooz Wolf was seeing something in this whole situation that remained invisible to Sondra Dearborn?

CHAPTER 4

Bey Wolf had chosen his home for its remoteness and its seclusion. Now it seemed as though the whole world was determined to beat a path to his door.

Or at least, to his communications portal.

He had hardly broken the connection to Sondra when the communicator was buzzing again. He decided to ignore it. He was amazed when it came alive anyway, and Jarvis Dommer's grinning face appeared on the monitor.

"I know, I know." Dommer held up his hand. "You didn't expect to see me again so soon."

"Ever, if I had my way."

"Ha ha!" Dommer's smile did not fade. "Well, you'll change your mind when you hear what I have to say."

Bey decided not to waste time on insults. Dommer clearly had a hide like a rhinoceros.

"I'd like to know how you did that," Bey said. "I mean, how you activated my system. I'm supposed to be protected from unwanted calls."

"I'm sure you are. But that word doesn't apply to *this* call." Dommer's face took on a look of grave reverence. "Behrooz Wolf, it is my privilege to grant you a rare honor. Trudy Melford wishes to meet with you—*in person*. I have here" —he held up his right hand— "your travel voucher to Melford Castle. Not by any standard method of travel, either, but by Mattin Link. Price no object!"

"I'm not interested."

Dommer's eyes popped. "You can't be serious. I'm talking about meeting Trudy Melford. *The* Trudy Melford, Gertrude *Zenobia* Melford, the outright owner of—"

"I know very well who Trudy Melford is. I've known all about her since the day she inherited Corly Melford's stock and became the Biological Equipment Corporation's majority owner. I've even met her. She was there when I signed the license with BEC to give you people the right to use the multiforms. She personally signed off on the purchase."

"But if she approved buying rights to your forms, then she's the reason you're a rich man today. If it weren't for Trudy Melford, you wouldn't own that island."

"Maybe. But she didn't buy my ideas as a favor to me. She and BEC have made far more from the use of the multiforms than I have. So you can tell her, thanks but no thanks."

"But Mr. Wolf, I can't do that! If I were to call Ms. Melford, and tell her that you refuse—"

Bey reached out and slapped the cut-off switch. That made two terminated calls in ten minutes. As an extra precaution he turned off communicator power completely. Jarvis Dommer and BEC might have enough clout to change an on/off setting remotely, but not even they could operate a dead system.

Frowning, he went once more to the form-change tank. The experiment in it was clearly failing. The hive cluster, despite everything that he could do, was breaking up. Individual bees were lifting lazily free of the swarm and seeking a way out of the basement lab.

Bey decided to try one more set of changes to the tank operating parameters. He set to work, but after a few minutes he muttered in annoyance and leaned back in his chair, the task incomplete. This wouldn't do. Only a small part of his mind was on a job that demanded full attention. Although Jarvis Dommer had not succeeded in persuading Bey to do what Trudy Melford wanted, he had certainly succeeded in interrupting Bey's work.

Trudy Melford.

Bey knew her rather better than he had suggested to Dommer. From his days at the Office of Form Control Bey was aware that she kept a complete file on his own activities. But that had been more than three years ago, when it made good sense for the owner of BEC to monitor closely the activities of the head of the Office of Form Control. Bey's office was one of the few organizations whose official decisions could have an effect on BEC operations. But why would Trudy Melford care what he did *now*, when he was long retired? And what possible reason could she have for wanting to meet with him *personally*?

Bey sighed, went back to his communications unit, and turned it on again. He placed a call to BEC. Not to Trudy Melford, or even to Jarvis Dommer. He needed to talk to Maria Sun. She was his oldest friend there, one of the few people whose opinions and talents Bey respected when it came to form change.

She was in. That was predictable. Maria was a workaholic, someone who was more likely to be in her office than anywhere else in the world. What was surprising was the unaccustomed neatness. The clutter was gone. In its place sat neat boxes and cleared surfaces.

She raised a casual hand when the call went through and two-way visual contact was established. "Hi, Bey. It's been a while."

She seemed not at all surprised to see him. That was itself odd, after such a long time.

"Hi, Maria. Has Dommer been over to see you?"

Maria was wearing one of her favorite forms, of an exquisite Oriental woman. When she was hard at work she swore horribly and continuously, but today she was obviously taking things easy. Her desk was completely clear. At Bey's question she merely twisted her mouth downwards and grimaced. "Jarvis Dommer? Not if I see him first. He's a prick. Why do you ask?"

"You seem to have been expecting my call."

"Not exactly. But all day long I've had one call after another from people wishing me well. So it's no real surprise to hear from you." She saw his frown. "Are you telling me you didn't know?"

"I guess I didn't. I still don't. What's happening?"

"I'm leaving BEC. Tomorrow's my last day." She smiled. "I'll be joining you in the idle ranks of the unemployed."

"You were *fired*?"

"Don't be an ass, Bey." Maria glared at the implied insult. "Of course I wasn't fired. I was just offered a retirement package that I couldn't refuse."

"But you're the best they have. You can't retire."

"I *was* the best. But you were the best the Office of Form Control had, and *you* retired. Or you said you did."

"I've always been lazy. And you've always worked your head off. Don't try to fool me, Maria, I've known you too long. There has to be more to it than that."

Maria sighed. She had been standing up, but now she flopped down into the chair behind her desk.

"I won't say you're totally wrong, but I really have been given more incentives to retire than you'd believe. And anything else that I say would be pure bitching."

"So bitch. You know me well enough."

"It's going to sound like the same old complaint of people who have been around too long. You know: BEC's going downhill, it isn't the way that it used to be. The top of the company is filling up with yes-men and yes-women. There's less and less real research going on. Nobody wants to hear my opinions any more. I'll be glad to go."

"If it's really that bad, you'll be better off outside. I know a hundred groups who'll fight for your services."

"We'll see." Maria was staring at Bey shrewdly, her head to one side. "Did they fight for yours?"

"I ran away and hid. But they tried. In fact, I think they're still trying. That's why I called you."

Bey summarized the recent conversations with Jarvis Dommer, including his own perplexity as to why Trudy Melford was personally interested. "And he made such a big deal about paying for my trip," he finished. "I wonder what's going on. I'm not as rich as Trudy Melford, nobody is, but I can certainly afford the price of a Link transition to Melford Castle."

"Are you sure?" Maria had a little smile on her face. "Bey, how would you propose to get there?"

"Take a flight from here to the Indian Ocean Link entry point." Bey knew he was being set up for something, but he couldn't imagine what. "A couple of Link transitions, then another flight the rest of the way."

"And where would that get you?"

"To Chetumal, of course."

"Of course. And where do you think Melford Castle is?"

"Don't play games, Maria. It's at Chetumal, in the Yucatan. Exactly where it's been for the past two hundred years."

"Not any more. Bey, I'm impressed. When you drop out of things you *really* drop out. Don't you watch newscasts? Didn't anybody tell you that the Empress moved?"

"Who?"

"Sorry. Now I *am* being bitchy. The Empress is Trudy

Melford. If you'd ever worked for BEC you'd know why she's called that by the insiders. She moved the headquarters, Bey, over two years ago."

"Why?"

"I don't know. She's not in the habit of consulting me regarding her actions. But the better question is *where*. She took the castle to Mars."

"For God's sake, Maria!"

"For God's sake, Bey. I know. To Mars, and Old Mars at that. Wall by wall, stone by stone, brick by brick. I haven't been to see it, but people who have say there isn't a stick or a slate different from the way it was on Earth. It's still Castle Melford."

"It must have cost an absolute fortune."

"More than you imagine. She didn't ship by any of the usual ways, because apparently she was afraid there might be damage in transit. She opened a Mattin Link and held it long enough for everything to be passed through."

"That's even worse. Maria, are you sure about all this? It's not just money. Opening a Link between Earth and Mars would need USF approval and the blessing of the Planetary Coordinators. What about quarantine? And holding a Link open with that geometry would cost more energy than you can imagine."

"I'm sure it did. But if you're the richest person in the solar system, little details like those don't matter. Anyway, now you can see why jackass Jarvis Dommer expected you to be impressed by Trudy Melford's largesse. The Empress is willing to link you out to Mars just for the pleasure of your conversation." Maria eyed Bey shrewdly. "When will you be going?"

"I won't."

"You're sure?"

"No way." Bey was silent for a moment. "But I still don't see any reason why she would want me there."

"Watch that bump of curiosity, I can see it swelling from here. If Trudy knows you at all she could be relying on it. But I'll make a guess as to why she's interested in you. People who have been out to see Melford Castle in its new location say there are some exotic forms on Mars now, shapes that BEC had nothing to do with developing. Maybe illegal forms, too. Trudy must have seen them, deep in the Underworld. If she thinks they have commercial potential, there's your answer. She wants you to evaluate the forms; see what makes them tick, see if they have fatal flaws, make them legal. She scents money and she'd like to chase it."

"Good luck to her. But it has nothing to do with me. I'm busy."

"Are you now." Maria pursed her lips. "You're making me curious. First you say you are retired, now you say you're busy. And you live alone on that island in the middle of nowhere. You always used to work like a dog—harder than me. What are you busy *doing*, Bey? I'll bet it's funny business."

"It's nothing." Wolf reached out as though to cut off yet another conversation. Then he shook his head. "Maria, you're too smart for your own damn good. When I'm ready to talk—if I ever am—you'll be the first to know."

"I'll hold you to that."

"And thanks for the information."

"Anytime. Say hi to the Empress."

"I won't be talking to her."

"We'll see about that. If you'd worked for Gertrude Zenobia Melford as long as I have, you'd know how pushy she is. Whatever Trudy wants . . . you're the one who'll need the good luck."

Maria nodded knowingly and cut the connection. She left Bey with a lot to ponder. After three quiet years on Wolf Island, he had suddenly found himself interrupted daily—almost hourly.

Coincidence?

Bey sat down at the circular table. Time to think.

He did not move for more than three hours. The failed experiment in the form-change tank in front of him, with its steadily dispersing swarm of bees, was ignored.

Sondra Dearborn had been correct in her assessment of Bey's personality. He was interested in ideas, things, and people—in that order. But people were not immune from natural laws. Such laws included the laws of probability. Bey understood very well that coincidences had to happen, that odd events involving people must sometimes occur in runs.

He had known that fact for many years. He would accept it now; but only when all other possible explanations for the sudden change in his own circumstances had been eliminated.

For the next two days it seemed as though Bey had been worrying over nothing. No one called. No one tried to visit. He had sixty quiet hours to think about and work on a different form-change experiment, one that he had been planning for a long time. Peace ended on the third day, when a major southerly gale brought biting cold air from the Antarctic ice-cap all the way to Wolf Island. A mixture of snow and sleet was falling by mid-morning. Bey had heard the rising gale from deep within the basement of the house. He went directly outside from the form-change lab where he had been working all night and set off along the shore. He walked three full circuits of his domain, bowing his head against the biting south wind. The hounds needed the break as much as he did. Janus and Siegfried, running on ahead, splashed into the water far enough to wet their paws. Then they retreated to the sand. Apparently even the sea was freezing.

✧ ✧ ✧

Bey hurried back to the house at midday. He was driven not by fatigue or hunger, but by the thunderstorm that swept in without warning from the open ocean. It brought with it a barrage of rattling hailstones as big as marbles. The sky was dark where it was not lit by lightning, and thunder rolled all around the horizon as Bey ran for home.

He heard the buzz of the message center as soon as he was inside the upper level of the house. He muttered to himself when he inspected the log. Five messages, in less than eighteen hours. Might as well be living in Chat City. He was more annoyed than interested when he called for playback.

The first three were sound-only. They were all from Sondra Dearborn.

"It arrived in Earth orbit," she said without introduction. "I have the initial reports, but Denzel Morrone won't let me send them to you! He says they're office confidential."

Until that moment Bey had felt little interest in seeing records of anything to do with the feral forms. Now he did.

The second message had been sent five hours later, in the middle of Bey's night. Sondra's breathless voice on the machine was saying, "I'm on my way to see it. I wish you could come with me."

And finally, six hours ago, "It's terrible, absolutely terrible." Her voice was nervous and quavering. "I have a lot more information about the Fugate Colony form, but I don't know what to do with it. Can I come and show you? If only you'd answer! Mr. Wolf? Bey? Are you there?"

There was a long silence, until he thought she must have disconnected. Then, in a more resolute tone: "You told me to warn you in advance if I wanted to come and see you again. So I'm warning you. I'm coming! I'll be at Wolf Island as soon as I can get there. Expect me around midday."

Before Bey had time to become furious the machine clicked again and the next message began reading out. It was just four hours old. This time it was audio-visual: Jarvis Dommer, grinning like a demented ape. "Hi, Mr. Wolf. I'm sure you'll agree that BEC—"

Bey slapped the Cancel-and-Delete button.

The final message had been left three hours ago, and it was again both sound and vision. Or it was supposed to be. Bey found himself viewing the image of a dark-haired woman. She stared serenely into the recording unit without speaking. Bey knew what she must be seeing. His answering system responded to incoming calls with his own voice message and picture, and they would be showing on her screen.

Bey stared also, analytically. Although Maria Sun had been right when she mocked his ignorance of general news, that did not include form-change fashions. From long habit he always studied those closely. This year's top female fashion represented quite a change. Low, broad foreheads and slanting devil's eyebrows were in. So were high cheekbones and slightly retroussé noses, along with a sullen, full-lipped mouth and firm chin. Eyes were brown and thick-lashed. Hair was black or honey-colored, long, thickly-growing and almost straight, tumbling down in profusion to cover large ears. Fuller breasts were recommended. Waists were not so slender, hips fuller, legs strong, long, and well-muscled. There was more sway and swing to the walk. The overall effect that the BEC designers had been aiming for was the sexy peasant look, a primitive woman deliberately far in image from last year's languid sophisticate.

Bey had been impressed when he first saw the form. Not by the problem of its design—he was beyond such trivia—but by the commercial cunning of BEC. The new shape was different enough from the old one for the change to be expensive. How much would it cost? He could guess: exactly as much as BEC believed that people could afford to pay to be in fashion.

At first glance, the woman who showed head and shoulders on the screen was following the new look. But a closer look revealed differences. Her nose was not quite straight and a fraction too big, her mouth too wide and generous. Eyebrows were thicker and darker than convention permitted. Most noticeable of all, her eyes were not brown but a clear, startling blue-green.

"Good morning, Mr. Wolf." The icon in the display at last came alive. "Before you disconnect me or delete me, let me say my piece. It must be obvious to both of us that Jarvis Dommer has been getting nowhere. So if the mountain won't come to Mohammed . . ." The broad mouth smiled. "That's right, Mr. Wolf. In ten minutes I will Link in from Mars to Earth. I will reach Wolf Island at midday. I hope that you can find the time to meet with me."

Bey was more surprised than he was willing to admit. Not so much by the quirky form—he had seen every human shape that could live, and many that could not—but by the fact that Trudy Melford was on her way to Wolf Island. When she had arrived three years ago for the signing of the multiform licenses he had been told that it was a unique event. The value of her time was incalculable.

And so, in Bey's view, was the value of *his* time.

She said she would arrive at midday. He glanced at the clock. Already it was well past noon, with no sign of Trudy. But suddenly a clatter of hard shoes came from outside, running like the devil through the storm.

A sodden Trudy Melford appeared, bursting in through the front door without knocking. Long hair hung down in black rats' tails, snowflakes whitened her thick eyebrows, water ran down her prominent nose. She stood dripping on the threshold.

"What a welcome!" She laughed, full-throated and infectious. "Head winds, thunderstorms, hailstones, snow, high waves, low cloud. If I had a suspicious mind I'd think you were hoping to keep me out with weather control."

She walked forward, wiping melted sleet from her forehead with the back of her hand. Her pale green dress was soaked and clinging. Bey could see that she was following current fashion when it came to body style, warm and sturdy and complaisant.

A peasant-empress? Incongruous, given the Melford reputation. Bey remembered their previous meeting. It was hard to imagine then that anyone would ever dare to touch the imperial Gertrude Zenobia Melford.

"Where can I change my clothes and dry my shoes?" She held up the grey bag she was holding. "I didn't expect anything like this, but I did bring a spare outfit."

No apology for arriving uninvited. Nothing about being late. No embarrassment at barging in without knocking. And no doubt in her mind that she would be offered hospitality.

Total self-confidence. That's what life must be like when you grew up with the solar system at your feet.

Bey nodded to the bathroom at the end of the hallway. "In there. Where's your pilot?"

"In the carrier, down on the beach. I told him to stay there. How about a drink for me? Plenty of ice. I'll be back in a few minutes."

She vanished. Bey was left to ponder the next move. This was his house, his property, his kingdom. He had a perfect right to throw Trudy Melford out, to tell her to get the hell away from Wolf Island. Already he knew he would not do it. But he did need to assert himself and throw her off balance. Trudy Melford rolled over people so easily, she must assume that it was her God-given right.

Bey hurried to the door at the rear of the house. In the closed porch, sheltered from the storm, the two mastiff hounds lay nose to paws. He spoke softly to them and they stood up and stretched. As he opened the outer porch door they went bounding off into the pelting rain.

By the time that Trudy Melford reappeared Bey was sitting comfortably gazing out at the driving sleet. A half-empty glass was in his hand and a full one sat waiting on the low table.

She was dry-haired and rosy-cheeked, dressed now in a full-length pleated robe of pale mauve with loose sleeves. Bare toes peeped below the robe's hem. Trudy Melford padded across to Bey, picked up her drink, and sat down across from him without waiting to be asked. "I'm glad you decided to be sociable. I wasn't sure, you know, even though I acted as though I was."

"I admire nerve. Of any kind." Bey raised his glass. "Welcome to Wolf Island."

She nodded, sipped, and gazed out of the wide picture window. "Nice place. This what you did with the money from BEC?"

"You know it is. You also know that the multiform licenses gave me enough to do anything that I want to do for the rest of my life. You should have realized that sending Jarvis Dommer after me was a waste of time."

"Maybe I did." The blue-green eyes sparkled at Bey. "So why didn't you turn me away the second I arrived at the house?"

"Curiosity." And another reason, one that Bey was not going to mention. "You knew I would say no to any suggestion that I work on new commercial forms. I knew you knew. And the answer is still no. But if you were to answer a few questions maybe I would reconsider."

"Ah. Ask, then." Trudy crossed her legs. One bare foot showed beyond the dress. Bey saw that it was well-arched, broad and solid. More peasant pattern. BEC was nothing if not thorough.

He nodded. "Just three simple questions. One, what do you really want me to do? Two, why *me*, when BEC retains a thousand form-change specialists? And three, why did you move Melford Castle to Mars? Maybe you should answer that one first."

Trudy had been quietly sipping her drink, but at the final question Bey saw a new expression flicker in her eyes. Surprise? Or anger? How often did people question the motives of the Empress?

And then she was once again in full control. "The move to Mars, that's an old story and a long one. BEC's form-control patents, as you know, are employed through the whole solar system. You may also know that patent violations are common, with pirate hardware and software in use from Pluto on out."

"I worked with some of those out in Cloudland. Pretty good equipment, I thought."

"But stolen ideas, you must admit. Five years ago I went to Earth's Planetary Coordinators and pointed out that BEC contributes as much to this planet through taxes and fees as a major government department. Revenue generated anywhere in the solar system floats through to BEC Headquarters. When BEC loses money because of patent violations in the Outer System, Earth loses, too. I asked for help in persuading the United Space Federation to cut down on the pirating. I know the USF. I felt sure that they would at least make an effort if they were asked.

"Well, I was right about the USF. It was the Planetary Coordinators, here on Earth, who wouldn't do one damned thing. A whole year went by. Nothing. And another year. I went to them again and this time we had a major fight. If you want to, you can check that for yourself. It's in the public record."

"I don't need to check. It was talked about within the Office of Form Control. For what it matters, I was on your side."

"All right. But that's when I got mad and went shopping. BEC Headquarters had been on Earth since the company started. It didn't have to be. I talked to Mars and the Belt and I even asked for bids from Europa and Ganymede. Mars gave me the best offer, and I signed a deal with them. They get a fraction of BEC royalties, with a much bigger piece of anything earned where the pirating has been going on.

"As soon as the contract was signed I was ready to relocate. But I was damned if I'd be driven from my home as well as my planet. So I included Melford Castle in the move. End of story. Does that answer your question?"

Trudy arched dark eyebrows at Bey while she calmly sipped her drink. He nodded thoughtfully. Just like that. Get mad, make a deal, move Melford Castle. A hundred-and-fifty-room mansion, built on bedrock, lifted and carried across fifty million miles of open space to be set down carefully on Mars. All it needed was gobs and gobs of money. And a formidable will. The Empress of BEC had both.

Bey heard a faint and excited barking from outside. The hounds were on the way back. "What about the other two questions?" he asked. "Why me? And what were you hoping I could do for you?"

"Easy. You, because you're the best there is, and since you retired you have time to spare and can focus on anything that takes your fancy. As for the other question, what you would *do*, I can't answer it—until you have a chance to see something for yourself."

Flatter me, then rouse my curiosity. But it could work. Bey knew he was responding. He needed his confusion factor to throw Trudy Melford off balance.

And at last it was here—the first part of it. Janus and Siegfried, soaking wet, pushed open the door and ran into the house. Their arrival told Bey that he had less than thirty seconds. He stood up and walked over to the door as though intending to close it. Behind him the dogs were shaking themselves vigorously, spraying water in all directions.

Bey took hold of the heavy door. Instead of closing it he swung it wide. Approaching the threshold, right on cue, came Sondra Dearborn. She was bedraggled, shivering, and even wetter than the dogs.

Bey took her by the arm and drew her inside. "Come in, Sondra. There's someone here that I want you to meet."

He turned. "Trudy Melford, meet Sondra Dearborn. Sondra, this is Trudy. Did you bring a change of clothes? I thought not. Make yourself a drink. And why don't the two of you get to know each other a little while I hunt up something warm and dry for Sondra to wear?"

Bey left the room without another word and headed deeper into the house, closing the door behind him.

Sondra stared after him in bewilderment. She was exhausted. After a horrible experience with the Fugate Colony form in low Earth orbit, she had been through another one almost as bad in fighting her way to Wolf Island. With smart planes and boats and self-correcting equipment, few people died any more during transportation. But that was only another way of saying that occasionally people *did* die. Sondra was hugely relieved when her solo transport landed on the wind-lashed beach. She stuck the data recordings made during her trip to orbit into the pocket of her dress and jumped ashore. She didn't take a second look at the other craft, farther along the shore, and she paid little attention to the two dogs whose frenzied howls greeted her arrival. She was no longer afraid of them. In fact she was glad to have their barks pointing the way ahead as she staggered toward the house through driven sleet so thick that she could hardly see.

All the way across the ocean she had wondered what Bey was likely to say to her. Here she was again, arriving at Wolf Island without invitation or adequate warning.

It was mystifying to find him greeting her at the door like a dear and intimate friend. And even more baffling when, after the briefest of introductions to Trudy Melford, he left her alone with the super-billionaire who controlled BEC.

To hide her confusion Sondra did as Bey had suggested. She'd been offered a drink, she wanted a drink, she *needed* a drink. Something strong with warmth and plenty of stimulants, to calm her chattering teeth and churning belly. She mixed, gulped, and gulped again until the glass was empty. Only after she had mixed a refill did she finally turn to face Trudy Melford.

The other woman was watching her with concentration and poorly-disguised irritation. Sondra knew why. She had broken up a tête-à-tête between Trudy and Bey. From the look of it, a very private one. A casual guest did not sit at ease and barefoot, in a lounge robe carefully designed to show off her lush figure.

Sondra returned the detailed scrutiny. Trudy Melford wore the current look, but at an age older than was fashionable. Sondra guessed it at thirty, but assessed Trudy's actual age as a good deal older. Mid-forties, for a bet.

Why wear neither one age nor the other, neither true age nor the early twenties that was the general preference? Sondra looked again, and saw other anomalies. She had studied the current fashion in great detail. Like Bey, she could catalog the minor differences.

And unlike Bey, she was able to make another deduction. Before ever visiting Wolf Island she had studied every reference she could find to Behrooz Wolf. Not just his technical work, but the personal details. She knew the name, age, background, and physical appearance of every woman with whom Bey had enjoyed a significant relationship.

So, apparently, did someone else. Because Trudy Melford's deviations from the standard form were far from random. They had all been chosen with infinite care—even, Sondra now realized, the age—to make Trudy Melford's appearance a subtle composite of Bey's former female companions.

It was ironic. Sondra had considered doing the same thing herself, until she made a rough estimate of how much it would cost. Nothing that she would need was off-the-shelf. The necessary form modifications called for complete custom-fitting, using specially-written and delicately designed programs. *Expensive* programs. She had been forced to drop the idea.

Sondra was suddenly aware of her own drenched hair and soggy appearance. And so, from the snooty look on her face, was Trudy Melford.

Sondra felt the rising tension between them. "I've never seen a form quite like the one you're wearing." She tried to sound casual, and failed. "How much does it cost?"

"A negligible amount." Trudy raised her dark eyebrows and again surveyed Sondra's clothes. "But rather more, I'm afraid, than you would be able to afford."

The tone was friendly enough. But the claws were out of their sheaths.

"Oh, I wasn't thinking of using it myself." Sondra glanced toward the door through which Bey had vanished. "I gather that I'm perfect for some people, just the way I am."

"I'm sure that you are, my dear." Trudy smiled, showing even white teeth. "Perfect. For some people."

Sondra smiled back, seething.

Trudy nodded. The two women turned away from each other. Nothing more needed to be said. There had just been a declaration of war; a statement as clear as if it had been written, signed, sealed, and delivered through official ambassadorial channels.

CHAPTER 5

Bey had watched the whole interaction with a good deal of satisfaction.

He had left the room, but he had not gone far. During his fifty-plus years with the Office of Form Control he had lived at the center of a web of data collection whose gossamer threads extended right through the solar system. It was unthinkable that he would give up that addiction simply because he had retired; and it was natural that his house communications center would track what was happening anywhere on Wolf Island.

The exchange between the two women did not make him feel sorry for either of them. They had invaded his privacy and interrupted his work. Sondra had done it twice. Trudy had done it once only, but she had also inflicted on Bey the unspeakable Jarvis Dommer. They both deserved a little suffering.

He was surprised and pleased with Sondra. It required real nerve to take on the most powerful woman in the solar system, and she had done it rather successfully. True, her mouth was quivering and her hands were shaking, but that could be more the chill of her arrival than a loss of nerve.

More importantly, the meeting had done what Bey hoped it might do. The Empress, clawing and snarling at Sondra, was less imperial. Trudy had lost at least a little of her absolute control.

When the two turned away from each other and apparently decided to speak no more, Bey at once headed back into the room.

"I'm sorry." He shrugged at Sondra. "I don't have anything in the house that would fit you." A perfectly true statement, as it happened. There were no women's clothes in his house at all.

Sondra glanced at Trudy Melford before she answered. "You know me, Bey. One of your old shirts will do just fine. But I have to dry myself before I freeze."

"Of course. Help yourself to anything you find in the guest suite." He gestured along the hallway. Sondra squelched away, turning only once to look back.

"An interesting young lady." Trudy arched her slanting eyebrows. "Your assistant?"

She was fishing. Bey ignored the bait. "You said earlier that you couldn't explain what you wanted me to do until I saw something for myself. You obviously don't have that something with you. Is it on Mars?"

"Of course."

"A new form?"

"That, and much more." Trudy Melford leaned forward. "Will you help me? This is more important than I can say. It's not a question of money, but if you do help you will find me . . . more than generous."

The Melford reputation was of a woman remote and quite untouchable. It was hard to accept that idea as warm hands enveloped Bey's and aquamarine eyes, deep and knowing as the sea, transfixed him. "Will you help me, Bey Wolf?"

"How long will it take?"

"On Mars? Just one day. If that is not enough to interest and persuade you, a longer stay cannot help. Will you do it?"

"I'm not sure. I'll let you know."

"When?"

"Within one week."

"But you have nothing to—" She stopped and took a deep breath. Bey could see the angry response being bottled up. An Empress must be accustomed to instant gratification.

"If you're hoping I'll say yes," he added, "you'd better keep Jarvis Dommer out of my hair. I don't want him pestering me for an answer."

"He is loyal and hard-working." Trudy was still holding Bey's hands. "Why do you despise him so?"

"My Persian ancestors had a saying: 'A stupid man is one who is willing to die for a cause that he does not understand.' "

"That could also be a definition of a loyal employee. You are not like that?"

"I guess not."

"Ah. A pity. Very well. One week, and if I have not heard from you I will call you myself." Trudy finally released Bey and stood up. She took her grey bag, opened it, and handed him a silver card. "To reach me at any time, use this on your message center. It will give you direct access, wherever I am. It will also cover any travel expense in reaching Mars. Do you wish to discuss other compensation?"

"No."

"I thought that's what you would say." Trudy managed to smile, a rueful lop-sided quirk of the mouth that Bey found highly attractive. "What a pity. It is much easier, don't you think, to deal with people who are motivated by money?"

Bey found himself walking with her toward the entrance. "Easier, and in my experience less productive. What you don't pay for is usually more valuable than what you do."

"And certainly more enjoyable." She waited as he slid open the door and held it. The wind howled in and around them, molding her robe to her body. The storm had become more violent than ever.

"Do you think it's safe to travel while it's like this?" He had to shout to be sure that she could hear him.

"Given the right staff and the right equipment, it's perfectly safe." Trudy gestured toward the beach. Bey saw, shining in the gloom, the pale violet outline of a mobile link entry point.

"I have to be back on Old Mars in half an hour." Trudy was leaning close. She patted Bey's arm in a proprietary way. "Goodbye. Next time we meet, I hope it will be there."

Bey watched as she bent low to face the wind and headed toward the beach. It was like a conjuring trick. Trudy reached and entered her carrier. There was a brief pause. Then the whole carrier lifted and moved into the Link portal. And finally the temporary portal closed, swallowing both the carrier and itself. There was nothing on the beach to reveal that either of them had ever been there.

Bey slid his outer door closed. That was what *real* money could do, as opposed to mere millionaire-class wealth. Trudy, bypassing the usual Link points, would have been transported instantly to Mars. Chances were she was already walking into Melford Castle, even as he headed to his living room.

He settled back into the chair where he had been sitting less than half an hour ago. His unfinished drink was waiting, its ice still only half-melted. Bey picked up the glass. The contents appealed greatly. He closed his eyes. He had been up all night and was beginning to feel it. He had earned a rest; and he had also earned the luxury of pondering a little bit on the curious behavior of Trudy Melford.

What did she *really* want? He was cynical enough to dismiss her compliments, and experienced enough to discount whatever oddities might be waiting on Mars. BEC kept a permanent staff to analyze just such future business potential. They could do anything that he could.

Well, almost anything. He smiled to himself. They couldn't say no to Trudy Melford.

He smelled Sondra before he saw her. A distinct, flowery perfume came wafting into his nostrils. He sensed that she was standing close to him.

He opened his eyes. And blinked.

He had told her to help herself to anything that she found, but her appearance went beyond eccentricity. She had found a short-sleeved purple shirt, long enough to cover her body only to mid-thigh. She had drawn it in tightly at the waist with a broad black belt, which made it even shorter. Her feet were bare, her long hair was carefully styled and piled on top of her head, and she was wearing make-up for the first time since he had met her.

Oddly enough, the combination worked perfectly. Bey nodded approval. "You didn't need to go to such trouble, you know, just for me."

Sondra gave him a withering glare. "Don't kid yourself. Where is she? Where did she go?"

"Trudy Melford?"

"Who else?"

"She already left. For Mars."

"Well, damnation." Sondra flopped into a chair opposite Bey. "All this for nothing. That bitch. Did you *invite* her to come and see you?"

"No."

"So what was she doing here?"

"Apparently not everyone who comes to Wolf Island waits for my invitation."

Irony was wasted. Sondra glowered at him. "What did she want?"

"To recruit me. To bribe me out of retirement. To get me to go to Mars and work for her."

"I knew it!" Sondra stood up again abruptly. "That fancy form she was using, and those sexy clothes. She was *stalking* you, couldn't you tell? If I hadn't arrived when I did . . . I assume you told her to go to hell?"

"No. As a matter of fact I told her I would think seriously about her offer."

Sondra put her hands on her hips. "You did *what*! You'd consider leaving here to work for *her*, for BEC and all its money?—when you won't even help one of your own relatives."

"We can talk about relatives later. Meanwhile" —Bey sighed and stood up also. Any hope of peace was gone. "I didn't think you came here to feud with Trudy Melford. I thought you came here to tell me about the wild form that was shipped from the Fugate Colony. Was I wrong?"

"No. I have all the records." Sondra clutched at her waist, and was briefly panic-stricken until she realized that the data device was still in her dress pocket. "I'll get them now and we'll go over them together."

"No!" Bey had to call after her—she was already racing off along the hallway, a flash of purple shirt and long bare legs. "You give them to me, and I'll review them. *Then* we'll go over them together."

He muttered to himself while he was waiting for her to return. What was the Office of Form Control coming to? Hadn't she been taught standard operating procedure? Everyone knew that separate reviews were performed *before* combined reviews.

Or they knew when I was there. Bey caught the logical next line before it could fully emerge, and grinned to himself. *The youngsters all knew better when* Bey Wolf *was running the show*.

The standard old-timers' complaint and boast. It had certainly been right to retire when he did.

✧ ✧ ✧

The Fugate Colony was one of hundreds of small groups scattered through a vast, near-empty region extending from the Kuiper Belt to the limits of Cloudland. All those groups were on the face of it extremely diverse; and yet in one way many of them were remarkably similar.

Bey had seen it happen a score of times. A colony would be founded because its core members shared some common oddity or belief that set them apart from the rest of humanity. After a generation or two, that singular world-view might fade. The colony would then dwindle and die, or be re-absorbed to the human mainstream. But sometimes separation *widened* the gap. Differences, physical or mental, became more extreme.

The Fugates were a fine example. Begin with the belief that the human brain could and should be bigger; add to it a requirement that bigger brains need bigger bodies; and after a century or two you would have—*this*.

Bey gazed at the image swimming in the field of view. The shape was undeniably human, with a soft, rounded body and shortened limbs. Its head was large in proportion, like a typical human baby.

But now came the differences. The body was nine meters long and massed more than four tons. The head was three meters from the chin to the top of the cranium. Two-thirds of that length—more than Bey's own height—was above the eyes. X-rays showed that the fitted bony plates of a normal skull had been usurped by a web of soft cartilage, bulging slightly from the pressure of the swollen mass within.

As Bey watched, the diminutive arms and legs moved in unison. The great head bobbed forward. His first impression was reinforced. *Swimming* was the right description. The immature Fugate form was curiously reminiscent of a whale, and he could imagine that in future generations those arms and legs might shrink away like rudimentary cetacean limbs.

The warning that had come from the Fugate Colony was also appropriate. The leviathan that Bey was viewing appeared so helpless, so harmless, so in need of care. But the record showed that the maximum-security chamber and the soft mesh of cables holding the form in position were fully necessary. The chubby body and dimpled limbs possessed a whale-like strength, while the bulging skull contained a brain of reptilian ferocity and random impulse.

It was fascinating; it was disturbing; and it was not at all revealing.

Bey finally sighed and leaned away from the viewer. He shook his head.

"Well?" Sondra had returned to his side, and she was looking at him hopefully.

"It's everything that you said it is. And I can't deduce anything more than you can."

"But you have so much more experience . . ."

"That's not the issue. If there has been post-natal form-change, what we are seeing is just the form-change *end-point*. There are a million ways to get to any given form. What you need is the whole record—every step of every interaction between the original form and the form-change programs. All the two-way information transfer. That should be in the permanent files. The form passed the humanity test, we know that. What we don't know is if there were marginal areas, places where the form showed definite oddities but just squeaked through. You also need something else that you don't have: you need to know the *typical* form and behavior of a Fugate Colony member. I think you have been regarding this one as a monstrosity. It isn't. Physically, I suspect it's very close to the norm for a standard Fugate modification. The differences are all in the brain—where we can't see them."

"So what do we do now?" Sondra's bright outfit contrasted with her dejected posture. She sat slumped forward in the chair, elbows on bare knees, chin in hands, staring at the viewer.

"We? *We* don't do anything. I told you already, this isn't my problem. It's yours. You have to find a way to persuade Denzel Morrone to let you make a trip out to the Fugate and Carcon Colonies."

"That's easy for you to say, but Morrone is already mad as a coot at me because I came out here to see you. A message just came through on your message center, chewing me out, while you were sitting here."

Bey was frowning at her, as though this was the most important news of the day. "For *you*? But I told you not to tell *anyone* that you were coming to Wolf Island."

"I didn't tell Morrone or anyone else. I chartered the flier myself. Seems Morrone found out anyway. But are you sure that going to the colonies is the right next step?"

"It's what I would do in your situation. Unless you have a bright idea?"

"I do. We should call Robert Capman on Saturn." And, when Bey did not respond, she went on, "I've read everything that you've ever written about him. According to you he was the absolute master of form-change theory, the greatest intellect of the century—and he became even more capable when he assumed a Logian form and moved to Saturn."

"All quite true. And all, I suspect, irrelevant. The Logian forms, deliberately, do not involve themselves in human affairs."

"Not the average human problem, maybe. But for a form-change problem, Capman's own special field—and if the request were to come from Bey Wolf, rather than Sondra Dearborn . . ."

"Ah. I see." Bey swung his chair around, to peer

knowingly at Sondra through half-closed eyelids. "Why didn't you admit this earlier?"

"Admit what?"

"That you tried to call Capman, *yourself*, before you ever came to see me."

"It didn't seem relevant." Sondra would not meet his eyes.

"Why not? He is still alive, you know that. Messages beamed to Saturn reach him. Your message must have reached him. If he were interested in your problem he certainly had the means to reply."

"That's not the point, is it?" She sat up straight and glared at him with new energy. "You are the one who worships the fusty old writers. You are the literature and quotation junkie. So try and finish this one. '*I can summon spirits from the vasty deep.*' "

"Maybe you have been doing some homework—at least on me." Bey leaned back and thought for a moment. "It's Shakespeare. Glendower says it. And Hotspur answers: '*Why so can I, and so can any man. But will they come when you do call for them.*' I see. Anyone can *call* Robert Capman on Saturn—"

"But only Behrooz Wolf will get a reply. I sent a message and I didn't hear one word back. But you would. You were his fair-haired boy. If you called him, he'd talk to you."

"He might. He probably would. But I think I know what he'd tell me."

"What?"

"Exactly what I am telling you. Go and solve it for yourself. I'm busy enough with my own work."

"You don't have any work. You've said it a dozen times, you retired three years ago."

"To pursue my own interests. Not yours, or anyone else's."

"You were ready enough to run off to Mars, when

Trudy Melford wandered in and blinked her big blue eyes at you. But you won't help one of your own relatives."

"That argument again?" Bey sighed. "Let's dispose of it, once and for all. Then I need rest—you may not care, but I have been up all night. *Working*. Come on."

He led the way along another hallway, to a part of the house that Sondra had not seen before. It was an odd combination of bedroom and study. The displays in the ceiling and the controls beside the bed would allow someone to work or sleep with equal comfort. Bey went to a wall unit, where a complex chart was displayed.

"You have assured me several times that you and I are related, as though this entitles you to special consideration."

"We *are* related."

"Indeed we are. But how closely? I took the trouble to determine that. Here is my genealogical chart, displayed together with yours. If we were identical twins we would share one hundred percent of our genetic material. If we were total strangers, unrelated in any way, we would share zero percent. From this lineage diagram you can determine for yourself our common genetic heritage."

Sondra stared at the family tree. She shook her head. "I don't know how to do that."

That earned another stare, this one more puzzled than knowing. "I am suitably appalled by your ignorance. But let me tell you how. Assuming there has been no inbreeding between distinct lines, the procedure is quite simple. Let's start with me. We go back through the tree, to every common ancestor that you and I share. Here we go." He stepped up through the generations. "Your great-great-grandfather was my great-grandfather, Dieter Wolf. He is our closest common ancestor. I was actually quite surprised to find that we share another, nine generations back, but that's so long ago I'm not sure I trust the results. Let's ignore it for the moment. We start with you. You share one hundred percent of genetic material with yourself. Now we go back toward our first common ancestor. At each generation, we multiply by one half. Your father was Soltan Dearborn. One half. His mother was Amelia Wolf. One quarter. *Her* mother was Cynthia Wolf-Stein. One eighth. And her father was Dieter Wolf. One sixteenth. You have one-sixteenth of Dieter Wolf's genetic material.

"Now we come back down the tree. And at each generation, we multiply by one-half again. Dieter Wolf was my great-grandfather. Dieter Wolf's son was Seth Wolf. We're now at one thirty-second, a half of one-sixteenth. Seth Wolf's son was Hector Wolf. One sixty-fourth. And finally we get to me, because Hector Wolf was my father. One one-hundred-and-twenty-eighth. You and I share less than one percent of our genetic material. If I throw in the other common ancestor, nine generations back, I simply add that to the other number. It makes hardly any difference—one part in five hundred thousand. Do you follow this?"

Sondra was scowling. "I follow it, but I'm not sure I believe it. Or see why it's relevant."

"Try it for some cases you know already. Brothers: two common ancestors—mother and father. Go back one generation from brother to mother, and down again from mother to other brother. That gives one quarter. Do the same for the father, another quarter. Add. Brothers share half their genetic material. Half-brothers share a quarter, cousins share one eighth. You and I share one one-hundred-and-twenty-eighth. Now come with me. I want to show you something."

Bey was smiling to himself as he led the way out of the bedroom and descended two levels to the basement laboratory. Sondra followed, totally confused. Bey had a habit of subject change and digression unlike anything she had encountered in her studies or in the Office of

Form Control. It sounded as if he were simply trying to annoy her, but she sensed that there was more to it than that.

He was walking along past a set of closed metal doors with external cipher locks. At the fourth one he stopped, dialed in a combination, and swung it open.

"Come in."

Sondra followed and squeaked in alarm and surprise when a small brown figure jumped across the room and grabbed her by the hand.

"Don't be scared. That's Jumping Jack Flash, and he's as friendly a chimp as you'll find anywhere."

Sondra looked down and found herself staring into a pair of solemn and knowing brown eyes.

"I just wanted to introduce the two of you," Bey went on. "And here's a question that I know you can answer, because it's in the standard form-control briefings. How much genetic material do a human and a chimpanzee have in common?"

"Ninety-nine percent. Actually, a bit more than that."

"Quite right." Bey reached down, and the chimp swung itself up his arm and to his shoulders in one easy movement. "That means you and I have less in common genetically than you and the chimp."

"That's absolute nonsense!"

"Of course it is, and I'm glad to hear you say so. I'll leave it to you to explain *why* it's nonsense."

It wasn't done simply to annoy. Sondra recalled another part of the Bey Wolf legend at the Office of Form Control. He was a unique teacher. Come to him with a problem, and he almost never provided a straight answer. Instead he did something apparently unrelated, something that made you think and figure out the answer for yourself.

He was trying to make her think. And she *was* thinking—but not about genetics and probabilities.

Sondra stared at the chimp, draped affectionately around Bey's neck. Jumping Jack Flash did not look quite right. His huge, grinning teeth were pure chimp, but his skull was higher than usual and his nose had more cartilage. Then she thought of the form-change tanks that they had passed as they walked through the basement lab, and another thought leaped into her mind from nowhere.

"Bey." (She was calling him Bey, just as if she was on the terms of familiarity with him that she had pretended to Trudy Melford. Why?) "Bey, don't do it. Please. Don't even think of it."

She expected an argument, perhaps a pretence that he did not understand what she was talking about. Instead she received a lightning flash from dark eyes that were suddenly wide open.

"How do you know what I was thinking of doing?"

"I'm a Wolf, too. I really am. All your genetic calculations don't mean a thing. I'm a Wolf."

He was studying her again, as though he saw her for the first time. "Maybe you are at that."

"Promise me you won't. It's a first step on the road to hell."

" '*Why this is hell, nor am I out of it*.' Sorry. Quoting is a lifelong habit, I find it hard to shake. All right, I promise you I'll put this experiment on the back-burner."

"Not enough."

Bey grimaced, with annoyance or resignation. "All right, I promise you I will not pursue experiments with Jack Flash—or with any other chimp that has been given a human DNA boost—unless I first discuss it with you."

"Any other *organism* with a human DNA boost."

"Any other *organism*."

"Thank you."

"No need for thanks." Bey stood silent for a moment, the chimpanzee lying silent like a great fur scarf around his neck. "And if you can tell me *why* I would make such a promise, I will be most grateful."

"I don't know." *But I think I do*. Sondra stared around the room. It was not anything like an animal cage. It was an apartment, as good as the one that she lived in. "I have to go now. I have to get back as soon as the weather allows. I'm going to change clothes, then I'm leaving."

What she did not say, what she could not say, was that she was suddenly hideously uncomfortable with what she was wearing. She was revealing too much skin, too much length of leg.

But too much for whom?

She headed for the door. As she reached it she turned. "May I come back and see you again?"

"If you wish."

"I may not have results."

Bey nodded. "I know. Come anyway. Keep me from the road to hell."

The moment stretched. Neither spoke. Then Sondra had turned and was fleeing—back to the upper level of the house, back to the psychological safety of the murderous storm outside.

CHAPTER 6

It was thirty-three hours since Bey had slept. He watched Sondra's departure, lifting off safely into dark afternoon rain clouds; and then he returned to his bedroom to rest.

Or pretend to. He lay staring at the ceiling, while the overhead displays flickered in spiraling colored patterns designed to soothe and relax. One touch of his right hand to the control panel by the bedside would take a more direct step. He would be eased into programed sleep.

His hand remained at his side. Too many mysteries; they were creeping around the base of his subconscious mind. He needed to name and catalog them before he could relax.

Begin with Sondra. He had checked her records at the Office of Form Control. She had done extremely well in everything theoretical, but her practical experience was woefully inadequate. And she was very junior. He would never have given her an assignment as difficult as a failure of the humanity test in a remote and unfamiliar location. The Carcon and Fugate colonists were notoriously tough on outsiders. Without help her chances of success were low indeed.

But she *was* seeking help—*his* help, as a family

member. Had someone else counted on that? Did someone in the Office of Form Control already realize that she and Bey were related when she was assigned to the case? That was unlikely. The connection lay so many generations in the past. Bey had noticed that her name in the official files was *Sondra Dearborn*, not *Sondra Wolf Dearborn*. She had identified herself to Bey as a fellow Wolf only because she was trying to enlist his support.

But if no one had known of their relationship when the project was assigned to her, it was Bey's guess that this was no longer the case. Sondra was now tagged as a Bey Wolf relative—with whatever that implied.

What else? He had told her to come and see him without telling anyone else in the Office of Form Control. But certainly someone had learned of her latest visit, because Denzel Morrone had known enough to send a message to Sondra *here*, on Wolf Island.

Mystery, or trivial incident? Bey had asked her not to talk about her visit—but he had not told her to keep it secret. A crucial distinction.

One person who had surely not known that Sondra would arrive on Wolf Island was Trudy Melford. Her surprise had been genuine. But how much else of what she had to say was true? If Bey's instincts were good for anything, Trudy held a whole hand of cards that she was not willing to show—until he did what she wanted, and went to Mars. Perhaps not even then.

Did she need him all that much? Bey had little false modesty, but he doubted that his skills exceeded the combined talent available within the Biological Equipment Corporation. Trudy surely had her own hidden agenda, of which he must form a part.

Bey reached for the control panel at the bedside. Not for programed sleep, not quite yet. He inserted the silver card that Trudy Melford had given him into the transportation module. Here at least she had not been deceiving him. The return showed huge available credit, beyond the number of digits that the machine could display. Bey instructed the module to arrange for a maximum-speed link from Wolf Island to Mars beginning in fourteen hours, with money no object. He asked for feedback only if Trudy balked at the cost.

At last he closed his eyes. He knew he would sleep now, and without the need for any program.

Had Sondra Dearborn or Trudy Melford been present in the room he would not have thanked them. But he should have. For if one thing in the world pleased Bey Wolf more than any other, it was the delicious sense of anticipation provided by new and perplexing questions.

Earth's permanent link system composed an exact twenty entry points, located close to the vertices of a regular dodecahedron. It had been conceived by its creator, Gerald Mattin, as an instantaneous and energy-free system of transportation in flat spacetime. Practical details had ruined that dream. Earth was not a perfect sphere, so the vertices were slightly off their ideal locations; spacetime near Earth's surface was slightly curved. Travel through the Mattin Link was still effectively instantaneous, but it came at a price.

That price, for travel around Earth, was nothing compared with the cost of maintaining a link with one vertex on Earth and the other on Mars. Trudy Melford, with a profligate disregard of expense that still amazed Bey, had been holding a link open for her personal use and convenience for more than three years.

How could she—or anyone, no matter how rich—possibly afford it?

Bey had part of his answer when he arrived in Chetumal, at Trudy's North American terminal point. He had linked in to the Yucatan on the east-bound route, traveling via Northern Australia, the Marianas, Johnston Island, and Portland, watching the sun flicker from horizon to horizon and morning turn to night in less than two minutes.

The people at each link stage were what he had learned to expect, nervous and harried guardians of goods too precious and too short-lived to be entrusted to conventional modes of travel. The cubes of bright red contained near-empty space. At their heart sat proprietary algorithms, embodied in microchips too small to see. The yellow lead containers held high radioactives, imprisoned behind their triple shields. Most urgent of all were the nano-flasks, their contents changing and evolving a thousand times as fast as their surroundings. The people who carried those also moved in more than real time, aware that a delay of half an hour could destroy their priority and the chance of a successful patent.

But at the Earth/Mars link point, all that changed. Travelers wore exotic forms and recreational clothing. They carried little or no luggage, and no commercial materials. There were scores of them, all apparently known to each other, and all chatting about earlier link trips that they had made to Mars. They had converged quietly and confidently on the Mars staging point, coming from all parts of Earth.

Bey studied them while he waited for the incoming link to operate. At last he realized what he was seeing. These were the super-rich of the Inner System, day-trippers who were using Trudy Melford's link to Mars not because of need, but to make a statement. A one-way link would consume the lifetime earnings of a normal person. These travelers did not *need* to go to Mars. They merely wanted to emphasize their own wealth and status. Trudy Melford could set the price of the link as high as she chose—and this group would compete to pay it.

They glanced at Bey and dismissed him. Their expressions said that he was not one of them, and therefore he was a nobody. It would have required a character more saintly than Bey's to feel no satisfaction when the incoming link door opened and a dozen BEC employees emerged, ignored the beautiful people, and converged deferentially on him.

"All ready for Mars, Mr. Wolf?" In spite of Bey's warning to Trudy Melford, the leader of the BEC group was Jarvis Dommer. He was grinning like Jumping Jack Flash, just as though he personally was responsible for Bey's presence at the link point.

Bey nodded. "I'm ready." He could hear the intrigued whispers from the glitterati around him: *"Who is he?" "They said his name is Wolf." "He's someone really important." "He must be traveling incognito using a new form."*

The whole group walked forward into the link transition area. They fell silent, waiting. The air pressure of the ante-chamber had already been cycled slowly down to an oxygen-rich mixture at half a standard atmosphere, exactly what they would encounter when they emerged within the boundaries of Old Mars. Before he left Wolf Island, Bey had also briefly entered a form-change tank. The adjustment needed to feel comfortable in Mars gravity was a tiny one.

If Bey had been less experienced he might have believed he could make it without the use of form-change equipment at all. Purposive form-change was no more than the machine reinforcement of human will. Why bother with the hassle of computer feedback and mechanical equipment, when it ought to be possible to do everything by pure mental power?

Maybe it was; but over many years Bey had investigated scores of Secret Masters, sages who claimed to have a command of form-change without the use of equipment.

Every one had proved to be a lunatic, a charlatan, or both.

The tension in the link transition chamber was mounting. The wall display flickered the last part of its count-down. There was a long final second, while the display showed zero and nothing appeared to be happening. Then came a dizzying instant as the link transition was performed. The chamber walls seemed to blur and shimmer. Ambient gravity dropped instantly to Mars equatorial, thirty-six percent of Earth standard.

Everyone swallowed hard, then smiled at each other. That gravity change was the indisputable proof that they were now on Mars.

There was one more moment of drama. To Bey's surprise, Trudy Melford herself was waiting outside the link transition point. She nodded to everyone who was emerging, as though she knew them all personally, but it was Bey whom she moved to and took by the arm. He received a special smile. Bey heard his own name coupled with Trudy's by the people around them.

"Ready to go?" It was not a question. Already she was leading Bey toward the Mars immigration area. She was wearing the same form as at their meeting on Wolf Island, but this time her dress was less conventional, a lacy white veil that floated around her body like gossamer in the lower gravity and thinner air.

Bey thought she looked terrific. He said nothing.

In his case the formalities had been disposed of in advance. He was whisked away to a long, sleek open car before any other arrival had been offered a first entry document. With Dommer in front and Trudy seated snugly at Bey's side in the cramped rear, the balloon-wheeled vehicle went snaking through a long, winding tunnel that steadily ascended.

It had been twenty-five years since Bey's last visit to Mars. According to all reports the place had changed beyond recognition; but he had a pretty good idea where he must be.

Two hundred years ago the first colonists had burrowed in close to the equator, down past the sterile rubble of the regolith until they were deep enough to tap the underlying permafrost. That had yielded ample supplies of water, enough to discourage much exploration and settlement close to the ice-caps of the frigid Martian poles. When a hot summer afternoon on the equator was already fifteen degrees below the freezing point of water, why seek out colder places?

Then the colonists and their machines had gone deeper yet, to explore the natural caverns that riddled equatorial Mars. The pockets had been discovered during the first seismic survey, early in the twenty-first century. The results of that analysis had been greeted with skepticism. Some of the caverns showed on the instruments as ten kilometers across and three hundred meters high. The tunneling colonists confirmed those readings, and learned that the cathedral heights were sustained by pillars and buttresses of igneous rock. They set their excavation machines to work, connecting the caverns by a system of branching tunnels far below the stark and frozen surface. The result was Old Mars, where everyone lived. It nowhere came closer to the surface than one kilometer, and in places the Underworld ranged as deep as seven. But no matter the depth, the populated caverns and burrows never strayed more than one degree—sixty kilometers—north or south of the Martian equator.

And few people saw any reason at all to wander the surface, which called for simple suits but elaborate precautions.

Cold. Arid. Airless. Everything up there was better done by smart machines, comfortable under the steady stars in an atmosphere that was still no more than one-fiftieth of the density of Earth's, and lower yet in oxygen and water vapor. Even the tourists, interested mainly in sight-seeing, confined their attention to the vast grottoes, natural and excavated, of the deep interior. Sunlight was piped in, conducted along loss-less fiber optic bundles to emerge as new miniature suns in cavern ceilings. "Rain" emerged from those ceilings at carefully planned (but seemingly random) intervals. The grottoes had become lush and magnificent, reduced-gravity jungles more riotous than any found on Earth.

With all of this, who needed—or wanted—the surface?

Not Trudy Melford, if Maria Sun could be believed. Melford Castle had been re-located to the Mars Underworld, three or more kilometers down. But now Bey learned that this was not the case. The castle sat only one kilometer deep, as close to the surface as anyone was likely to go. It was also in the extreme north by Martian settlement standards, situated in a previously-empty natural grotto almost seventy kilometers from the equator. The link entry point sat much deeper, ten kilometers closer to the equator.

The castle's location offered another couple of small mysteries for Bey to ponder. If Trudy Melford wanted to explore new forms in the Mars Underworld, why not choose a deep location close to them? She surely had enough money to put her home anywhere that she wished. But she had picked a bleak spot that was by Martian standards far from the comforts and company of civilization, and farther yet from the Underworld. She must have been forced to install her own air compressors and light pipelines, and then grow the vegetation to make the Melford grotto hospitable rather than merely habitable. The committee that controlled the living space of Old Mars should be paying Trudy, rather than the other way round.

The car they were in followed its own programed route. Their course wound its way through a maze of well-lit tunnels and broad highways. Bey felt the decrease in air pressure and knew that they were steadily ascending. He saw a handful of other cars and occasional cargo barges, but no settlements. They did not pass through any large grotto or agricultural cavern. Apparently Trudy controlled a private road between Melford Castle and her link entry point.

After her first warm greeting she had not spoken to him. She surely knew that he had not been to Mars for a long time, and understood that he needed time to adjust to the changes. But with the car's snug seating it was impossible to avoid more physical forms of contact. Bey was aware of her hip and warm shoulder, touching his. Her dark hair gave off a faint scent of roses. Jarvis Dommer, up in front, looked straight ahead and was mercifully silent—the result, Bey suspected, of direct orders from Trudy. If she was the Empress of BEC back on Earth, how much more was that the case here on Mars, where the controls on her actions were fewer?

For the past couple of minutes the tunnel had been steadily widening, changing from a two-lane highway to a broad plain of dark rock forty or fifty meters across. A row of floor lights now marked the car's path. The walls and roof of the chamber were far-off and no longer visible.

Then the road illumination ended. The car's lights also dimmed and faded to nothing. Bey was suddenly in limbo. The car's motor was inaudible, but he had the feeling that their forward motion was slowing. He felt a hand on his, and heard Trudy's soft voice in the darkness beside him, "Melford Castle, Bey Wolf. Welcome. I hope that you will choose to remain here for much longer than one day."

It had been carefully staged, of course—whether for him alone, he could not tell. A diffuse light appeared, high and far-off. At first it was like the glow of an Earth sunset, soft-edged and tinged with red. As the car moved steadily forward the light strengthened and changed, to become the white blaze of Mars noon. Bey knew that it was exactly that—piped light, carried in to form a new sun in a cavern roof high above them.

Still there was no sense of scale. That came only when they had moved another half kilometer and Bey could see what lay ahead. Melford Castle had been transported from the Yucatan peninsula stone-for-stone. Walls of white limestone glimmered now in front of him, shining in a light bluer than they had ever seen on Earth. The atmosphere of Mars was thickening—slowly—but the short wavelengths of the solar spectrum still came through here far more strongly than they had ever been seen in Castle Melford's original setting.

Bey had never visited the castle, but he had heard of the eccentric tastes of Ergan Melford, founder of BEC and amateur architect. The topmost blue-and-gold octagonal spire of the fourteen-story, hundred-and-fifty room mansion stretched ninety meters above the castle's foundation. The light source in the roof of the Melford cavern shone high above that.

Bey looked, measured with his eye, and decided that he was in an open space maybe two hundred meters high and two and a half kilometers across. The transformation of the grotto had begun, but obviously it had far to go. Thin lines of greenery petered out a few hundred meters from the castle walls. Beyond them hundreds of machines were at work converting bedrock to fertile soil by seeding it with bespoke bacteria and algae. For at least another few years, oxygenated air must be brought into the cavern—at a price—from supply points deeper in Old Mars.

The car was easing its way silently forward, on a road that in its final hundred meters was bordered by sweet-smelling bushes. It led straight to an arched entrance to the castle itself. And there, in an English-style interior courtyard of cobblestone floor and red brick walls, the car stopped. Jarvis Dommer at once jumped out and disappeared through a wooden door that led inside the ground floor of the building.

Trudy climbed out more slowly and turned to Bey. "Are you tired or hungry?"

He realized that it was only the third time that she had spoken to him since his arrival on Mars. He had to pause and think about the answer to her question. With so many time zone shifts he had little idea what his own biological clock was doing. But improbable as it seemed, less than three hours ago he had been sitting in his living-room on Wolf Island, eating breakfast and staring out at the calm waters of the Indian Ocean.

"Not tired. Or hungry. Suffering from sensory overload, maybe."

"Do you want to rest?"

"That's not why I came to Mars."

"Good. Dommer will find a couple of suits." She saw his expression. "Don't worry, they're not for you and him. They are for you and *me*."

"That's not what was worrying me. What's this about suits? I didn't think we would need them. Why should we wear suits in the Underworld?"

"No reason at all. But we're not going there." Trudy's blue-green eyes glittered. "We're going *up*, Bey, not down—up and up, all the way to the surface."

CHAPTER 7

"I assume it's safe?"

Even shielded by a kilometer or more of rock and twelve hundred kilometers of distance, Bey had felt (or imagined) a planetary surface in massive tumult. Soon it would be much closer.

"Safe as can be. Nothing hits this near to the equator. But it's still spectacular. Wait and see." Trudy stood a step in front of Bey on the spiral escalator, built in oddly-connected discrete segments, that bore them steadily up through a wide shaft in the compacted rubble of the regolith. They had ridden a little rail car to the foot of the escalator direct from Melford Castle, and put on their suits at a way station halfway up the kilometer-long rise. The lock of that station signaled a sharp change in outside conditions. According to Bey's suit indicators the temperature was now twenty below zero and the pressure had dropped to forty millibars. Three hundred meters more, and they would be at the surface.

Bey had asked his question about safety more from curiosity than real fear or discomfort. The suits were lightweight, but for all practical purposes foolproof. He had also been in far stranger and more threatening environments than the surface of Mars—even if that surface had now become one of the most active in the solar system, rivaling Io's sulfur-spitting vulcanism.

The vibration at his feet was certainly not imagined. It brought signals that did not carry well in air so thin. When they emerged onto the surface Bey took one glance at the rising sun to orient himself, then turned north-west.

"Other way." Trudy placed gloved hands on his shoulder and spun him around, just in time to see one to the south. A ball of fire came flaming across the southern sky from west to east. It vanished from sight in twenty seconds. One minute later a brighter flash of crimson light lit the south-eastern horizon. The sky in that direction already glowed with incandescent streaks and plumes.

"Now the other." She had Bey's arm and was turning him again, this time toward the north. "Get ready for the quakes, they come every few minutes."

A second fireball ripped the northern sky, again traveling from west to east. Before it could pass out of sight the shock of an earlier impact was arriving. A surface wave came rippling in from the south and shifted the ground beneath Bey's feet in a double up-and-down that had him swaying and sent the rubble-strewn desert into new patterns of cracks and small fissures.

Bey hardly followed the trajectory of the second object. The ground beneath your feet was not supposed to move like that. He felt much less safe.

"That was a big one." Trudy still had her hand on his arm, steadying him. "Close to maximum size, at a guess."

Which meant it was about a hundred meters in diameter; a rough-edged chunk of water ice, dirtied throughout with smears of ammonia ice, silicate rock and metallic ore, had smashed into the surface and vaporized on impact.

"What's the energy release?" Bey felt a second, smaller ripple of movement.

"About a thousand megatons, for one that size."

Like a really big volcanic explosion back on Earth. Bey was watching events that were equal in energy to several Krakatoa eruptions—except that these were happening every few minutes rather than every few decades. It was the hail-storm of the Gods, with hail-stones the size of Melford Castle hitting the ground at forty kilometers a second; and mortal humans, not gods, were responsible for it.

The chunks of ice had been on their way for a long time. Even with a strong initial boost the journey in from the middle of the Oort Cloud, a quarter of a lightyear out, took a comet fragment at least thirty years. And even with the most precise direction by the Cloudlanders during the first phase of the trajectory, a fragment's fusion motor usually needed a small corrective burn as it came closer to Mars. The specification was a tight one: tangential impact along a due west-to-east line of travel, striking between latitudes twenty and twenty-five degrees north or south of the equator. The thin atmosphere of Mars ablated a little from the bolide, but most of it would make it all the way to the surface and strike at over forty kilometers a second.

Space-based lasers in orbit high above Mars watched for correction rocket malfunction. At the first sign of a guidance problem the fragment would be disintegrated in space, long before it could become a danger to dwellers on the planet.

The rain of comets had begun a century ago and continued ever since. It was slow work. Even with a hundred years of added volatiles from orbit and the help of bespoke ground-based organisms to split oxygen from iron oxide, it took a Martian eye to see much difference in the planet's atmosphere. The water vapor was up to only a thirtieth that of Earth, the oxygen content one fortieth.

The contribution of the comet fragments to changing the Martian day was even harder to appreciate. Arriving tangentially at forty-two kilometers a second, every one made an addition to the planet's angular momentum. Mars was gradually being spun up like a gigantic top, whipped by infalling chunks of frozen volatiles; but a century of impacts had shortened the period by less than a second. If anyone hoped to see a time when the Mars day of twenty-four hours and thirty-nine minutes was reduced to exactly equal that of Earth, they would have to be prepared to live a long, long time.

Bey scanned the horizon. The sky to both north and south was streaked and filmed with white haze. Most of the added dust and water vapor in the air came not from the comet fragments themselves, but from surface *ejecta*, vaporized rocks and permafrost of the upper few hundred meters blown high into the stratosphere.

As a spectacle it was astonishing, just as Trudy had promised. But since Bey was strictly an amateur in all science except his own form-change specialty, it was clearly not the reason for the trip to the surface. He was not surprised when she nodded to him and started to walk across the powdered and rubble-strewn surface. As he caught up with her he noticed that the ground was not quite as desolate as it seemed. The grains of rock were coated with a varnish of dark green. More bespoke organisms, hardened against solar ultraviolet, eking out an existence using dissolved minerals and captured water vapor; their photosynthesis was making its own contribution to the oxygen in the Mars atmosphere.

A surface structure—the first that Bey had seen—lay a hundred meters to the north. An aircar was waiting inside.

"Put up with the bumpiness for twenty seconds." Trudy motioned Bey inside. "After that it will be all right."

Even with outsized tires the run to takeoff was rough.

The landing strip had presumably once been smooth and flat, but continuous ground movement had created pits and potholes ranging in size from fist-sized to big enough to swallow a house. The pressurized car was more than smart enough to note the obstacles and choose a safe course to reach flight speed, but it had less objection than its passengers to sudden swoops and swerves and changes of direction. The promised twenty seconds seemed much longer to Bey before they were at last safely aloft.

Melford Castle had been placed in a location at the extreme northern edge of Martian development. To Bey's surprise they now set a course that took them farther north, due north, toward the danger zone of comet impact. He was paranoid enough to reflect that if he were to vanish somewhere in the broken wilderness below it would be a long time before anyone found him.

Then his sense of humor returned. He was no great prize. It would probably be days before anyone bothered to look for him. But they would certainly search for Trudy Melford. Bey had noted Jarvis Dommer's discomfort when Trudy headed for the surface. Dommer was a company man (Bey knew no worse insult) and the Empress of BEC was his guaranteed lifetime meal ticket. If Dommer had his way he would keep her in a maximum safety environment and coddle her all the time. It must be hell for him, working for someone as independent and impulsive as Trudy.

Bey, on the other hand, approved of her more and more. They had exchanged only a handful of remarks and questions since arriving at the surface, but that was good. He liked people who did not feel a need to talk.

He worried a little about that, too. Start to like a woman, and you became vulnerable to other forces. It had happened to Bey too often in his life for him to pretend that he was immune to manipulation.

Another flash of fire appeared in the sky to their left. This one struck close to the western horizon. Bey realized that if an arriving object was to strike Mars at a west-to-east tangent, it had to arrive close to local sunrise. As the day wore on the turning planet would take them clear of the impact zone until the dawn of the following day. The firework display at this longitude was ending.

He turned to Trudy. "How far north are we going?"

She had been sitting companionably at his side, watching the ground glide past beneath them. She had lifted the faceplate of her suit right after takeoff and motioned Bey to do the same. They were flying low, at no more than three hundred meters.

She shrugged. "I don't know. Sometimes very close to here, sometimes almost all the way to the impact zone. Dawn is the best time."

She did not volunteer any more information on what they were looking for. Bey did not need it. He had guessed. But he was certainly curious to see for himself.

It took another few minutes. Then as they were flying over a broken terrain of rock spires and deep crevasses, Trudy suddenly pointed east. "The Chalice and the Sword. We're in luck. See them?"

Bey stared into the sun. He saw a narrow spire of rock, jutting straight up, and next to it a curious shallow basin forming the top of another rock tower.

"This is one of the best places," Trudy continued. "See? There."

Bey saw nothing. He squinted harder into the rising sun. The ground shadows were long, dark, and confusing, and he needed a few seconds to make out movement next to them.

"Can we land?"

"No. Too rough."

"Can we get closer?"

"Doing it now."

Trudy had taken over manual control. The car banked to the right and descended. Bey leaned forward as they swooped in low, wishing that he had some kind of telescope.

There were five of them. Large-headed, fat-bodied, thick-legged, and bipedal, they bounced across the ground with the long, springing leaps of kangaroos, covering fifteen meters and more at each bound. Chameleon-like, their skins were black on the side that faced the sun, white everywhere else. Good strategy for heat absorption and conservation. Their feet seemed to be both hoofed and clawed, for insulation from the frozen ground and purchase on slippery thawed rock.

They showed no sign of alarm. As the car passed right overhead two of them stopped and stared upward. Bey saw big deep-sunk eyes fringed with thick lashes, bulging noses, and ear cavities with padded flaps that could move to cover them.

Trudy was turning the car to make a second run. But she was going to be too late. Bey saw the five creatures take a last look in their direction, then move toward the shadow of a ledge of rock. One of them gave a little wave as they disappeared from view. The thin Mars atmosphere scattered very little light. Even flying directly above the rock shadow, all that Bey could see below was blackness.

"Is it worth sticking around?" He was hungry for more.

"Not today. When they head out of sight like that it means they don't want visitors."

"How about on foot?"

"That's possible. But not if you stay on Mars for only one day."

Bey shook his head. Trudy had set the bait. Now she wanted to see how firmly he was on the hook. "I have to get back to Earth."

"You realize what you were seeing?"

"Sure. I won't pretend I'm not fascinated. It's a form-change job, no doubt about it—you'll notice that there were no signs of air-tanks, and there's no way that an animal form could adapt so fast to such extreme conditions. Those are humans down there."

"BEC had nothing to do with this."

"I guessed as much."

"But we might like to."

"I guessed that, too. I thought before I came that it would be new forms down in the Underworld, but this is much more intriguing."

"And potentially valuable." Trudy had returned control to the car, which was arrowing back to the south ten times as fast as it had headed out. The ground was a blur beneath them. "Illegal, do you think?"

"Sure." Bey did not bother to offer his personal philosophy: illegal forms were always the most interesting; and legality was often no more than a matter of being willing to plow through the right application process. "The big question is the form-change tanks. Where are they? Where did they get them?"

"I'm more interested in the second question. Either they were stolen from BEC, or they infringe on our patents." The car was already descending for a landing. Trudy reached up to drop her faceplate back into position, but before she closed it she turned to Bey. "I might be willing to reach an accommodation on the question of theft."

She said nothing more. She did not need to. It was a standard BEC strategy. The question of theft would never be pursued—provided that BEC could make the right deal with the developers of the new form.

Bey followed her out of the car onto the raw Mars surface. He peered around him with a new eye. The place when he first saw it had seemed wild, harsh, frigid, and inhospitable. It was still all of those, but now he knew that it was far more. It was *habitable*. Something could live here, something far more interesting than the veneer of tailor-made photosynthetic algae or oxide-breaking microorganisms that clung to the naked rock. He wanted to know a lot more about the Mars surface forms.

Bey had swallowed the bait, all the way down. But he was not about to admit that to Trudy Melford. "Very interesting. Now I have to head back to Earth."

And if she was disappointed at his response, she was not about to show it to him, either. "Of course. But won't you at least stay at the castle long enough to have a meal with me?" She sensed his question before he had time to voice it. "*Alone* with me. I value the services and loyalty of Jarvis Dommer, but not his company."

"That sounds fine."

Bey had traveled a hundred and twenty million kilometers since breakfast, give or take the odd few hundred thousand, using everything from his own legs to the Mattin Link.

He had earned an hour or two off.

Back at the castle Bey realized that Trudy had certainly not given up trying. She dropped him off at a suite on the twelfth floor, suggesting that he relax for half an hour while she changed and gave final instructions for their lunch.

It took him only a couple of minutes to realize that the whole suite he was in had been designed and equipped for Bey's particular taste and convenience. Trudy had not only visited Bey's house on Wolf Island—she had taken careful notes there. Everything from bathroom fixtures to wall decorations had been modeled on what she had seen, presumably with the idea of matching his personal tastes. Trudy didn't want to give him any reason to refuse to stay.

Bey was smiling to himself by the time he had been through every room of the suite. What Trudy did not and could not know was that Bey didn't care what his surroundings were like. He didn't inhabit a material world. The decoration and arrangements of the house on Wolf Island owed more to prior occupants and gifts from friends than they did to Bey's own tastes. The thing that he liked best about this castle suite was the view from his windows, of strange illuminated rock spires and spears that jutted up and down from the grotto floor and roof. And he liked that because it was so totally different from Wolf Island.

Well, it was only money, and Trudy surely had oodles of that. She could afford to decorate a new suite or a new house for a visitor every day of her life and never notice the expense. But what were her own tastes? He would never deduce it from his immediate surroundings.

Bey decided that he had the time and inclination to see the rest of Melford Castle. Particularly, if he could locate them, Trudy Melford's personal quarters.

He left his suite and headed for the nearest elevator. Up, or down? Would Trudy choose to be high up on the fourteenth floor among the glittering spires, like a princess in a fairy-tale, or would she prefer the greater convenience of the lower floors?

The second, if Bey was any judge. She might be the Empress, but she was a highly practical one. Wasted time was no more to her taste than wasted words; which again raised the question as to why she was willing to devote so much of the former to him.

He was no nearer to answering that than he had been before their first meeting on Wolf Island. The Martian surface forms were fascinating, but Trudy Melford had many others working for her who would jump at the chance to come to Mars and investigate them.

Bey arrived at the elevators, changed his mind, and

headed for the stairs. He would still go down, but he wanted to see every floor.

It was impossible to do a thorough job in half an hour, or even half a day. Melford Castle was reputed to have a hundred and fifty rooms. Bey soon learned that this number did not include ante-chambers and bathrooms and interconnecting corridors. There seemed to be subsidiary staircases on every floor, walk-in closets the size of Bey's Wolf Island study in every bedroom, little nooks and crannies everywhere that housed treasure troves of priceless curios of old Earth.

After the first few minutes he gave up the idea of a systematic tour and headed down from floor to floor by the most convenient staircases. By the time he reached the fifth story he had decided that the big surprise about Melford Castle was not its size, or its opulence, or even its odd setting in a Martian grotto. Its principal oddity was its *emptiness*. He had encountered plenty of cleaners and polishers, smart enough to roll out of his way and delicate enough to handle fine silver and eggshell porcelain. But he had met not a single human being, in eight floors of random wandering.

Just who lived here? Not Jarvis Dommer, who spent most of his time back on Earth. Not the BEC research staff, who remained in their superbly-equipped labs.

Bey was beginning to suspect the answer, and to add it to his growing list of mental queries, when he descended a little crooked staircase carpeted with a thick-piled green rug and found himself where he was not supposed to be.

The stairs were not intended for general use. They brought Bey down right into a little changing-room that formed part of Trudy Melford's private wing. He saw the dress that she had been wearing when she met him at the link terminal, dumped unceremoniously on the floor together with underwear and shoes. The launderers would take care of those—they had stood waiting for Bey's clothes until he shooed them away—but logic said that Trudy must be here, probably beyond the inner door of white enamel.

Bey was clearly in private territory. He should go no farther. He peered at the panties, which he was delighted to see bore a repeating printed pattern *Empress of BEC*. Trudy had a sense of humor. How many people got to appreciate this particular demonstration of it? He went to the white door.

It was still another ante-chamber, or maybe a study. A great wooden desk stood in one corner and the walls were lined with old paper books. Bey started for them—books were one of his own addictions—but he paused halfway. On the wall by the desk hung a series of framed pictures. One showed a baby, fat-faced and frowning at the camera. The next was the same child with a little more dark hair. This time it was smiling. In the final image it was clear from the clothing that the baby was a boy-child. But the same picture was black-edged, and bore along its lower boundary the grim legend: *Errol Ergan Melford. In Memoriam, sweet baby. Sleep in peace.*

Bey knew that he had intruded on a very private place. It was almost a relief when the inner door opened and Trudy Melford emerged. She saw Bey, gasped, shivered, and looked around her before she spoke.

"My God, you startled me. Where did you spring from?"

"I didn't feel tired. I thought I'd look round the castle."

"But this is my private suite. I mean, I had no idea you were even on this floor. This is my dressing-room. I might have wandered out here stark naked. That's why I was so shocked."

Nice try; but not persuasive. "I'm sorry."

It was the conventional reply. Bey wasn't sorry, not in the least. Trudy had been shocked, no doubt about it, but not at the prospect of being caught nude. She was not far from it now, when she presumably considered herself appropriately dressed for lunch and all she had on was a short and tight-fitting sleeveless blue tunic that left her arms, midriff, and most of her legs and breasts bare.

"I guess you're not used to having people around here."

Now Bey was fishing, but Trudy had recovered her composure. "Not usually. I'm like you. Company is fine, but unless it's with just the *right* person" —those startling eyes stared into his— "it's usually too much of a good thing."

A deliberate distraction, intended to set his mind running along other tracks. Bey decided to play along and see how far it would go. He stared hard at Trudy's body before he offered her his arm.

"I didn't meet anyone on the way down," he said. "Just how private is this place?"

"I'm like you." Trudy slipped her arm through Bey's and snuggled close. "I prefer to live alone. The castle is as private as you want it to be."

So there you have it. Bey allowed Trudy to lead him down one more floor, to a small and intimate dining-room where a sumptuous meal stood ready for two people. The whole fairy-tale. Come and work for BEC on Mars. You will be given more money than you know what to do with. You will face the intriguing challenge of the Martian surface forms. You will live in a legendary castle, in a suite adapted to fit your personal tastes and convenience. And you will if you desire it enjoy the company, bed and gorgeous body of Trudy Zenobia Melford, Empress of BEC.

No one in all of history had ever been offered such a package.

Now for the big question: why was it being offered to Bey Wolf?

✧ ✧ ✧

Although his day was no more than half over, Bey would have bet that there could be no more surprises. He had been given enough of them since breakfast to last a month or two.

He would have lost the bet.

First it was Trudy Melford. She had deliberately dressed to show off her body to Bey, and used words in her private quarters to suggest that it was available to him. But as soon as the meal began she backed off. Although her voice remained warm, everything else about her said that her mind had moved somewhere else. She sounded thoughtful and abstracted, even melancholy.

Bey knew of nothing that he had said to cause the change. There had to be another reason—and he had an idea what it might be. He couldn't wait to get to his data center and begin his own investigations. He ate and chatted about nothing, but as soon as he could politely do so he nodded at Trudy and pushed his chair away from the table.

"That was delicious." (Not really a lie. He had hardly noticed the food, but he was sure that Melford Castle served only the system's finest.) "Now I have to be getting back to Earth."

Trudy came really alive for the first time since they had sat down at the table. "You'll consider my offer?" She was staring at him anxiously.

"I am already considering it."

"If there is anything else that you need to know, or want to add to make it more attractive . . ."

"Nothing. I would like one small favor before I leave. I'd like to place a call to Wolf Island."

"But you said no one is there."

"True. I want to check my message center."

"No problem." Trudy stood up. "You can use my personal communication system." She led the way out of the dining-room and back up to the fifth floor, this time taking the other direction when they came to the top of the stairs. Bey realized that her living quarters must consist of the whole fourth floor. Only blind luck had led him earlier straight into her private dressing-room.

They walked along a hallway filled with Melford family portraits, most of them dark and brooding, until Trudy stopped and opened a paneled door of polished oak. She smiled and ushered him in. "This is it. Make yourself at home. I think you'll be pleasantly surprised."

She stayed outside, closing the door.

Surprised? Bey walked over and examined the console. It was a conventional enough communication system, no better than the one installed on Wolf Island. He sat down and queried for Earth-Mars response time. He expected to see a number around thirteen minutes, the round-trip travel time for bodies that were currently about a hundred and twenty million kilometers apart.

What he got was nonsense. The Earth-Mars response time was cited as 1.5 seconds.

Bey shrugged. If this element of the system was not working, there was a good chance that the rest might be no better. He entered his personal code and sat down to wait for an indication that the query was being relayed through to Earth. Before he knew it, the system was responding. His own ID appeared on the screen and his message center's voice was saying, "There are three messages for you. Do you want to hear them, or do you need some other service?"

"I'll hear my messages. Oh Lord. I get it!"

Sondra Dearborn's face appeared on the screen, but Bey hardly noticed her. He had realized what must be happening. Trudy was making use of her Earth-Mars link to provide signal communications. His outgoing message would be sent to a recorder on Mars, right next to the link; then the recorder shuttled through the link and down-loaded to an Earth-based planetary communication system for transmission to Wolf Island. The response would be stored on the same recorder, shuttled back through the link, and placed into the Mars system. Finally it would be sent on to him.

The process could be done almost instantaneously, since the main reason for delay in shipping humans was the simple need to equalize ambient air pressure. Message units didn't require that. They would operate happily at any pressure, even in vacuum.

Why had no one used the same sort of system for communications on Earth? Simple. Even using satellite relays, the signal delay was only a fraction of a second, and satellite transmission was a lot cheaper than a Mattin link. But there would be a real market when the natural signal travel time was minutes or hours—as Bey knew from experience, there were few things in the world more frustrating than waiting ten minutes for the answer to an urgent question. Trudy Melford had again showed the Midas touch. In opening an Earth-Mars Mattin link for her own convenience, she had tapped a whole new potential market. The United Space Federation would certainly want to use it for urgent USF business.

Bey realized that Sondra was still talking. He had not been listening. He sent his own signal, telling the processor at his house to start over.

It didn't work. She went on talking, and she looked ghastly. He swore, hit the command sequence again, and finally noticed that he was receiving a real-time transmission. It was not a recording. Sondra had somehow managed to over-ride his house system and replace its signal with her own—even though Bey's earlier experience with Jarvis Dommer had led him to make a specific change to rule out that form of interruption.

"Sondra? How did you manage to *do* that?"

There was a delay, of perhaps two seconds. In that interval Bey had another revelation. In the background, behind Sondra's framed head and shoulders, he could see a wall-chart.

He recognized it: it was a taxonomy of form-change routes. He had made the chart himself. And hung it on his own study wall.

"What the devil are you doing inside my house?" he burst out. "You're supposed to be on your way to the Carcon and Fugate colonies."

This time even the two second delay was intolerable, until Sondra finally answered. "Weren't you listening to me at all?" There was horror on her face but no hint of embarrassment. "There's been *another* one—in the same region of the Kuiper Belt." Her voice rose to an anguished squeak. "Bey, I just have to talk with you about this—as soon as you can possibly get back to Wolf Island."

CHAPTER 8

Sondra's mood had changed on her way back to the Office of Form Control. Her meeting with Bey Wolf—or maybe it was her spat with Trudy Melford—had been the final straw. She steadily became more and more angry. She was going to prove she was as good as anyone, in BEC or out of it, when it came to solving form-change mysteries. As for Denzel Morrone, with or without his permission she would head for the Kuiper Belt just as soon as she could arrange a flight. She would do it with her own savings, and on her own time, and to hell with the office.

She did not go to headquarters as she had originally intended, but hurried instead to the apartment that she shared with two other Form Control employees. The place was supremely disorganized—as usual—and locating the must-have items for her trip took a little time. She was still hunting and cursing when her partners in messiness walked in.

"Well?" Gipsy and Dill came into the bedroom and perched on the high stool by the dressing table. They were testing an experimental multiform and had finally reached the stable commensal stage that preceded body cross-over. The combined form watched Sondra as she pawed through a big pile of freshly-laundered clothing, heaped randomly on the floor. "So tell us. How was he?"

"What do you mean?" Sondra knew from the question that Gipsy was speaking, even though the commensal was in Dill's body. Dill herself must be in dormant mode. "How was who?"

"That's what me and Dill are waiting for you to tell us. Who?"

"I don't know what you mean."

"Oh, come off it, Sondra. All of a sudden you get secretive with your friends about what you're doing. You disappear for days at a time without telling anybody, then you come back all wild and woolly like you just spent a weekend with Tarzan. Go look at yourself in a mirror. You're flushed and straggled and wiped out. If that doesn't spell s-e-x, I don't know what does."

"You've got it all wrong." Sondra thought for a moment. She had not told anyone where she was going, but they had known it anyway. Denzel Morrone had reached her easily enough. Secrecy was a waste of time. "I've been to visit Behrooz Wolf. Twice."

"Really?" Gipsy eased Dill's body off the stool and walked over to help Sondra assign the underclothes to their right owners. "The Great Bey himself. We always thought you were kidding when you said he was one of your relatives. I repeat the question with even more interest. How was he?"

"If you're thinking along your usual one-track, I have no idea. We did nothing but talk about the problem that I've been assigned at the office."

"The mystery problem that you can't talk about to *us*. Hmm. But you talk to Wolf—or you think you talk. Let me remind you of something. Studies in Form Control, Lesson Three: *A human being is at least ninety-eight percent subconscious mind and at most two percent conscious mind. The conscious two percent spends much of its time trying to explain, after the fact and in logical terms, what the ninety-eight percent subconscious mind decided to do and did. Speech is a function of the conscious mind. It is impossible for the whole transfer of information during a meeting of two humans, or even the bulk of such transfer, to be limited to speech alone.* You *think* you just talked, but from the look of you Wolf did a whole lot more to you than that."

Sondra had never been too impressed with that particular section of the training course, and Gipsy hadn't quoted it correctly; but she could not forget those intense final few minutes on Wolf Island. "He's not at all the way you're thinking. He's *old*."

"How old?"

"Middle seventies, according to his file."

"And he's dropped his form-conditioning?" Gipsy suddenly sounded horrified. "That's suicide."

"I don't think so. He looks like he takes regular sessions in the tanks. He's strange, but he's not crazy."

"Then he's good for at least another fifty years. Plenty of mileage left in him once you get him going."

"Don't be crude. Anyway, you don't understand. He doesn't *look* old, his form is maybe thirty and very fit. But he *acts* ancient. Cold, and remote and superior, and sort of turned off."

"Maybe women turn him off." Gipsy went wandering across toward the message center as though she had lost interest in the conversation; but one eye was still on Sondra. "Maybe he prefers men."

"No way!" Sondra raised her head and glared. "I'm sure he doesn't."

"Well, if you're *that* sure." Gipsy seemed pleased with herself as she bent over the center. "There's still hope. Hey, don't you ever check for messages? You've had one waiting here for hours."

"From Bey Wolf?" Sondra had not even thought about messages when she rushed in.

"Dream on. It's from the boss. Wonder what dear Denzel wants with you. Like me to call it out?"

They knew Sondra's code, just as she knew theirs.

"Sure. Go ahead."

Sondra moved to Gipsy's side, waiting for the message to be recalled. Typical of Morrone, it was in written rather than oral form.

From: Headquarters, Office of Form Control.
To: Sondra Dearborn.
Subject: Failure of humanity test.

My office received news four hours ago of another unfortunate situation in the Carcon Colony. Offspring successfully passed the humanity test but was proved non-human by its subsequent behavior. This is, as you know, the third such failure, others having occurred in the Carcon and also in the Fugate Colony.

Earlier today I received a query from the United Space Federation via the Planetary Coordinators, asking why there has been no on-site investigation of this case. That question seems very appropriate. It is two months since the case was assigned to you. Why have you not visited either the Carcon or the Fugate Colony in person?

I look forward to your prompt reply and explanation. It will form part of your official record with the Office of Form Control.

—Denzel Morrone, Office Head

"The bastard! The absolute bastard."

"What has he done?" Gipsy could hear rare rage in Sondra's tone. The message meant nothing to her.

"Screwed me."

"Since it's Denzel Morrone, I know you're being metaphorical. Screwed you how?"

"First he refuses me permission to go out to the Kuiper Belt, says it's not necessary. Now he turns around and *blames* me because I haven't already been."

"Covering his ass. See there, he says he had a query from the Planetary Coordinators. Standard creepy-Denzel operating procedure. What are you going to do?"

"Head for the Kuiper Belt and the colonies. But first—"

"Watch it, Sondra. Don't throw your job away."

"It's all right. I'm not going after Morrone—that slimy scum can sit and fester until I'm ready to talk with him. But I need help, bigtime. Before I leave I have to take one last shot at Bey Wolf."

"We'll help you pack." The hands and head of the commensal gave a sudden twitch. Dill was awake and had joined the group. "Mm. Looks like I arrived just in time—before you do your usual trick and run off with all my clean underwear."

"I don't know why you worry, Dill." Sondra started to throw bits and pieces into a travel bag. "By the time I get back you should be through body crossover. You won't be my size then—Gipsy will."

One last shot at Bey Wolf. It felt more and more that way when Sondra reached Wolf Island and found it deserted.

She had contacted Bey's message center, just as he had told her to, but only a machine had answered. And when she arrived at the lonely beach after a top-speed flight from the Cocos Islands link point, only the two hounds greeted her.

Sondra grabbed her travel bag and her thin brown satchel of data records and headed along the jetty. Before leaving the apartment she had downloaded everything on the new form-change problem and booked a rapid transit to the Carcon Colony. In less than fourteen hours she had to be at the spaceport and heading for orbit.

She peered at the two mastiff hounds as they gambolled

about her on the beach. Something looked different about them. Or about one of them.

"Here, Janus! Good dog." Sondra grabbed the hound by the collar and made a closer inspection of its underbelly. Hadn't both dogs been *male* on her previous visits? But those nipples told a different story. Janus was now certainly a bitch.

Well, it didn't prove much. Sex-change didn't imply form-change experiments; it could be done easily and routinely with pure chemical treatments. Sondra headed on up the beach.

The house when she reached it was silent and deserted. It was also unlocked and open, as though Bey was either somewhere inside or had stepped away for a few minutes. Just when she urgently needed to see him.

She called his name at the front door. No response. She went inside and called again. After a few more minutes of waiting and prowling the main floor she helped herself to a drink and a sandwich—it felt like days since she had eaten.

Still no sign of him.

Maybe he was in his basement lab. Retired or not, he certainly spent a lot of time there, and it might be pretty well sound-proof. Feeling like an intruder—but even more impatient and annoyed at the owner's absence—Sondra descended to the house's lower levels. There she confirmed the impression of her earlier visit: the basement's form-change tanks had seen some odd modifications, surely put in by Bey, but they were as sophisticated as you would find anywhere. Unfortunately there was no sign of the man himself.

She returned to the main floor and went back to the message center. The lights were blinking. One of the messages would be from her. Maybe one of the others would tell where Bey was, and when he would be back. She reached out one hand, then stood dithering. She had no right in the world to read Bey Wolf's private mail. But time was short, and she couldn't afford to waste it.

A difficult decision was avoided when the machine became active without any touch from her. She found herself staring at Bey's startled image on the display.

The surprise was mutual. Sondra pressed the transmission button and started to explain why she was inside Bey's home, but before she was halfway through he cut her off. He didn't sound impatient. Just super-furious.

"Wait there," he snarled. "And don't touch anything else in my house!"

It was an order, not a suggestion. Sondra opened her mouth for a second try at explanations and found that he was gone. As his image faded she made a quick check for the point of origin of the call. The reply was a stream of unfamiliar numbers. Bey was making a call from a point outside the whole communication system. He could not be anywhere on the land surface of Earth, or within its oceans.

Wait, he had said. But for how long? Where was he? She had to be on her way to the Carcon Colony in just a few hours.

Sondra grabbed the brown satchel of data records and went back to the terminal. Bey's order not to touch presumably did not apply to general computer access. She loaded her new data from the colony and began to study it.

The story was by now familiar. A new-born infant, strange in appearance even by colony standards, but given as always the benefit of the doubt (some of the system's finest minds had emerged from the womb looking like teratomas). The standard humanity test, and its successful passage. And then the horror, as the supposed human was shown to be pure animal, incapable of reason, incapable of learning, capable only of savagery.

Sondra peered at the most recent failure. This one did not look like a ferocious beast. It was placid and unresponsive, dull and unmoving. Staring at it she was able to ask a question that the horror of the other two failed forms had blanked from her mind. Here was a non-human result of human couplings. Random mutation would always produce such a genetic mistake from time to time; but what were the odds of such a result? If it were more common here than elsewhere in the system, the problem lay in the physical environment of the colonies, forcing mutations faster than elsewhere. She pulled the statistical data files and made the comparison. The mutation rate was indeed unnaturally high.

But that merely created two mysteries in place of the original one. Why were mutation rates higher in these colonies, leading to the birth of non-human babies? And then, if that could be explained, why were the humanity tests *passing* those non-human creatures, insisting that they were in fact fully human?

Sondra struggled on, comparing the Carcon Colony records with those of other colonies. Once she got into the swing of it the work was surprisingly interesting. She was amazed when she heard the outer door slide open and looked up to find that more than three hours had passed since she sat down.

It could hardly be Bey—only a few hours ago he had not been anywhere on Earth. She jumped up and hurried through to the entrance hall.

It couldn't be Bey; but it was. He was glaring at the table with its leftover food and dirty crockery.

"Nice to see you made yourself at home."

She had intended to give instructions to the cleaners to take the dishes away, then forgotten to do it. "I'm sorry. I had to come. There's been another one—Carcon Colony again."

"So you said." Bey hardly seemed even mildly interested.

"You know what I told you last time you were here. Go out to the Kuiper Belt. My advice hasn't changed—and don't bother trying to show me what the failed form looks like this time, because I told you that externals are useless."

"I'm heading for the colony in just a few hours. I'm not on Wolf Island to talk about the new form."

"So why are you here?"

"To ask you to do what only you can do. I want you to make a call to Robert Capman on Saturn. What's happening in the colonies might be just the beginning. Suppose that it spreads and affects form-change everywhere?"

"I don't think that will happen."

"You have fewer facts about it than I do."

"My opinion isn't based on fact. It's based on intuition—what's left after fifty years of facts have all evaporated."

"Intuition can be wrong. One quick call, it would be so easy. Won't you please call Capman?"

"No. I'll do something better." Bey walked across to the message center and sat down at it. After a few moments of interaction he turned to glance over his shoulder at Sondra. "I'll warn you, you might not like some of what you are going to see and hear."

The two-way record of an earlier call was being drawn from memory, appearing split-screen in the display volume. The right side was Bey Wolf himself, in profile. The other showed a chamber filled with swirling greenish-yellow gas.

Sondra guessed it, even while the chamber was still empty. "You already called him!"

"Right. I had an hour to kill at the last link point before I could fly back to the island. Here he comes."

The general appearance of the figure who emerged from the green mist in the left side of the display was familiar to Sondra, as it was to everyone in the solar system. She stared at the broad skull, dominated by the Medusa of ropy hair, the jeweled eyes with their nictitating membrane, and the wide, fringed mouth. Below it sat a massive, wrinkled torso, with a smooth central panel that changed constantly in color and could be used to send or receive data to another Logian a thousand times as fast as any human transfer. The arms jutting from the heavy shoulders were powerful, long, and triple-jointed.

Sondra had read and heard a lot about the Logians. But like most humans she had ever met one. With the whole of Saturn off-limits and the Logian forms showing no interest in living anywhere else, Bey Wolf was a rare exception in his Logian experience and his access. Sondra did not even know how deep the Logian forms lived within the atmosphere of the gasgiant planet, and she suspected that the information was available only to a chosen few.

The great grey-skinned figure sat down and bobbed its head forward, in what Sondra knew to be a Logian smile. "Hello, Bey. It has been a long time. I received your call just minutes ago. Something interesting, you said."

"Possibly." The icon of Bey in the display volume sounded more cautious than Sondra had ever heard him. She could not tell one Logian from another, but the other shape in the split viewing volume could only be the transformed Robert Capman. "It is unusual enough that at least I thought you might want to hear about it. Problems with the humanity tests."

"Ah." The broad head nodded. "We have certainly seen that before. Continue, if you will."

"I'm going to edit. Stop me if at any point you want more details." Bey in the display volume leaned back and started to talk. After a few seconds Sondra realized that she was hardly understanding a word. He was employing a cryptic, compressed vocabulary that seemed to reject discussion of specific form-change in favor of a general definition of envelopes of the physically possible.

Whatever he was saying, it apparently went down well with Robert Capman. The Logian form offered not a word of comment until Bey was finished. And then what he did say seemed to Sondra to come from a wholly unexpected direction.

"Describe to me the individual who has been assigned to resolve the problem."

(Bey, standing at Sondra's side, shrugged. "You won't like this bit, Sondra.")

The icon of Bey Wolf seemed startled by the question as it replied: "Her name is Sondra Dearborn. She has a decent theoretical background, but very limited practical knowledge. By conventional measures she is not much above average intelligence, although I realize that neither you nor I place much stock in that parameter as a useful guide to achievement."

"Do you give her high marks in any field?"

"If we agree that stubbornness is a field for which marks can be given, yes. She is also young, hard-working, and enthusiastic. And she cannot be suborned."

"Do you believe that the last fact is relevant?"

"I do. And I believe that it was not realized by her superiors when she was assigned to the case. I also believe that they had no idea that she would seek help from me."

"Do you know what that implies?"

"I do."

"Intriguing." Capman was rubbing at his ropy locks. "Most intriguing. This is not relevant to the present discussion, but on some future occasion I would like to meet Sondra Dearborn."

Sondra had sat up rigid when she heard her own name mentioned, and the last comment made her shiver. To meet with Robert Capman, the senior deity of form-change! She had found it hard to evaluate some of the other exchanges she was hearing, but it was clear that Bey was telling Capman something he did not want to say outright.

Capman's next words seemed to confirm it. He had allowed his head to sink onto the great chest, and his eyes were covered by a milky membrane. "As you know very well, Logians do not interfere in human affairs. For good reason."

"I understand."

"And I cannot break that rule. I will tell you only what I believe you already know: your intuition has not led you astray. This is a problem which owes less in its origin and its solution to natural events than it does to human actions. And that is all I will say."

"It helps."

"To confirm, rather than to inform." The Logian sat straighter and his head bobbed forward. "And now, are you ready to change to a superior form and come to work with me on Saturn?"

The icon of Bey Wolf smiled and shook its head. "Not yet. Maybe someday."

"The usual answer. Very well." Capman stood up, moving easily in spite of his great mass. "It was good to hear from you again. Have you ever looked into the early history of the theory of elliptic functions? If not, you might want to do so. It would possibly enlighten you. Farewell."

The Logian figure nodded and stepped away into the mist. A starred icon in the display region showed that communication had been terminated.

To Sondra, the final comment had been even less intelligible than Bey's remarks. After looking forward for so long to hearing from Robert Capman, she felt bitterly disappointed.

"Is that all we get?"

"It's more than we have any right to expect. You heard

Capman and you know the Logian policy: they realize they are far smarter than humans, but they refuse to do our thinking and decision-making for us because they say it's bad for the human species. He was already stretching it in what he told us."

"He didn't tell us one thing!—not that I could understand."

"Wrong. He went out of his way to give us information. I think I got most of it."

"Why did he say he wants to meet *me*?"

"There I'm as puzzled as you are. That's one thing I didn't understand at all. I've got to think about it."

"And what was that weird comment about studying the history of elliptic functions? It had nothing to do with anything."

"It didn't seem to. But I believe he was revealing far more to us than he should have."

"Elliptic functions are some sort of math. Are they something else, too?"

"Not that I know of. That's not the point. Capman was giving an important clue, sure as I'm standing here. You just have to learn how to interpret it."

"I can't do anything—I head for orbit in just a few hours." Sondra glanced at the clock. "In fact, I should be leaving right now. Can't you work on this while I'm gone?"

"I admit that I'll certainly *think* about it—I've been doing that ever since I spoke to Capman, I can't help myself." Bey turned off the display unit and began to call other files from storage. "But let me point out again what I've told you over and over: this is *your* project, not mine. I have other things to do."

"But you'll be here if I need to talk to you?"

"Probably not. I think I'll be on Mars."

"Working for Trudy Melford?"

"That, and doing some other things."

"You're selling out!" Sondra felt a hot rush of anger, fierce and inexplicable. "You're going to be just like everyone else and let that bitch Trudy Melford own you body and soul."

"Body if I get lucky. Soul I doubt. Look at it that way if you want to." Bey quietly went on working at the terminal.

His calm was almost more maddening to Sondra than her own strange anger. "You won't help me—because I can't *afford* you!"

"Exactly right." Bey lifted his head and gave her a cool stare. "You can't afford me, Sondra, and Trudy can't afford me, and nobody can afford me. Because I'm not for sale. And I *am* helping you, ungrateful as you seem to be." Bey turned from the terminal with a program card in his hand. "This is a diagnostic routine of my own devising. It is better than anything you will find in the library of the Office of Form Control. Use it on the form-change programs in the Carcon Colony. My bet is that you will find the source of the problems there is a simple software malfunction."

Sondra took it without a word.

"Second," went on Bey, "I can be reached on Mars, or anywhere else, by using Wolf Island as a relay point. My access code is written on the same card. Third, you will find on the same card your introduction to a Cloudlander called Apollo Belvedere Smith. He is currently working in the Kuiper Belt. Aybee is an old acquaintance of mine. I strongly recommend that you visit him before you go to the Carcon or Fugate colonies. My letter asks him to help you."

Sondra looked at the card she was holding. "Why are you doing all this for me?"

That stimulated Bey's biggest sign of emotion since he had seen the dirty dishes. He growled at her, "Make up your mind, Sondra *Wolf* Dearborn. You keep insisting that you are my long-lost relative. Do you want me to help, or don't you?"

"I do. I *need* help. Thank you, Bey." Sondra had to force the words out. Her own feelings were too complex to fathom. *It is impossible for the whole transfer of information during a meeting of two humans, or even the bulk of such transfer, to be limited to speech alone.* "I am grateful for the help, really I am. But I have to go now, or I'll never make the shuttle. And thank you for the introduction, too."

To add a final touch to her confusion, he was now smiling at some private joke. "Maybe you should wait until you meet Aybee before you thank me for that."

"Why? what's wrong with him?"

"Wrong? Nothing at all. Aybee is a genius in mathematics and physics. A good guy, too." Bey beamed at her. "The rest, I think I'll let you find out for yourself."

CHAPTER 9

Anyone who believed that time proceeded at a uniform rate had to be crazy.

Bey sat alone in his living-room, cupped his chin in his hands, and gazed out at the red day's-end splendor of an Indian Ocean sunset.

Today was a perfect example of the time problem. Since breakfast he had linked to Mars, wandered its surface with Trudy Melford, explored the interior of Melford Castle, and been actively recruited with an offer that came close to seduction.

All that, by mid-afternoon. Then came the return to Earth, the conversation with Robert Capman at the link exit point, and finally the meeting with Sondra before she rushed off to the North Indian spaceport.

All of this strange, and all worth thinking about. He knew now, for instance, how the Logians could send and receive messages instantly anywhere in the solar system. It had to be done by establishing a virtual link, similar to the link that Trudy had set up between Earth and Mars but somehow without the use of a physical link chamber.

He was no closer to understanding Capman's comment about elliptic functions, but he knew Robert Capman, and a little of how the Logian mind worked. That provided at least a starting-point for exploration. He would turn the problem over to his subconscious, and let it go to work while he worried about more immediate issues.

Immediate issues, like Sondra's new data about the peculiar failed form on the Carcon Colony. She had left a copy for him and it deserved at least a quick inspection. No help from the subconscious mind there, at least not until he had done the hard grind through a mass of detail.

Strangest of all, though, was the event that did not happen.

The car that had carried Bey from Melford Castle to the Mars link point was automatically controlled. Since the trip demanded no attention on his part he had time to look all around, including behind him, and to notice that he was being followed by another car for the whole second half of the trip.

At the link embarkation point Bey got out of his car and waited. The second car stopped fifty yards back. A short red-headed man with a bushy red beard stepped out and stood looking in every direction except at the car in front. When Bey headed for the transition zone, the other man trailed along behind. When Bey moved into the transition chamber itself, the man came closer.

But they had reached the point of no return. Bey heard the sudden blare of a siren and a loud warning message from hidden speakers: *This chamber will seal in twenty seconds for air pressure and composition modification to Earth standard. Anyone inside when this chamber is sealed will be linked to Earth. LEAVE NOW, OR BE LINKED TO EARTH.*

The man hesitated on the far side of the threshold. He lifted one hand toward Bey; and then the door between them slid into position with a hiss of finality.

It could be some form of Mars Underworld security, making sure that a visitor did not stray into dangerous areas—parts of the deep Underworld certainly had a bad reputation. It could be a BEC employee, sent by Trudy to make sure that he got to the link point without difficulty. It might even be a BEC act undertaken without her knowledge, Jarvis Dommer perhaps making sure that Bey was out of the way before he sought his own session at Melford Castle.

The last explanation was the most plausible. Bey had worked most of his life in a big organization, and he knew the ferocity of fights over turf and guaranteed easy access to the boss. But the red-bearded man's final wave of the hand didn't fit any of the possibilities. He had actually *wanted* to talk to Bey, but he had made his move a little bit too late. By implication, he was unfamiliar with the mechanics of the Earth/Mars link.

Bey sighed, and stared unseeing at the vanishing rim of the setting sun. Plenty to think about, and no clear place to begin.

So make it chronological order. First things first.

Bey stood up and went over to his main data center. He tapped into the general banks and began his search. It took less than fifteen minutes to be sure that he was getting nowhere. Every key-word that he could think of came to a blind end. At least that explained why he had never heard before of the event that interested him.

It was time to consult an insider. Bey called Maria Sun's old number at BEC and waited impatiently while the system tracked her to her present location.

She appeared on the imager frowning and rubbing her eyes. Her usually perfect make-up was smeared and she was dressed in an exquisite but rumpled brocaded robe. She nodded blearily at Bey. "What's at?"

"Hi, Maria. I'm sorry. I didn't realize it was the middle of the night for you."

"It's not." She yawned and stretched. "Park Green came by. He heard I retired, so last night he dropped in from

Luna City and dragged me off partying. The man's a lunatic. I just got back. Tell me what you want quick, so I can get some sleep."

"I need another favor."

"Yeah? I'm keeping count."

"Trudy Melford. Is she married?"

"Isn't, never was. Why, are you getting ideas?"

"Not the ones I need. How about children? I saw a picture of a child in her rooms. The name on the picture was Errol Ergan Melford. I wondered about his relationship to Trudy."

"You went to her rooms in Melford Castle? You *are* getting ideas."

"The border of the picture suggested that the child was dead. I never heard anything about a Melford baby."

"No. You wouldn't." Maria pursed her lips and thought for a while before she went on. "It's a sad story, and I'm not sure I should be telling it. You might say it's something from the classics: the person who has everything, but fate still steps in and does what it likes to them. Trudy did have a child, a little boy, maybe four years ago. He died when he was just a few months old. People who know Trudy say that death almost killed her, too. She blamed herself."

"Do you know how it happened?"

"Just from rumor inside BEC—the whole thing was hushed up. I guess if you're willing to spend enough money you can switch off media interest."

"I didn't know there was that much money in the whole solar system."

"You're not Trudy Melford. It was apparently a freak accident. Not out in the Belt or Cloudland, either, where accidents are supposed to happen. Here on Earth, of all places. Trudy and the kid and a couple of nurses were on vacation aboard one of the Melford auto-yachts, cruising around the islands in the Aegean Sea. The weather was good, sea a flat calm. Trudy was up on deck, the baby in a carrycrib next to her. Safe as you could get. Except there was a minor sea-floor quake a few kilometers away from the yacht. Not enough to be called dangerous, but enough to cause a big swell with no warning. The yacht rolled, the crib slid across the deck and tipped over the rail. Trudy and one of the nurses saw it happen, they jumped in after it. Got the crib, got the blanket. But no baby. Never found the body."

"Terrible. Where was the father?"

"Wrong question. You mean, *who* was the father. Trudy wasn't saying, and as far as I can tell no one ever found out."

"Any suggestions?"

"Sure. Sperm bank."

"The old Melford tradition."

"Right. Keep the line pure, don't admit outsiders into the family. That's another reason you shouldn't get ideas." Maria was studying him. "What's happening, Bey? You've gone cross-eyed."

"That's because I finally *am* getting ideas. Not the sort you think, either. Thanks, Maria."

"Any time. Now I need sleep. Be careful, Bey. You're playing out of your league."

"I'll remember that."

As Maria vanished, Bey wondered what league she put him in. The league of cynical opportunists? The league of retired, over-the-hill form-change specialists? The league of nostalgic, backward-looking literature buffs?

Certainly not the Trudy Melford super-rich beautiful-people power-players league. Still less the league of love's young dreamers. Maria might cast Bey in many roles, but that of Trudy Melford's soul mate was not one of them.

He remembered Maria's earlier comment. *Whatever Trudy wants . . .*

Except, maybe, the one thing that she had wanted most. And Bey could in no way see himself as a baby substitute.

What *did* Trudy want from him?

CHAPTER 10

Civilization ends at Ceres.

Or should that be Saturn, Pluto, or Persephone? It all depended how deep you lived within the solar system. But when you came this far you'd better stop having thoughts like that—or at the very least, keep them to yourself. Out here, the inhabitants of the Outer System tended to see things the other way round.

Sondra glanced at the ship's indicator board. All the familiar worlds of the inner system lay far behind. She was moving into the unknown—to her—region of the Kuiper Belt, three hundred and some astronomical units from the Sun, where a really "large" habitable object was a celestial peanut no more than fifty kilometers across and had a mass maybe one ten-millionth of the Earth. The preferred forms of the region were as alien to Earth humans as their preferred habitats. Half the hundred passengers on the hi-vee vessel *Serendip* had entered the form-change tanks before breakout from Earth orbit. They were intending long stays in the Kuiper Belt, or even farther off in Cloudland, and they wanted to make their personal form adaptation as soon as possible.

Sondra watched the first of them as they emerged from the tank compartment, and wondered again if she was really suited to a job in the Office of Form Control.

As a specialist she ought to be comfortable with and sympathetic to all legal forms; but the Cloudland standard, with its skinny elongated torso and arms and diminutive legs like a cross between a stick insect and a starved giant albino ape, left her profoundly uncomfortable. The hairless, eyebrow-less head on the stalk of a neck didn't help. But no one else seemed to notice.

By the time of the docking with Rini Base it was Sondra herself who seemed the oddity. Everyone else on board had changed, with the exception of the crew who would fly the circuit of the Belt and then head back for the inner system. Sondra noticed the stares of the other passengers as she disembarked and peered around her looking for Apollo Belvedere Smith.

Bey Wolf had described him to Sondra before she left. Typical of the man and his twisted sense of humor, Bey had not bothered to point out that his striking description would fit every second person in the entry lobby. Sondra stared around in bewilderment, until a great, gangling figure appeared from nowhere at her side.

"Hey! You gotta be Sondra Wolf Dearborn." He was grinning down at her, white teeth and deep-set brown eyes in a skeletal face. "You're little and fat enough, I'll admit that, but you don't look nothing like the Wolfman. Thought you're supposed to be his relative?"

"*Distant* relative. I presume you are Apollo Belvedere Smith?"

"Presumed correct. 'Cept everybody calls me Aybee." He was staring at her now with even more interest. "*Distant* relative, eh? Well, that explains a lot. Come on."

"A lot about what? Where are you taking me?" Sondra hurried after him, uneasy in a gravity field that varied at every point.

"Gotta educate you, the Wolfman says." Aybee glared

at her, as though questioning whether that was possible. "Teach you stuff about the Kuiper critters you'll never find in books. Well, there's lotsa that. You'll see."

If the Rini Base was anything to go by Sondra was seeing it already. That changing gravity field, she knew, could only be the product of kernels, the shielded black holes that formed the home of the Rinis after whom the base was named. According to Bey, Aybee Smith had actually been the first person to understand that the Rinis were a living and intelligent life-form, inhabiting the bizarre and unreachable interior of the kernels. Rini Base (RINI—Received Information Not Interpretable, the human first impression of the inscrutable life-form) had been established specifically to study them. It held the system's biggest concentration of kernels, communication links, computer hardware, and raw brains. Looking around her, Sondra could understand hardly anything of what she was seeing.

"Don't let it get to you, Wolfgirl." Aybee had noticed her confusion. "No need for you to cotton any of this. You're not staying here, you're heading first thing in the morning for Meatland."

"The Carcon Colony . . . meat? I thought they favored inorganic components . . ."

"They do. I mean meat*head*land. I've looked at the results of their work. Useless. All right!" Aybee had somehow navigated his way through an incredible jumble of equipment to an open space where an empty desk and chair sat in isolated splendor. "Here we are—my office."

"No computer? No data tap?"

"No way. They're crutches for people whose heads don't work right." He motioned Sondra to a seat, while he prowled up and down. "We'll use a display when the time comes. First, though, tell me how old Wolfman is doing."

"He's doing fine." Sondra gave the conventional reply, then had second thoughts. "Except that he really isn't. He retired, you know."

"I heard that. Bad deal. You shouldn't have let him."

"I had nothing to do with that."

"Glad to hear it. He's not an idiot, you see, like most people."

"You're not the only one with that opinion. Gertrude Melford thinks so, too."

"Trudy, the one and only."

"You know about her? Anyway, she's trying to hire him."

"What for?"

"I hesitate to speculate." Sondra bit back her next catty remark. "But I don't think retirement's good for Bey. He's acting *old* now, really ancient since he left the Office of Form Control."

"Physically old? You been wearing him down?"

"*Mentally* old."

"No worries. Don't let him fool you. He does that on purpose. His mind's as young as yours—and I bet it works a whole lot better. But I got a question for you. What's the Wolfman have to say about *me*?"

"He says you're brash, arrogant, opinionated, and insensitive."

"Ah." Aybee smiled beatifically. "That was the old me. *Before* I had sensitivity training."

"But for some strange reason he seems to like you."

" 'Course he does. Why wouldn't he? Just a mo, though, I have to do one thing before we get down to your business. Got a personal call waiting."

Aybee sat down on top of the desk and fiddled with a dark band on his left wrist, while Sondra wondered what she was supposed to do now. He'd said it was a personal call, but she had nowhere to go. She stared around at the jumbled piles of cabinets and cables that formed the barrier of his office, and decided that it was his own fault if she overheard private discussions. She heard a discreet buzz of comment from the wrist set, then Aybee's loud reply.

"Sure, Cinnabar. I did it already. It's on the way."

Cinnabar? If that was Cinnabar Baker, Sondra was impressed. Baker was the most powerful person in Cloudland. And Aybee Smith was on an easy first-name basis with her. What else about Aybee was Bey allowing Sondra to find out for herself?

"Sure, she's right here." Aybee winked at Sondra. He seemed to have his own idea of a private conversation. "I told you she was coming. That's why I'm gonna be *incommunicado* for a few hours." And then, after an inaudible comment from the other end, "I dunno, he never told me. The usual reasons, I guess. You know the Wolfman and his bimboes, seems he's as bad as ever."

Bimboes. Sondra didn't bother with the rest of the conversation. She sat and seethed, waiting until Aybee fiddled again with the band on his wrist and she heard the beep of a severed connection.

"Is that what Wolf told you?" She was up out of the chair and standing right in front of him. "That I'm a bimbo? That he and I are—are *sexual partners*?"

"Hey, don't get your knickers in a twist. The Wolfman never said one word like that. Never even hinted at it."

"So why did *you* say it? 'Wolfman and his bimboes!' You and your sensitivity training."

"Don't knock the training. Maybe it don't work for everything, but it sure works for some things. The Wolfman never said one wrong word, never talked about you—but I listen to what *you* say, and the way you say it. That means more than the words."

"Bullshit! I never said a thing."

"All right, all right." Aybee held up his arms, enormously long and thin. "You never said a thing, agreed. Forget I spoke. We got work to do. Can't do it when you're up in the air."

"I am not up in the air." Sondra made a tremendous effort and lowered her voice to a normal speaking level. "Aybee, I came here to do a job and I am going to do it. I'm not going to let innuendos and insults put me off. We can start as soon as you are ready. But we'll do it with one rule."

"You name it."

"No more talk about me and Behrooz Wolf, okay? No matter what you imagine we're doing and not doing."

"No problem. You got it. To work, Wolfgi" —he saw the danger signal just in time— "Sondra. I promise you, by the time you leave here you'll know more than you want to know about the Carcon Colony."

Aybee's promise was easy to keep. Long before the *Serendip* went spiraling out around the Belt toward the independent colonies, Sondra had decided that she knew far more than she ever wanted to know about the dreadful Carcons.

"Carcon horribilis," in Aybee's phrase. His coaching had a special style that took some getting used to. Always he said it clearly, always he said it fast, and always he said it *once*. At first that wasn't too bad, because what he was offering was more like a refresher course. Sondra had heard most of it before.

"Except you were probably told it with an Earthside spin." Aybee wouldn't sit down. He prowled backward and forward, never looking once at the imaging area where a sequence of tutorial materials would appear for a few seconds and then flash off. "There's a Cloudland joke for you. It shows an Earthling's view of the solar system."

The imager displayed a cartoon. A substantial Earth sat at the center of the frame, its continents clear and labeled. Next to it, quite a bit smaller, sat Mars, Ceres, and the moons of Jupiter. Saturn was a little misty ball with a Logian head sticking out from the mist. Far away at the edge of the image area, sketched at about a tenth the size of Ceres, little vague patches were labeled "Kuiper Belt," "Kernel Ring," and "Cloudland."

"Whereas if you drew it to physical scale it would look like this."

The cartoon changed. At first sight Cloudland filled the whole scene, a vast spherical array of tiny dots. The Kernel Ring sat at the center, a little flat torus only a tenth as wide as Cloudland. The Kuiper Belt lay within that, a tenth as small again. Finally the planets of the solar system, everything from Mercury out to Persephone, formed a little bright dot at the very center.

"But empty space isn't the important thing." Sondra felt obliged to protest. "It's *people* that count. The whole Oort Cloud is nearly empty."

"You bet. Let's hope it stays that way." Aybee was a true Cloudlander. "Now, you'll notice one other thing. In neither the Earthside nor the Cloudland view of things do you see the independent colonies. They're little, unimportant to the big guys. But that's where you're going, so they're important to you. Let's take a look at 'em."

The imager was gradually zooming in. The outer parts of Cloudland vanished from the edge of the image volume. The zoom continued, and soon the Kernel Ring was gone. The Kuiper Belt filled the screen, another donut shape with Rini Base marked as a dot on its inner left edge.

"The independent colonies." A blurred patch appeared on the right hand side of the Belt. "Independent why? Because they fight to stay that way? Nope. Independent, because nobody in either the inner or the outer system wants to lay claim to a bunch of worlds inhabited by raving loonies. We'd both rather disown 'em."

"Aybee, they can't *all* be crazy."

"Maybe not, but they come close. Trust me. I've been there. There's nearly three hundred independent colonies, three fifty if you count the far-gone ones who won't even talk to anyone else in the system. You only need to know about a couple of them, but you should see one or two others to get the flavor. I'll save Carcons and Fugates 'til last. Here's a goodie for you to start with. Be thankful you won't be visiting the Socialists."

The imager displayed the interior of a hollowed planetoid. A pink caterpillar stretched its way along most of the inner surface. It took Sondra a few seconds to realize that the segments of the caterpillar were individual humans, bloated in body and with each one's arms and legs partially absorbed into the next section. Their heads were atrophied except for the very front segment, where a huge naked cranium with bulging white eyes swiveled on a long stalk of a neck.

"The Wolfman developed multiforms," said Aybee. "He was smart and he did it right. This shows what happens when you're dumb and do it *wrong*, try to use regular form-change methods to achieve form fusion. I give the Socialists another ten years. There there'll be no more problem."

"They'll give up?" Sondra felt nauseated.

"Never. The Socialists are all true believers. They'll exercise their right to die. There used to be eighty thousand of them. Now they're down to about twelve hundred."

"That's terrible."

"Nah. It's evolution. Non-survival of the unfittest. Evolution never quits, even in the independent colonies. Their multiform dies off from the back. See?"

It was obvious once it was pointed out. At the tail end of the caterpillar the bodies were shriveled and brown and the heads had almost disappeared.

"Mind you," Aybee went on cheerfully, "the Socialists haven't done bad by independent colony standards. Some of the real losers went dodo-bird inside five years from colony formation. Not this next lot, though. They've been around for a long time. How'd you like to live in Heaven?"

Another image was already on the display. It showed a great hall, filled with gaudily-dressed men and women who whirled and swayed to the sound of a stately waltz provided by a score of musicians on a dais at the side of the room. Laughter and animated chatter competed with the music.

"Happy, healthy, and rich." The display zoomed in on one couple, a man and woman a head taller than everyone else. "Especially the king and queen." Aybee glanced across to see Sondra's reaction. "What do you think? Look like a good place to live?"

"It looks like a great place if you like dancing and ceremony. Which I don't."

"Good for you. Me neither. But most people do. They think it's the way Heaven ought to look. This one was started a century and a half ago by Tomas Dicenzo. He was a religious leader back on Earth who used Biblical arguments to prove to his followers that by definition Heaven and Earth had to be in different places, so an off-Earth colony out in the Kuiper Belt could actually become Heaven. Tomas was an honest, well-meaning man, and he was lucky enough to lead his flock to a big planetoid rich in volatiles and metals. Under his rule the place was probably as close to Heaven as people ever get. It was a couple of generations after his death before his descendants turned the succession into a monarchy. Then they introduced the Divine Right of Kings. Notice anything odd about them?"

Sondra was studying the scene closely. She noticed that one of the musicians had a withered leg, and another was peering near-sightedly at the music. "They don't seem to use form-change equipment."

"Hey, that's pretty good for a quick look. Maybe you are the Wolfman's relative after all, and not a—" Aybee coughed. "Actually, they do use form-change, but it has to be consistent with their social standing. Notice that the king and queen are taller and better-looking than anyone else, and the courtiers are bigger and healthier than the musicians. Appearance has to fit pecking order. Even so, nobody is really sick or deformed and miserable." There was a flicker of movement behind Aybee, and the display changed to become a blur of white. "*Inside* the palace, that is. It's not so good outside. This particular King of Heaven really likes winter. Keeps it year-round in the colony."

Sondra was looking out across a bleak plain that seemed absolutely flat and endless. ("Curvature optics," Aybee added. "Infinite depth and flat field effects. Pretty neat trick on something only forty kilometers across.") The plain was thickly covered with snow, from whose untouched surface leafless trees jutted black against a white sky. More snow was falling, in big, soft flakes.

It took a little while to see the human figures, struggling along in the middle distance. They were bare-headed and poorly-clad, pushing their way through drifts that already came to their mid-thighs. As the imager zoomed in on them Sondra could see the blue and white of frozen fingers, the starved, twisted limbs that would barely support their owners.

"Gathering fallen wood," Aybee said softly. "Completely unnecessary, of course—Heaven uses kernel and fusion power, like everyone else in their right minds. But the king is a stickler for tradition. There have to be peasants and wood gatherers, and there have to be a few deaths from freezing now and again. That way everyone at the top will know how well-off they are and appreciate the king's bounty. Heaven is a wonderful place to live, see—provided that you're king and queen and live in a palace. Being a courtier isn't quite so good. Fail to kiss the king's ass in the right way, and next thing you know you're stuffed into a form-change tank. You come out short, sick, crippled, and *outside*, begging in the snow for shelter and a meal." He glanced slyly at Sondra. "Still think it would be a great place to live?"

"It's absolutely awful."

"Not for the king. And Heaven is stable, at a hundred thousand people. It could go on that way for another couple of centuries. I'm not sure I'd say the same about the structure of society on Mars or Ceres. All right, enough of the fun stuff. Time we got on with the Carcon Colony. How much do you already know about it?"

"I know when the colony was started, in 2112. I know that its founders set out to create combined organic and inorganic beings, carbon-silicon fusions that would use both human and machine intelligence. I know what the results look like."

"That it? What about history and social habits?"

"Those weren't in the Office of Form Control data bank."

"Then you know nothing." Aybee started to stalk Sondra, circling menacingly around her chair. "The colony moved into the Belt back in 2112, but for nearly a century they just futzed around getting nowhere. They tried to make carcon melds, but there was one slight snag: they all kept dying. Then they had bit of luck. Ever hear of Jonathan Watanabe?"

"Why, yes. He worked for the Office of Form Control, a long time ago. He's used in the training courses as a dreadful warning."

"You know what he did?"

"I know what the record says." Sondra was becoming more cautious. She had a lot to learn when it came to off-Earth activities, and Aybee seemed to take a special joy in playing *Gotcha*! "He ran up big debts and started dabbling in illegal forms to make money. Then he got caught."

"Wrong. He got *found out*, but he never got caught. He made it away from Earth and hid in the Belt—and ended up in the Carcon Colony. Turned out he was just what they needed, because he was able to add modern form-change methods to the carbon-silicon combines. After a few hundred failures and deaths—no big deal, the Carcons were used to that—he hit on the right trick. He made the first successful Carcon intelligence. Happy ending, right?"

"If you say so." It was clear to Sondra that there was more to come.

"Trust me. Happy ending for the Carcons, and even happier ending for BEC. You know the ground rules for a successful form?"

"Better than you do: viable, stable, and legal. I'd add that in my opinion a really successful form must have a decent life-ratio, but that's not a formal requirement. If people want to burn out fast, like the avian forms, that's their choice."

" 'Specially out in the colonies, where everybody's wacky to start with. Anyway, Jon-boy did his thing and hit two out of three. His Carcons have a normal human life expectancy and they're not an illegal form. But they sure has hell aren't *stable*. Leave 'em out of a form-change tank for a few days and *bingo*!, you've got an expensive sort of fertilizer. But form-change dependence is no big deal, when you can always buy more tanks and make sure everybody has one whenever they need it. And it's real good news for BEC—a ton of sales from one small colony."

"How many Carcons are there? How many form-change tanks are you talking about?"

"Rather a lot. There's maybe fifty thousand Carcons—and at least that many tanks." Aybee grinned as though he had just brought Sondra especially good news. "You're going to have real fun out there. You're on your way to form-change paradise."

On the way, and shortly about to encounter paradise at first-hand. Sondra was poised at the entrance lock while the crew of the *Serendip* hovered around, grinning with anticipation. It was not their first run to the Carcon Colony with an unfledged Earthling as passenger.

This time they were due for a disappointment. Sondra stood calmly waiting for the lock to operate, fortified by the knowledge that Aybee, in an attempt either to prepare or disgust her, had shown her one after another of the Carcon forms. Not just the successes, either. There had been plenty of misses even after Jonathan Watanabe had his technique under control, and those failures loomed large in Aybee's catalog of yuckies.

The lock opened. Sondra stared, gulped, and looked away. The ship's crew won. There was a world of difference between viewing a Carcon form in the display volume of an imager, and facing the living, breathing reality.

There had been recent advances—if that was the word for it—in Carcon forms. The man waiting for her at the lock was naked, with no sign of hair on either head or body. His arms and legs carried the odd bulges that she had noticed on the first images she had seen, back on Earth. But in addition to that the whole body surface was covered with bright points of silver, as though thousands of small studs had been hammered into it. The eyes were also bright, silvered, and empty of all expression. The effect was of a human-shaped robot, over which a human skin had been draped and attached by thousands of tiny bolts.

"Dearborn Female? Terran Office of Form Control?"

The voice, cool and expressionless, helped Sondra to regain her self-possession.

"That's right. I am Sondra Dearborn."

"Good. I am Shoals Male. I am eager to cooperate with you. Do you have questions before you proceed to the form-change tanks?"

Aybee had warned her: she would not be given a free run within the Carcon Colony. It was hard to imagine that they might have any secret worth stealing, but the Carcons disagreed.

"I have two questions. First, is the equipment that you use at this colony made by BEC, or are there other manufacturers?"

She did not spell out what that meant, but anyone hearing the question would know what she was getting at. Was this genuine BEC hardware, with all its warranties and guarantees and detailed testing? Or was it a rip-off of BEC equipment, with who-knew-what shortcuts and compromises in design and manufacture.

Shoals stood silent for a long time. Sondra noticed that he lacked eyelids, but a transparent membrane flickered up and down over his naked eye surfaces every few seconds.

"The equipment used with the feral forms that were sent to Earth was all manufactured by BEC," he said at last. "It is new, and it is still covered by warranty."

He had not explicitly answered Sondra's question. There must be at least some pirated designs around in the Carcon Colony, but the only equipment she really cared about was the genuine BEC article.

"And the software?"

"That used with the feral forms was also provided exclusively by BEC."

"None of your own, developed by the colony itself?"

"None of our own is used until the end of the first year."

In other words, not until long after the humanity test on a form was over and done with. Sondra's task had suddenly become orders of magnitude easier. With only standard BEC hardware and software involved, she would not have to worry about whatever strange form-change deviations were practiced to create a form like Shoals'. She felt a moment of huge elation. She knew the BEC systems intimately. In just a few hours of work, she would know exactly what had happened and be ready to go home successful.

"I would like to see complete records of the birth of the feral forms. I would also like to see all form-change records from the time of first tank entry. Raw data, as well as reduced evaluations. Is that going to be a problem?"

Shoals was scowling at her. "I am confused." The skin of his forehead wrinkled upward, emphasizing the absence of eyebrows. "You talk as though two different data sets might be involved. Surely you know that all Carcon births take place within a form-change tank?"

She had not known. Sondra started in to work on the form-change records with Bey's words reverberating as a loud inner voice. *You have to go the colonies and see things at first-hand.*

The only problem with such advice was that Bey had left out a key variable. It was one that would never have occurred to Sondra, either. Carcon Colony visitors from Earth were *rare*. In colony terms she was the oddity, the interesting freak that people wanted to stare at.

While she struggled to analyze data sets and concentrate on complex computer displays, scores of Carcons wandered by just to gawk. They ranged in age from infants, dragging their mobile form-change tanks along behind them, to beings so changed and augmented that Sondra could not even guess at their ages. The prizewinner for oddity was a being of indeterminate gender, who seemed determined to explore the inorganic limit of humanity. Arms and legs were steel-and-silicon prostheses, while the torso was a pleated barrel-shaped tube that breathed vertically. The chest section moved up and down with each breath like an upright concertina. The Carcon stood close to Sondra. It stared at her in apparent curiosity, with eyes compound and crystalline in a shiny cranium of plastic metal.

Strangeness all around. Everywhere—except in the records that she was analyzing. After four hours of work the frustration began. The Carcons were peculiar enough for the most eccentric taste, but their form-change equipment could not be more normal. The tanks that had been used to administer the humanity test to the feral forms were a standard BEC model. The seals were unbroken, indicating that they had not been opened since the day they were shipped from an Earth production plant.

Sondra had next examined the software programs that had been used, reviewing both the intermediate data outputs and the code itself. She had found nothing out of the ordinary, using her own programs or the one that she had received from Bey himself.

The situation was as clear as could be. Sondra reviewed her results:

✓ two births, odd-looking but not much more so than a thousand others born in the Carcon tanks within the past few years.

✓ a humanity test, delivered routinely when the subjects were two months old.

✓ clear passage of the test, without even a suggestion in its results of a marginal case.

✓ total failure, after that first success, to interact in any way with form-change programs.

✓ increasing evidence, day after day, that the forms were not merely non-human, but wild, vicious, and dangerous.

The Carcons, eager to proceed as soon as possible with the modifications needed for any form they would consider satisfactory, had been a little more impatient for results than another group might have been. But that was a detail. If the births and tests had taken place on Earth itself, or anywhere else in the system, the same failure of the humanity test would have been recorded by now.

Sondra didn't like to admit it, but she had reached a dead end—already, so soon after her arrival. The problem was not the peculiarity of the data trail she had followed at the Carcon Colony. It was the *normalcy* that was so frustrating. The remoteness of the independent colony, which led to the feeling that procedures and events would be different here, was an illusion. So far as the purposive form-change needed for the humanity test was concerned, the same results would have been obtained anywhere.

Sondra hated to think about what came next. All this way, after her loud insistence to Denzel Morrone that the journey was absolutely necessary to solve the mystery of the feral forms. And then all the way back, without even a suggestion of an answer.

Worse than Denzel Morrone would be Bey Wolf. He wouldn't harangue her and gloat over her, the way Denzel would. But his quiet nod would in many ways be harder to take than any number of harsh words. She could imagine that nod now, and interpret it— "Just as I suspected. Second-rate brains, she'll never solve it!"

Sondra was suspecting the same thing herself. Somewhere, somehow, she was missing a key insight. Her only hope was that the next stop on her flight path, at the Fugate Colony, would provide it. After what had happened with the Carcons, Sondra didn't have much confidence in that prospect.

CHAPTER 11

On the road again; and not sure where it would lead.

Bey stood within the link zone during the final spasm of transition, and wondered. Trudy Melford had urged him to return as soon as possible to Mars and investigate the surface forms. And here he was, reporting for duty just like any other brain-washed BEC employee.

But what had prompted him to quote to Jarvis Dommer an arrival time one day later than he planned to travel?

Bey could answer that, after a fashion, except that his reply had a great big hole in it—or rather, a hundred thousand holes.

The standard Earth/Mars comparison cliche, still trotted out by USF politicians after centuries of use, was the area logic. Earth is largely a water world. Mars is a smaller planet, but it has as much *land area* as Earth.

Bey had been puzzled by that statement the first time that he heard it. What did total land area have to do with anything? No one on Earth lived at the summit of Mount Everest, just as no one on Mars lived on top of Olympus Mons. No one on Earth lived out on the surface at the North or South Pole. Still less would a sane person try to reside at the Martian poles, where most of the snow was solid carbon dioxide and midsummer was a cold winter's day in Antarctica, minus air. In any case, land *area* was almost irrelevant. Humans inhabit three dimensions, not two, and a large planetoid like Ceres, suitably re-structured in its interior to provide thousands of habitat levels, could in principle be the home of more people than lived on Earth.

The colonists on Mars had known all this. With the aid of their machines they had worked not the harsh surface, but the more tractable interior. It was not difficult for the tunneling machines to connect the gas-filled hollow pockets of subsurface Mars so that chamber led to cave led to cavern. After a century of work, a gigantic, multiply-connected, hundred-thousand node network of living space had been created: Old Mars, fully navigable only with the help of a computer.

The exit point for the Melford link lay close to the surface, above most of Old Mars. Bey, emerging from Immigration, stood motionless and stared around him. There were plenty of people greeting arrivals from Earth, but none showed any interest in a plainly-dressed and silent visitor.

That ought to be enough to prick the bubble of curiosity that had brought him early to Mars. Somewhere within the convoluted maze beneath his feet he might find red-beard, the man who had tracked him from Melford Castle to the Mattin Link entry point. But more realistically Bey would not find the man, no matter how hard he searched. The population of Old Mars was tiny by Earth standards, just a few millions—but a million is a big number. Examine the ID of each resident, one after another, and you would be at it for months. And as Bey knew from his work on illegal forms, there were plenty of people in the deep Underworld whose ID's were, to put it charitably, unreliable.

Bey placed the light knapsack that formed his entire luggage on one of the benches of polished synthetic that lined the link exit chamber. He sat down next to it. He was not happy. His vaunted intuition had led him badly astray. What was he going to do now? Back on Earth, he had made two assumptions: that anyone who had knowledge of his movements during his previous visit to Mars would have just as good information now; and if they had been eager to talk to him then, they would still be just as keen.

One of his assumptions was not valid. No one in the chamber was taking the slightest bit of interest in him. On his last visit Bey had been favored by the presence of Trudy Melford herself, so all the staff had been falling over themselves to offer assistance and advice. Today he was a nobody. He had not invoked the power of the Melford name, and so he was on his own.

Bey leaned back. The bench molded itself to his body. He wondered. What other benefits came to you when you were smiled on by the Empress? Was Trudy Melford's smile just the grin on the face of the crocodile, moments before the jaws gulped you down? Bey recalled a furious Sondra, glaring at him and shouting: "That fancy form she was using, and those sexy clothes. She was *stalking* you, couldn't you tell? If I hadn't arrived when I did . . ."

It was a good thing Sondra had not been at Melford Castle with Bey, to see Trudy's tight-fitting and brief costume and the warm look in those startling blue-green eyes, or to hear the tone in Trudy's voice when she told him that the castle was "just as private as you want it to be."

Bey lolled on the bench, musing on the memory. He lacked the energy to find an auto-car to take him again to the castle. Half an hour passed before he was finally lifted out of his daydream by a loud clatter of footsteps. The man with the red beard had come running into the chamber. He skidded to a halt by the information board about twenty yards away from Bey and bounced nervously up and down on the balls of his feet. He was scanning the entries. His shoulders slumped when he saw that the link transition had been completed a while ago.

Bey walked across to stand beside him.

"You're late," he said quietly.

The man turned. "Yes, I am. I was delayed by the—" He stopped and stared open-mouthed at Bey. "Behrooz Wolf! I thought I'd missed you."

"I hung around. Who are you?"

"My name is Rafael Fermiel." After a few awkward seconds the man held out his hand and smiled at Bey.

Bey grinned back at him. He had never been more pleased to see anyone. He didn't know who Rafael Fermiel was, or what he might want, and for the moment he didn't particularly care. What mattered was that Bey's hunch as to what would happen if he came to Mars had been right after all.

Bey regarded Fermiel fondly while he waited for the next step. He knew that in spite of everything that the form-change machines could do in the way of body maintenance, the urge to sin changed as a person got older. Some sins, like lust, often vanished completely.

Maybe. But in Bey's own case, he suspected that the Sin of Pride would be with him undiminished until the day he died.

"We seem to be going *downward.*" Bey had assumed they would be heading for the surface and a meeting with the new forms who now lived there.

"Certainly we are." Rafael Fermiel nodded as the auto-car they were riding glided its way around a steeply descending curve. "Did you imagine that we might be going *up*? We will be heading all the way to the deep Underworld, where you will meet with the most important party on this planet."

"Trudy Melford?"

It was the wrong thing to say. Rafael Fermiel lifted

his nose in the air, as though he had suddenly encountered a bad smell. "No! Gertrude Zenobia Melford represents all that is *wrong* with Mars. In the long-term future of the planet she is of no importance. I am aware that she brought you here, and that she wishes you to work for her. However, in the next few hours I hope to persuade you that such an action on your part would be a great mistake. There is a higher cause."

Bey wasn't much into higher causes. "If she didn't give you my name, then who did?"

"I am not at liberty to discuss that." Fermiel refused to look at him. "However, let me assure you that your abilities have been described by that individual in the most complimentary terms. See there, Mr. Wolf." Fermiel nodded ahead. "We are now approaching the real Mars. Not the barren wilderness of the outer surface, nor the unnatural import from Earth of Melford Castle, but the true heart of this planet. Prepare to be amazed."

Bey recognized a deliberate change of subject when it was pushed in his face. If Fermiel was hoping to make a convert to his cause he was going about it in a very strange way. Bey was tempted to tell him to go to hell, explain that he had been recruited unsuccessfully by better men than Rafael Fermiel, and demand to be taken back to the link exit point.

But if he did that, he might never find out what was going on. And he did have most of a day to kill before he was expected at Melford Castle.

Go with the flow.

Bey leaned back in his seat, stared out of the car's front window, and waited to be astonished. He was not optimistic. Mars had been explored by humans and machines for two centuries and permanently settled for three-quarters of that period. The surface forms that Trudy had shown him seemed to be new, but what could be radically different about a maze of caves and tunnels?

The car had continued its steady descent. It was emerging into the biggest caverns that Bey had seen so far on Mars, running its way along a black-top road that might have been found in a million places back on Earth. High above, in the roof of the cave, three artificial suns mimicked the solar spectrum.

The air was warm and humid. Standing water covered the level fields that stretched out on both sides of the road toward the distant cave walls. Bey saw a handful of smart supervisor machines, rolling along by the narrow irrigation canals that marked the field boundaries. They were monitoring the work of thousands of small laborer robots, who in turn were tending countless millions of narrow green stalks that poked up from the shallow water. There was no sign of people.

"Rice." Rafael Fermiel glanced smugly at Bey as he spoke. "Grown in the traditional way. It is alternated through the growing season with legumes and root crops."

Bey nodded. He was beginning to wonder if there had been a bad case of mistaken identity. He was a form-change specialist. He could think of nothing less likely to interest him than a guided tour of mud farming.

The auto-car went rolling on, back into another connecting tunnel. They were still descending, deeper and deeper into the Underworld. The atmosphere was noticeably more dense. A shimmering heat haze hung in the air of the next cavern that they entered.

The black-top road and the multiple artificial suns were here again, but everything else had changed. The surface of this cave was bare broken rock and fine white sand. Jutting upward here and there were occasional stunted bushes and fat, spiny cacti. Bey saw no animals, except for one bird like an outsized crow that flapped slowly away from the moving car on lazy black wings. He glanced at Fermiel. The other man nodded in a satisfied way. The car rolled on.

And on.

By the eighth and last cave—a turbulent body of water, with a strong wind blowing salt spray across the narrow causeway that they were crossing—Bey understood. He had seen steaming wild jungle, desolate high veldt, salt ocean, gloomy moss-strewn swamp, hot desert, scrubby tundra, carefully-tailored agriculture, and bare snowy hills. Every cave was different. Every cave had its own balanced ecosystem. Every cave appeared empty of human life.

"Well?" Fermiel was staring expectantly at Bey.

"It's very interesting. It's a long time since I've really followed what's happening on Mars, but I had no idea—"

"Everything you have seen is recent. Twenty years ago, each one of these deep caves was nothing but unbreathable air and dark, empty rock."

"Which makes what you have done even more surprising." Bey stared ahead as the auto-car left the cave, accelerating sharply up the steep gradient of an unlit tunnel. He felt his ears pop at the change of pressure. He swallowed hard. "But I still don't understand why you showed this to me. I realize that you are simulating a variety of Earth ecosystems, but if you know my specialty you also know that I can't offer better comments on the caves than any casual tourist."

"I know. Do not worry about it. That is not why we wished to meet with you."

"We?"

"You will have the answer to that question very soon now. We are almost there."

The road that the car traveled had leveled off, while total darkness was giving way to a diffuse glow ahead. The car was emerging to an environment much more familiar to Bey. They were no longer in a natural cave, but approaching the side of a well-lit four-story building that filled the whole end of the tunnel. A dozen autocars were parked outside, in front of double doors of frosted glass. Their own car rolled forward to halt at the end of the line.

"I said you should prepare to be amazed. I know you were unimpressed by what you have seen so far." Rafael Fermiel had descended from the car, and he motioned Bey to do the same. "But I was not referring to the habitats. Follow me, please. You are about to see something quite unique."

The glass doors swung open, to reveal a lobby beyond, escalators, and a bank of elevators. Fermiel went in, but he remained right by the entrance. A great cube of grey stone stood there, as tall as a human. He pointed to one face of it, where a plate of hardened transparent plastic had been set into the rock.

"The original." Rafael Fermiel tried to sound casual, but the reverence showed through. "There have been millions of copies, but this is the *original*."

Bey stepped closer. Behind the impermeable plastic sheet stood an oblong piece of yellowed paper. He could see the printing and the couple of dozen signatures scrawled at the bottom, but the words were almost too faded to make out.

"Be it known by all who follow . . ." he read aloud.

And then he knew. "The Declaration! I thought it was lost—a century ago."

"It was. It was buried when the Ladnier Cavern collapsed. We found it last year during a secondary excavation. Are you amazed now, Behrooz Wolf?"

"More than amazed. I am overwhelmed." Bey leaned close. Of the original Mars colony, three men and three women had died during the first few days. The remaining twenty-four signatories were all here, immortalized by far more than a crumbling piece of paper a century and a half old. Their names were engraved on the memory of every child born on Mars.

Rafael Fermiel reached forward and touched his finger to three of the signatures. "Ilya Mahajani, Mira Alveida, and Dilys Chang," he said proudly. "I am a direct descendant of each of them. But I did not bring you here to boast of that. Nor, indeed, merely to show it to you. Come along, Mr. Wolf." He tapped Bey, who was still crouched forward in total absorption, lightly on the arm. "Mr. Wolf! I was informed of your interest in historic writings, but there will be time later for a fuller examination. In any case, you will see the Mars Declaration—or at least a far more readable copy of it—again in a few minutes."

He led a reluctant Bey to the escalator. They ascended two stories. The arrival of the car must have been noted on some automatic routing board, because a group of men and women stood waiting for them in silence at the top of the escalator.

If Rafael Fermiel did not actually preen himself, he came close to it. The red beard jutted out, and he squared his shoulders. "Ladies and Gentlemen, allow me to present Behrooz Wolf, former head of the Earth Office of Form Control."

He turned to Bey. "Mr. Wolf, you are in the presence of the policy council, leaders of what is popularly referred to as 'Old Mars.' Our enemies in the media often use a different term— 'The Rulers of the Underworld.' So far you have showed remarkable restraint in asking questions of me. But now you will have answers."

Fermiel waved Bey forward, following him into a long room whose grey table held places for precisely twenty-five people. The twenty-three others came crowding in after them and moved to pre-assigned seats. Bey found himself at the head of the table, facing two long lines of intent faces. Rafael Fermiel sat at his right hand. At the far end, occupying most of one wall, the first section of the Declaration was engraved in huge letters.

Fermiel waited until Bey was settled in his seat before he leaned closer. "Before we perform introductions and begin in earnest, let me ask Mr. Wolf if he would like to say anything. I assume that you know nothing about us?"

Any colleague of Bey Wolf's would have recognized that as a dangerous question. Fifty years with the Office of Form Control was a long time, enough to master a few party tricks.

"Very little." Bey's voice was deliberately casual. "Of course, most of you restrict the use of form-change to medical functions, rather than to cosmetic ones. Nothing wrong with that, so do I. I'm pretty happy with the shape I was born with, and like you I feel content to stick to it. But I note that" —Bey glanced along the line of name plaques, which sat in front of each member of the policy group— "that Ms. Beulah Cresz needed remedial work in the form-change tanks as a child, for kidney problems. Mr. Willi Moskewitz spent time in a tank very recently, after an accident that broke his left arm and produced facial scars. Ms. Katerina Dussek suffers a hormonal imbalance, one which requires monthly corrective sessions. Seth Stein, like me, is naturally myopic. And like me, he tends to put off remedial work rather too long with the form-change equipment. Tomas Sedgwick has a hereditary chromosomal defect, which calls for occasional treatment now and will need more frequent ones later. While Janos O'Mara" —Bey paused and gave the man next to Rafael Fermiel a long, thoughtful stare. O'Mara gasped, turned white, and put his hand to his mouth. The two men gazed into each other's eyes for five seconds.

"I think that's probably more than enough," Bey said at last. "Let's agree that I really know very little about any of you—or about the reasons why you brought me here."

No one seemed to be listening. The members of the policy council for Old Mars were staring at each other and past each other, throwing in an occasional venomous glance at Rafael Fermiel.

Bey reflected that there was no justice in the world. After all Fermiel's efforts in snaring Bey and bringing him to the Council Headquarters, the red-bearded man would be given little credit for that work on the basis of the meeting so far.

"Perhaps we should proceed without further introductions." Rafael Fermiel cleared his throat and looked at Bey. "Although I must say that I should hate to hear your comments, Mr. Wolf, about a group you *do* claim to know something about. Let us get right down to business. That" —he pointed to the engraving on the far wall— "was not placed in this room by accident. The Declaration guides and motivates all the council's work. We begin and end each of our meetings with its words. I now ask that we do so again, familiar as it may already be to most of us."

Be it known by all who follow . . .

The Mars Declaration was indeed familiar to Bey, and to the whole solar system—as a unique historical document. But no one else, in Bey's experience, treated the words with anything like the reverence accorded them here.

Be it known by all who follow that Mars is now a home for humans. We, the surviving crew of the exploration ship Terra Nova, *pledge never to leave this world. We will not obey any order to return to Earth, no matter how or by whom delivered. We will venture no more into space. We will remain here to live, to labor, and to die.*

Since we will not survive to see the end of our work, we give our dream to those who come after. This we believe:

That Mars, before our arrival, was barren of life.

That Mars will never after this be without the life forms of Earth.

That Mars is destined to be one day fertile and blooming, as a second Earth.

That human children will breathe the air of this New Earth, and sit at ease beside its flowing rivers . . .

Its flowing rivers. Bey was sure that the crew of the *Terra Nova* had known nothing of the deep caves of Mars, had never imagined a Mars Underworld of simulated Earths like the ones that he had just seen.

Their vision had been of the surface. Its flowing rivers. Bey saw again in his mind's eye the old, dried-out water-courses and jagged, rusty rocks, the desolate wilderness beneath a thin, dry atmosphere and a diminished sun. But on that frigid red desert, without life-support equipment, stood a handful of long-legged bipeds. How did Mars appear to *them*, the new forms that Trudy Melford had shown him?

Bey tried to make the mental shift of viewpoint, to look on Mars through other eyes. He was still struggling when he became aware that everyone else at the long table was sitting patiently waiting. And he was less than a third of the way through reading the text of the Declaration.

"We know what you must be thinking, Mr. Wolf." Rafael Fermiel spoke softly and sympathetically. "You have seen our work, creating the ecosystems for New Earth within Mars. On your last trip you visited the surface, and saw our progress in the Mars conversion process. Day-to-day changes are too small to notice, but the atmosphere constantly thickens and every year holds a little more water vapor. Had you gone farther north, you would have seen temporary pools of surface water near the cometary fragment impact points. The goals of the Declaration are being realized. Full terraforming will one day be completed. But there are complications."

"The new surface forms?" Bey had made no promise of secrecy to Trudy Melford.

"Exactly. Not so much their existence and present numbers as their implications. There are powerful groups on Mars who insist that the new forms point the direction of the future. 'It is far easier to change humans,' they tell us, 'than planets. Why not do as the Cloudlanders and Colonies do, and adapt *form* to *setting*?' We know and reject those arguments. We also believe that the most powerful voice in those dissenting groups is the newest one, and the one with most to gain from the use of form-change."

"She employed me to help her."

"We know that, too. We assume that you are the creator of the new surface forms, and we do not blame you for accepting a new and novel assignment in your chosen field. You could not have known its implications. Also, we do not ask you to deceive or betray Trudy Melford. We ask rather that you resign from her staff—and work with us."

"Doing what?" Bey glanced along the double line of intent faces. "I know of nothing I could do that would be useful to you."

"We will gladly give you whatever Trudy Melford is paying you, to do *nothing*." Rafael Fermiel sounded desperate.

"You have no idea how much she *is* paying me." Bey was on sure ground with that—he didn't know himself, and he didn't really care.

"Mr. Wolf, money is not an issue." Beulah Cresz spoke up from the far end of the table. "Whatever she is giving you, we can more than match it."

"More than match Trudy Melford? She's the richest woman in the solar system."

But the others were all nodding assent. "Take our word, Mr. Wolf," Fermiel said. "Our available resources at least equal those available to BEC."

"I am flattered that you place so high a value on my services." Bey leaned back in his chair and put his hands behind his head. "But I can't give you an immediate answer. I need time to think about all this."

That was the understatement of the century. Trudy and BEC, suggested as the *developers* of the surface forms? Although Trudy denied it, and insisted that the forms were nothing to do with her, it made both technical and economic sense. She had access to the right equipment. She had more than enough money to fund experiments indefinitely. And BEC would benefit most if Mars were *not* terraformed to look like a new Earth.

But if that were true, why bring someone all the way to Mars, to investigate those same forms? Bey's mind was on fire with paradoxes and conjectures.

"Of course you need time," Rafael Fermiel was repeating. "We have no intention of rushing you to a decision. Like the original framers of the Declaration, we have learned to operate on a time-scale of centuries rather than days or weeks. Take as much time as you need. And if you want to discuss this further, with us or even with Ms. Melford, we understand. From everything that we have heard about you, you are an honorable man."

Bey nodded. He was hardly listening. A few weeks ago he had been happily unemployed, a retired man pottering about on his own private business. Now everyone seemed to want him.

He hadn't changed. So what had?

And he knew one other thing, from half a century of experience. When a whole lot of people wanted you, it was almost never for *your* benefit.

✧ ✧ ✧

Rafael Fermiel offered to drive with Bey to Melford Castle. Bey refused. He needed an opportunity for private thought.

He promised to be in touch with Fermiel "soon," without specifying what that meant. And as the autocar snaked its way up from the deep Underworld he leaned back, closed his eyes to the endless succession of caverns and tunnels that rolled past him, and turned the pieces of the puzzle over in his mind.

The trick, as always, was to ask the right questions. Do that, and clarification would usually follow.

So. Question One: Why did Trudy Melford suddenly want him to come to Mars, when she had not contacted him in the three years since he left the Office of Form Control?

Answer: To explore the surface forms.

It was the obvious reply, but it did not feel like the right one. Particularly if, as the Old Mars council insisted, Trudy and BEC were themselves the agents behind the development of the new forms. Accept, then, that Bey lacked the information to answer the question.

Try Question Two: Were the new surface forms on Mars indeed a BEC/Melford product?

Answer: Trudy had suggested that they were not, but her statements were suspect. There was no way for Bey to determine the truth without more data. In particular, he had to examine the forms directly. From such an examination he was pretty confident that his own knowledge of BEC's work would tell him at once if their labs had been involved.

Note, then, an action item: he needed to meet the surface forms as soon as was feasible.

Question Three: Was the Old Mars policy council *for real*? Bey struggled to phrase that vague thought more precisely. He had been exposed to some of the real power centers of the solar system. Movers and shakers all had a certain ineluctable feel to them, an unpleasant electric force that ran through their meetings like an underground current. Robert Capman had it. Laszlo Dolmetsch had it. Cinnabar Baker had it. On the other hand, they also had the ability to turn it off when it suited their purposes. Did the current Old Mars group possess that hidden engine?

If they did, it was amazingly well-disguised. Bey had received rather the opposite impression, of a rather old-fashioned and ineffectual historical society, obsessed by a nostalgia for distant ancestors and an old vision of Mars as Bey suspected it would never be.

The original framers of the Mars Declaration could not be blamed for that. In their time the science of form-change had been in its infancy, so the only way they could imagine the human habitation of Mars was through the planet's transformation to suit human needs. However, from what Bey had read of that tough-minded early group, if form-change had been available they would have grabbed it with both hands and run with it as a perfect tool for colonization.

Over the generations, the bloodline had been diluted. That early drive and vision had been lost.

Question Four, then: Did the policy council really control such huge resources that they could out-bid Trudy Melford and BEC for Bey's services, no matter how much those services might cost?

They certainly *believed* that they could. At that point of the meeting Bey had seen nothing but total certainty on every face.

So. Question Five: Where was the funding coming from to support the Old Mars council?

Bey sighed to himself as he phrased the question. It was one he had been forced to ask again and again in his career. When in doubt, follow the money trail. People could lie, motives could be disguised, even acts could be misunderstood. Money was as constant as human nature.

The auto-car had moved up and up. At last the road was leveling off, with the towering bulk of Melford Castle coming into view ahead.

Bey reviewed his list of questions one more time. Was he satisfied that it was complete? He had just about convinced himself that it was when he found another question poking its way unbidden into his mind.

Question Six: Is Sondra at risk, out in the Kuiper Belt Colonies?

Bey shook his head. What was going wrong with his brain? The new question was totally ludicrous and irrelevant. Sondra's assignment had nothing to do with the Mars surface forms, nothing to do with the warring factions of New Mars or Old Mars. It was unrelated to every thought that had gone before.

So ignore it.

The car pulled up in the deserted courtyard of Melford Castle. Bey prepared to dismount. Then he paused and leaned back on the car's soft cushions. He had defined *intuition* for Sondra: it was what remained after all the facts had been forgotten. But intuition could also be something else. Sometimes it was the subconscious mind, establishing deep connections long before the thinking part of the brain could explain them.

Bey descended from the car and entered Melford Castle. The castle's security system recognized him and allowed him in without hesitation, but no one was there to greet him. At the moment that was a relief.

Sneaking along in silence and feeling like a thief, Bey headed for the elevators. He did not, however, go to the suite prepared for him or to Trudy Melford's floor. Instead he headed at once for the fifth floor—and the castle's communication center.

CHAPTER 12

Real-time conversation with the Kuiper Belt colonies was out of the question. The round-trip delay from the Carcon Colony, for example, was more than a day and a half even if the party at the other end responded at once. Bey didn't have that much time, and anyway he didn't know who to call. His best bet was a kernel-to-kernel connection with Aybee, working through the Rini net.

The only trouble with that was the unpredictable nature of the linkages. Despite Aybee's best efforts to pin down the sources of uncertainty, response time still varied between seconds and weeks.

Bey set up a top priority six-node routing, Melford Castle to Mars link to Earth link to Earth-orbit, then kernel to kernel on Rini Base and into Aybee's personal line. He initiated the message transmission. Then there was nothing to do but stare at the clock and wonder how long he would sit there before he gave up.

It felt like hours. It was actually less than six minutes before Aybee's glowering face appeared in the display volume in front of Bey.

"Hey, Wolfman. What's all this stuff about a high-priority chatline? You're too cheap to pay for that level of service."

Bey glanced at the monitor. The message had zipped

through every node in a few seconds. Almost all the delay had been waiting for Aybee's reply. "Assume I'm not paying for this call myself. What kept you?"

This time the reply came in a couple of seconds.

"I'm a busy man. The fate of the whole Outer System depends on my unceasing labors." Aybee grinned. "Actually, I was on the pot. Got to keep the priorities in order. Anyway, what you want? Keep it short, because I really do have lots of work."

"Did you brief Sondra Dearborn?"

"Better believe it. If she took it all in, she knows as much about the colonies as I do."

"Have you heard from her since she left?"

"Not a thing. Was I supposed to?"

"I'm wondering if she got to the Carcon Colony all right, and what she found there."

"I can check that for you easy enough. The transportation data bank for the Kuiper Belt will tell me who's where." Aybee paused, studying Bey's image on his display. "Look, if there's something funny going on here you might as well tell me now an' get it over with."

"I don't know of anything going on that you don't know already. But I don't feel good about this. I was the one who told Sondra that she had to go to the colonies. I said she had to be there to find out why things are passing the humanity test that should be failing it. As for *why* I don't feel good . . ." Bey shrugged.

It was a weak and unpersuasive answer, but Aybee was nodding sympathetically. "It's the wee, wee witch. The one who sits on your shoulder when you have a really tough problem to solve, and whispers in your ear, why not try this? I don't know about you, but I never ignore her."

"Well, she's telling me that I should never have let Sondra to go out to the colonies alone."

"It wasn't just you, Wolfman. Sondra told me that her boss said the same thing to her."

"If you knew Denzel Morrone, you wouldn't take much comfort from that." Bey studied Aybee's intent face, and finally realized why he had called. "Would you do a favor for me—a big favor?"

"Probably. I'm known through the whole Outer System as a gullible idiot. What you want this time?"

"I'd like you to take the fastest Rini ship in the fleet and zip on out to the Fugate Colony. Get there, if you can, as soon as Sondra."

"Probably can't do it that fast. She might be there already. What am I supposed to do when I get to Fugate Central? Protect her? I mean, the average Fugate citizen probably masses two hundred times as much as me, and I'm a theoretical physicist, not a professional bodyguard. Obviously I could beat 'em all up easy enough" —Aybee flexed a long, skeletally thin arm, and a tiny knot of muscle appeared at his biceps— "but then they'd complain formally, and I know you don't want that."

"If anything does happen, it won't be official. I don't expect you'll need to do a thing. Just the fact that you are there, watching, should be enough to protect her."

"Yeah. Or else I'm a witness, so Sondra and I *both* get killed." Aybee shrugged wide, bony shoulders. "All right, Wolfman. I got a million things to do here, but I'm a sucker. I'll do it. But can I ask you something personal?"

"Nothing ever stopped you before."

"Are you having it off with Sondra?"

"Certainly not! What the devil put that into your head? She's related to me, and anyway she's fifty years younger than I am. I'm too old for that sort of thing."

"Yeah. Sure. But to coin a phrase, nothing ever stopped you before. What am I supposed to tell her when I get there? She won't be expecting me, and if she's nothing special to you it's weird for you to be trying to protect her. Come to that, why aren't *you* on your way to the Fugate Colony, yourself?"

It was typical Aybee, asking a question so simple and obvious that anyone could ask it—yet no one did. And asking the right question usually clarified everything.

"I think Sondra might run into trouble out in the colonies, but I feel absolutely sure that the problem didn't start there. I need to focus on the real cause. That's somewhere *here*, in the Inner System."

"I'll believe that. The closer you get to Sol, the more trouble you run into. But what about my other question. What do I tell Sondra?"

"Tell her—" Bey swore internally. "Tell her I am worried about her, but say you don't know why."

"You are worried about her. Fine. Very persuasive. Are you *sure* you're not having it off with her? All right, all right." Aybee pushed his hands, palm outward, toward Bey. "I'll tell her. Is that it?"

"Yes." Bey paused. Aybee's finger was on the disconnect. "No, wait a minute. One other question on the same subject. What do you know about elliptic functions?"

"The *same* subject!" Aybee's eyebrowless forehead wrinkled. "Wolfman, you could sure have fooled me."

"I know. I felt the same way when I heard it. But if I understand anything at all about Robert Capman, it has to be relevant. Listen."

As Bey summarized his conversation, Aybee sat totally still and silent. At the end he shook his head. "If Capman says it, you hafta take it seriously. He's still wearing a Logian form?"

"He was when he talked to me."

"Then you have to assume he's a lot smarter than you. Hell, he's even a lot smarter than *me*. Maybe he's so smart, he thinks he's helping you when he isn't. Elliptic functions!"

"What do you know about them?"

"I know so much that I don't know where to start. Wolfman, we're talking here about a whole major branch of mathematics. There are scores of books and treatises and thousands of papers, all about elliptic functions. I can name a dozen great mathematicians who worked on the subject—Legendre, Abel, Jacobi, Weierstrass, Cayley, Riemann, Hermite, Poincaré—and that's just the pure theory, without even getting into applications. Did I mention Kronecker—and Gauss, too, of course, though he didn't publish what he had discovered—"

"Capman didn't just say 'elliptic functions.' "

Aybee had been in full stride. At Bey's interruption he stopped and stared. "Then what did he say?"

"What he actually asked me was if I had ever looked at the *early history* of the theory of elliptic functions. Does that make a difference?"

"All the difference in the world. It means we don't need to worry about work done after about 1830. And it means something else, too." Aybee paused, and sat frowning at nothing. "You sure that Capman said elliptic functions, and not *elliptic integrals*?"

"Quite sure. Though I hardly know the difference."

"Well, shame on you. Let's get you educated. The whole business started out by people trying to find the length of an arc of an ellipse. That gives you a certain sort of integral, and naturally it's called an elliptic integral. A mathematician called Legendre spent a good chunk of his life writing down bunches of related sorts of integrals, and reduced them to three basic forms. He had done all that pretty much by about 1810.

"But he never saw to the bottom of the problem, or realized that he was studying it the wrong way round. Nor did anyone else at the time—except maybe Gauss, he had this horrible habit of discovering major stuff and putting it in his notebooks, then keeping quiet about it until somebody else came up with the same results. Then he'd say, look here, boys."

"That sounds a bit like Apollo Belvedere Smith."

"Could be. Easy to hate a guy like that, eh? Anyway, about 1820 along comes a younger mathematician called Abel. He dies of starvation and tuberculosis when he's twenty-six years old—which isn't as bad as it sounds, 'cause mathematicians usually do the good stuff in their early twenties and geeze along for the next century. Anyway, before Abel kicks it he finds the right way to handle elliptic integrals. He *inverts* the problem. Switches the roles of independent and dependent variables, if you want to get technical. That inversion of outlook starts the whole theory of elliptic *functions* off and running."

Aybee paused to frown at Bey. "I may be wrong, but I get the feeling that you're not overjoyed to hear all this. There's lots more."

"I'm sure there is. And I know you're going to be disappointed and disgusted to hear that it all makes about as much sense to me as if you were singing folk songs in Cloudland Chinese. Let's keep the rest of the inversion story until I'm feeling smarter."

"I won't hold my breath for that. Don't you at least want to hear about elliptic modular functions, and how Hermite used them to solve the general quintic equation?"

"Naturally. There's nothing in the whole universe I'd like better—*after* you get back from the Fugate Colony, and we know that Sondra is all right."

"Some people got a one-track mind. Okay, I'll go check her out. One more thing, Wolfman, then I'm on my way." Aybee waited, his finger once more on the disconnect, until he had Bey's full attention. Then: "Are you really hanging out close to home because you're having it off with Trudy Melford?"

He grinned horribly. His finger stabbed down and he was gone, before Bey had time for even one cuss word.

Bey decided that he ought to talk with Aybee more often. The Cloudlander was rude and uppity, but a conversation with him was as good as a tonic. Also, it always clarified Bey's own thoughts. Aybee had put his finger on a basic question: Why was Bey *here*, and not out in the Carcon and Fugate Colonies?

One part of the answer was his insistence that he was retired. He had his own interests, his private projects. Why should he become involved in Sondra's problem?

That logic did not satisfy. After all, he had allowed himself to be drawn to Mars by Trudy Melford, when he had plenty of work to do back on Wolf Island. And he could not blame Trudy for everything. She had brought him here the first time, but he had only himself to thank for today's meeting with the Old Mars council.

He knew what was happening, even if he did not want to admit it. Maria Sun had warned him: *Watch that bump of curiosity. I can see it swelling from here.* Somewhere, deep inside, he knew that he was involved in the unfolding—or concealment—of a major mystery. People and events were being manipulated. If that included Bey himself, or even if it didn't, he had to know how and why.

Bey placed a call to Trudy using the castle's internal communicator. There was no reply—not even an invitation to leave a message. He went to the elevator, intending to ride it down to Trudy's floor. The controller refused to obey him, sliding by the assigned destination as though that level did not exist.

Bey returned to the fifth floor. As before, it was deserted. He tried to walk down the flight of steps that had led him on his first visit to Trudy's dressing-room. The stairwell was blocked by a Roguard, which gently and mutely refused him entry.

He returned to the elevator and rode it all the way up to the twelfth floor. That was accessible with no problem. So was the suite he had occupied on his last visit. The decor still displayed the misguided attempt to match Bey's personal tastes.

The good news, for the moment, was that it was empty. He would try to find out later what was going on with Trudy. For the moment he wanted a working data terminal and access to his own information sources.

He hesitated for a moment when the service asked him if he needed an encrypted line. Twelve hours earlier he would have thought it unnecessary within Melford Castle. Now he was not so sure. Finally he called for a scrambled signal that could be decoded only with his personal key.

Then the difficult part began. He had to convert thoughts, some of them vague and tentative, into queries specific enough for a semi-smart information system to be able to handle them.

Easy ones first.

What are the financial resources available to the Old Mars policy council?

When the answer came, Bey sagged in disbelief. The council was shown as the source of funding for the whole Mars terraforming activity. For over a quarter of a century it had paid for the purchase of thousands of Outer System cometary fragments, including their delivery to precisely defined target areas on the surface of Mars. As an incidental expense it had funded the space-borne security system that blew to atoms anything with the wrong final trajectory.

Next question, then.

What is the source *of Old Mars funding?*

That drew a blank from the information system. There was nothing in the files.

So try a different one: *Did Trudy Melford and BEC—*

Bey stopped before the question was fully framed. The beginning of the terraforming effort had *preceded* Trudy's move to Mars by over twenty years. More than that, it went back to a time long before Trudy had inherited control of BEC. She couldn't be the sponsor.

How about the surface forms? Were they the result of an investment by Trudy, either on her own behalf, or as an investment by BEC?

He might be able to check that—if the Melford Castle information service would permit him. It called for access to the local data bank, particular to users within the castle, but that should be routine.

Bey felt his way along, relying on the fact that Trudy would expect him to make use of local entry. He had been dealing with restricted data bases for half a century, and this one was nothing special. Five lock levels, and it was done.

The surprise was the place where he finally found himself. He was sitting deep within a data hierarchy that delimited the BEC empire. Only a real insider ought to be allowed here.

Was that another Trudy Melford carrot—a lure, designed to draw Bey in deeper yet?

Accident or design, there were far more data pointers than he expected or needed. The temptation to browse here, deep within the secret heart of BEC, was great.

Too great, for someone of Bey's temperament. He began to cross-index, wandering up and down the data branches. One key structure told of BEC failures, providing full chapter and verse for forms too awful to mention outside the BEC inner circle. Another lead wormed him into a bank of BEC's most precious commodities, new commercial forms that would not be announced for a decade or more. Bey found pointers there to new avian forms, to piscine forms, even a deep penetration into the hidden (and forbidden) invertebrate arena. The latter structures had been so long separated by evolution from the vertebrate branch that common thought patterns were usually considered non-existent. BEC was now about to question that. Bey itched to examine the details of the actual form-change programs, and learn the approach that was being used. It had to be something radical and ingenious.

After a few minutes he leaned back in his chair and took a deep breath. He could happily spend days—weeks—wallowing in the BEC data banks.

But not today. Bey made the ultimate sacrifice, and turned his back on the temptation of the new BEC forms. He set up a data search on a handful of specific key words: Mars surface, aerobic tolerance, temperature tolerance, oxygen compression and storage methods, and radiation tolerance. He found the usual C-forms, developed for in-space use, along with form experiments for the Europan deep ocean. But there was nothing relevant to Mars.

He varied parameters half a dozen times, with the same negative results. If BEC and Trudy had any knowledge of the surface forms, their own private data bases lacked that information. They suggested that no human form had been developed able to survive unaided on the surface of Mars.

Bey would have said the same thing, a few weeks ago. But he had seen them with his own eyes.

Maybe the data system was telling Bey more than he was asking. *If you want to solve the puzzle of the Mars surface forms, you must go to the surface and investigate.* It was Bey's own form of inversion; his advice to Sondra, turned back on him.

And it was good advice in both cases.

Bey sighed. Data base interaction was pleasant and addictive. At the moment it was a denied luxury.

Time to stop playing, and do some real work.

He retraced his steps, ascending at each stage to operating system level and wiping out the evidence of his presence within the data base. When that was completed he switched off the terminal and headed for the long spiral escalator that would take him up to the surface of Mars.

Trudy had made herself inaccessible to him. She could hardly complain if he accepted that fact and went on with the job that he had been brought here to perform.

CHAPTER 13

Bey had said nothing good about Sondra's brains, but he had given her top marks for stubbornness.

She clung to that thought. She needed every scrap of obstinacy that she could muster, just to persuade herself to keep going.

All the way to the Fugate Colony she had warned herself to expect an environment stranger than anything she had found with the Carcons. They, whatever their oddities, had retained standard human size. That bond with Earth would vanish, the moment that the ship's docking was complete and Sondra eased forward into the main Fugate entry lock.

She had been advised to remain in a suit all the time that she was in Fugate territory. Now it was easy to see why. As new air hissed into the lock she found herself floating within a foggy chamber whose nearest wall began to drip with moisture. The atmospheric pressure rose to twice Earth normal. Her suit informed Sondra that the outside temperature was 33 degrees Celsius—almost blood heat. The chamber's far walls, at least fifty meters away, were soon barely visible through thick swirls of mist.

But Earth had its fogs, too, and its hot, steamy jungles. Sondra's sense of alienation came not from heat or humidity, but from scale. She stared around her and felt dwarfed and diminished. By Fugate standards she was insignificant, a mouse who had strayed into a human house. The lock was automatic and that was just as well. The manual controls were fifteen meters up, far above her head, and in an emergency she would need to use her suit's jets and fly to reach them.

She headed for the far side of the chamber. As the lock cycled and its inner door slid open, Sondra for the first time saw her reception committee.

She had spoken to them on her trip through the Belt from the Carcon Colony, but it had been a low-capacity line with sound-only communication. The Fugate voices, two of them, proved easy to understand and yet not quite right in their timbre. Slightly thin, slightly fluting, they did not seem to be a local accent, understandable in a colony established a century ago and living in relative isolation from the rest of the solar system. It was something else, something that Sondra could not put her finger on.

And now, looking at the two great forms floating in front of her, it became obvious.

Examining the Fugate that had been shipped to Earth orbit, Sondra had known very well that it was a baby and that the adult Fugates must be a lot bigger. But that was an intellectual understanding. Confronting the reality was far different.

The two forms waiting beyond the airlock were not wearing suits, and their clothing was limited to a blue tunic that covered only the main torso. Sondra estimated that it was at least seventy feet from the top of the thinly-haired heads to the bare feet and stubby pink toes. The arms and legs were short in proportion to the body, which was in turn dwarfed by the head and thick neck. The heads themselves were pear-shaped, dominated by the bulging cranium. Even so, the mouths that now smiled a greeting to Sondra must be at least six feet across. There was no way that such lips, tongues, and vocal chords would produce the same range and type of sounds as the midgets of Earth.

The smiles did a little to establish a more comfortable feeling. Sondra smiled back at them, not sure that they could see her face through the foggy visor of her suit. She lifted her arm and waved. They ought to be able to follow her movements all right because their eyes were not that much bigger than hers, tiny compared with their heads.

She felt as much as heard a peculiar rumbling, at the same time as a familiar female voice spoke in her suit receiver. "Welcome to Fugate, Sondra Dearborn. We are Maria and Mario Amari. If you would like to begin work at once, the equipment that led to the anomalous result of the humanity test is waiting. If you would prefer to rest before you begin, a special area has been prepared for you."

Normal Fugate speech from those great vocal chords was not subsonic for Sondra, but it was close to it. The female Fugate was using a frequency converter, which must also have been in operation when she spoke to Sondra on board the ship. It presumably worked both ways, lowering the pitch of Sondra's voice to a standard Fugate range.

But the woman—*think of her as a woman. Maria Amari is human, as human as you are*—was coming closer, and continuing: "Or, if you prefer it, we will arrange for you to see something of this world before your work begins."

The urge to blurt out "No way!" was close to overwhelming. Sondra wanted to do her work and then leave as soon as possible. Only the knowledge that background information about the Fugate Colony and the general life-style there could be important allowed her to grit her teeth, nod, and reply, "I would be honored to be shown your home."

Before she could change her mind, a stubby-fingered hand big enough to enfold her whole body was reaching forward. "If you do not object, this is the easiest way for you to travel. If you wish to observe without being observed, this is also by far the best way."

No matter how alien the Fugates were in appearance, they certainly understood human psychology—hers as well as their own. Sondra nodded and snuggled down into the soft hand. The index finger close to her head was about three feet long. The whirls of fingerprint on the final joint were those of a normal human finger, written a dozen times larger.

Sondra had not said anything in reply, but the Fugates must have seen the nod of her head. She was suddenly in motion. It was an oddly comfortable ride, although she knew that with one sharp contraction of the muscles in the hand that held her, her insides would be squeezed out like tomato paste from a tube.

"We were chosen to meet with you." Mario Amari spoke for the first time since Sondra's arrival. To Sondra's ears, the male Fugate sounded no different from the female, a bass rumble she felt more than heard. "Chosen, because we were judged typical of our colony in both body and mind. But we would like you to know that we also *volunteered* to meet with you. Our own efforts to solve the mystery of a human who is clearly not human have not progressed. We need someone far more familiar than we with the failures of the form-change process. Your willingness to come here is much appreciated."

Sondra nodded again. Now she felt like a real fake. Change theory, yes. But when it came to the analysis of problem forms she could think of dozens with better practical experience. And that was just within the Office of Form Control. BEC must have scores, if not hundreds, of more experienced people working for them.

Why weren't *they* here, since their company's equipment was involved?

Before Sondra had time to pursue that thought they were out of the first chamber and entering what must be one of the main agricultural centers of the colony. A huge cubic room, a kilometer or more on a side, was filled with a three-dimensional lattice of smaller cubical tanks, thousand after uncountable thousand of them. The six faces of each tank were of transparent material, glass or plastic, and the tanks were complexly connected by meter-thick tubes emerging from the center of each face.

A second lattice, offset from the array of tanks, contained ribbon illuminators. Each one streamed with hellish light, an eye-damaging blue actinic glare that penetrated every cubic centimeter of every tank. The single-celled organisms who filled the cloudy interiors seemed to thrive on it. They were greenish-black in color, designed to drink in every available photon and use its energy to convert simple nutrients to high-level food materials. Like the Cloudlanders, the Fugates took their food from single-celled organisms, avoiding the unnecessary and wasteful step of a food chain to the multi-celled forms of a traditional Earth diet.

Sondra wondered if exposure to that short-wavelength deluge of light might be the cause of the mutations leading to the creation of the feral form. She threw that thought away before it had even taken root. Even if the Fugates had not planned for their own protection, the worst that the radiation bath might do was to produce skin cancer, and even that was unlikely given the thick epidermis of the two Fugates she had seen.

In any case, there were few Fugates within the monster room. She saw only three of them, far-off in the foggy distance. The workers and caretakers of the agricultural center were not humans, but machines. There were many thousands of them and they did not operate at the same scale as the Fugates. None bigger than a rabbit, they went scurrying along the lines of tanks, reading tank temperatures and chemical balance, tightening connections, and adjusting connector tube positions.

The Fugates took no notice of them, nor the machines of the Fugates, except to remain well out of the way of the giant visitors. The machines were not smart enough to talk. Had they been able to do so, Sondra felt sure they would have agreed that the Fugate supervisors were nothing but a pain—quite unnecessary, and a hindrance to good, efficient machine operations.

That prompted another thought, this one about form-change tanks. It was obvious that the Fugate tanks would be on a monstrous scale, with monitors, feedback attachments, and nutrients built large enough to serve their twenty-five meter occupants. But the physical plant in the tanks was really the trimmings, the necessary peripherals. The true heart of a form-change tank remained its computer hardware and its associated unique software. And those, assuming that they were BEC equipment rather than pirated versions, meant that they were designed to be serviced and repaired by *humans*, closer to two meters in length than twenty-five.

Put that another way: the three-foot digits enclosing Sondra in their cozy embrace might be able, with difficulty, to remove the cover from a form-change controller. But they would no more be able to manage the delicate work of changing form-change functions than Sondra could sit down and weave a spider's web.

They had almost reached the far end of the agricultural center. The single Fugate they had passed, a woman even larger than the one who carried Sondra, took little notice of them. She raised one hand in casual greeting, rumbled something that was not translated by the frequency converter, and went on her way. It was doubtful that she even saw Sondra.

"Shall we continue, Sondra Dearborn?" The Fugates had paused, and Sondra found herself lifted toward a great questioning face, its expanse of brow creased by six-foot horizontal lines of query. "If you would prefer to rest . . ."

"Let's keep going. I'd like to see more." The colony was totally different from any place that Sondra had ever been, yet she was feeling more and more at home there. For the first time, she felt that she understood the central dogma of form-change: "*Humanity is defined not by appearances. It is defined by actions.*"

(Bey Wolf was not there to offer his personal point of view. "The central dogma of the Office of Form Control adds one more sentence. *Be kind, be polite, be nice—and watch out for the nasty surprise.*)

The two Fugates were proceeding without hesitation, out of the agricultural plant and on through a corridor wide enough to pass a fair-sized space freighter. Sondra had noted long ago, on her first examination of the Fugate data base, that the colony occupied one of the largest planetoids in the Kuiper Belt. Occupied it, and needed every cubic meter of space. A Fugate could reasonably claim to need for comfort a thousand times as much living space as the average Earth human. Presumably a thousand times as much food, too, to go with their mass. A middle-sized Fugate weighed as much as a big Earth whale, and had the same nutritional needs.

In fact, when they first emerged into another chamber Sondra assumed that it was another agricultural plant. There was a similar lattice of vast cubical tanks, the same interstitial array of ribbon lights.

Then the difference hit her. She gasped. These were

tanks all right—*form-change* tanks. Thousands of them, enormous, each large enough to hold a Fugate.

"For adults only, of course," said the combination of deep rumble and its thin, high-pitched modulation. "The tanks that will be of most interest to you are the ones employed in humanity tests. They are located in the children's creche section, which follows Earth convention and has been placed well away from here, on the other side of the world."

"But so many!" Sondra waved her arm at the array, trying as she did so to make a rough estimate of numbers. The tanks were far too numerous for her to actually count them. "How many? I mean, *why* so many?"

It was hard to read expressions on faces so large and so near that her eyes could not take their features in all at once. The Fugates were frowning, in either annoyance or perplexity. The woman held Sondra even closer, until every separate pore and bristly hair was visible on her plump cheeks.

"So many? Is this many? We do not think the number of tanks excessive to our needs. With our current population, and a session for each person every two days . . ."

She went on speaking, but Sondra had moved to an internal space where no external sound meant anything. *Every two days*. A session in the form-change tanks, every two days. That was something Aybee had not mentioned—probably had not even known, although he had given her similar data for the Carcons. It made physiological sense. Those huge bodies, so far from human normal, would be enormously difficult to stabilize in that form. Blood flow, internal temperature control, digestion, breathing, circulation—a hundred body variables would have to hold values wildly far from those natural in humans.

The Carcons and the Fugates, so different in so many

ways, had one important thing in common: The continued existence of their colonies depended on the availability of form-change equipment all the time. And that meant they were critically dependent on BEC; or else—far more likely—they were employing pirate form-change equipment to avoid that dependency. The Carcon representative had pretty much admitted that they did use illegal equipment, although he had assured Sondra they did so only after a child was one year old.

At the time Sondra had felt sure that he was telling the truth. Now she felt just as sure that he had been lying. The Carcons and the Fugates were surely using cheap form-change tanks, suspect in both hardware and software. Despite BEC's best efforts to wipe out such patent violators, rip-off manufacturers for cut-price form-change equipment kept popping up all over the solar system.

But then—

Sondra felt her first twinge of doubt. It made sense for a colony to use cheap pirated equipment as long as they had no trouble with it. But the Carcon Colony had now encountered *two* cases where a supposedly human baby who had passed the humanity test later proved to be non-human. Would any group be stupid enough to keep using the same flawed equipment, when it would be so easy to put it aside and use only tanks that had never given trouble?

It ought to be easy enough to answer that question.

"The tanks employed in the humanity tests—you said they are over on the other side of the colony. Could you take me there? Immediately." Sondra's body had gone rigid, and the Fugate holding her must have noticed. Both of them were peering at her in surprise. She had to offer at least a word of explanation for her frozen silence. "I've just had an idea," she stumbled on, "an idea as to what might be causing the problem with the failed form."

Two giant heads were nodding in unison. "We will go at once," said the man. The Fugate woman was already moving, her massive body setting a pace across the chamber that Sondra could never have matched. "Can you give us some idea what you think is happening?"

They deserved the truth, but Sondra was not ready to give it to them. Suppose she was wrong? She didn't think she was, but it would be awfully embarrassing to accuse the Fugates with no real evidence.

"I think it may be the signal multiplexer. That device mixes and unmixes the multiple input data streams to and from the computer. If it were to go wrong, there could be a recursive signal to the main decision algorithm, and that would create a resonance in the purposive feedback loop."

She was spouting gibberish, pure and simple. But when Sondra looked up at the Fugate woman's face she saw that the hurrying giant was nodding respectfully.

If anything, that confirmed Sondra's suspicions. When waffle like that, made up and delivered off-the-cuff, was enough to snow the Fugates, a real professional salesman of junk form-change equipment would find this colony an easy mark.

Or maybe not. The man, close behind, was speaking. "We did not arrange for our own form-change staff to be present for the initial meeting with you. As you will surely understand, there are questions of ego and self-esteem involved here. Our own people failed to discover the problem, but they were not happy with the idea that an outsider should be brought here, all the way from Earth. Not even when that outsider comes from the famous Office of Form Control. But when we tell them that you have almost certainly identified the source of our problems, they will surely be more than willing to work with you.

Just tell us when you need their assistance—at once, perhaps?"

Sondra felt goose bumps break out on her skin. What combination of ignorance and arrogance had allowed her to assume that the Fugates lacked specialists in form-control, even though they were too big to work directly with the equipment? It was sheer blind luck that the people with her now had not seen right through her flim-flam.

"Not at once." Sondra's throat felt tight, and she had to clear it a couple of times before she could continue. "Better let me have a look at the equipment by myself before we pull anyone else in on this."

"There will also be engineers from BEC, arriving here in a few days for routine machine maintenance. If you need help at that point . . ."

"We'll see." BEC engineers, too. With so many form-change machines in use, regular visits from them would be natural. But maybe they had not seen the tank that produced the wild form. The Fugates would presumably not be willing to ask BEC employees to service pirate equipment that violated the company's own patents.

Sondra's rapid ride through the interior of the Fugate world would in other circumstances have caused her to marvel, and many times to ask her bearer to slow down. In the century since its first colonization, the home of the Fugates had been subjected to vast internal reconstruction. Sondra was whisked through a series of great chambers carved in the interior of the planetoid, each with its own carefully-planned functions. Some, like agriculture, form-change, and nanoculture, were easy to understand. Others had a tantalizing mixture of the familiar and the strange. The presence of half a dozen kernels in one great room indicated that it was the main energy-producing center for the colony; but why so many kernels, when one ought to suffice? And why were the kernels' triple shields all linked together, to form a matrix of interlocking dumbbells?

She saw and wondered, but with only half her mind. The other half was already rehearsing the task that lay ahead. She was mentally taking apart form-change equipment and running a detailed history of its use for the past year. Few people not directly involved in form-change realized that the control computer for every tank maintained a log of all executed instructions and every piece of subject bio-feedback measurement. It took years of experience to read efficiently that avalanche of raw data. Bey Wolf would probably do it twenty times as fast as Sondra, and might be able to skip whole sections of data because he could see at a glance what they were doing. But Sondra would get there eventually, no matter how long it took her.

"If we agree that stubbornness is a field for which marks can be given . . ." Bey Wolf was going to learn that it was.

They were finally at their destination. Sondra knew it the moment that they entered a chamber, smaller than any she had seen so far, and she took a first look at its contents. These were form-change tanks, enormous by Earth standards, but still tiny compared with the others that she had seen in the Fugate Colony. They were designed to hold babies between one and two months old. That was the critical age, the time of the humanity test. Pass, and you were defined as human; fail, and you soon ceased to exist. Somewhere close by stood the chamber where failures of the humanity test were absorbed into a general organ pool.

"Stop for a few moments, just here."

At Sondra's command, the Fugate woman paused on the threshold of the chamber.

Long ago, Bey Wolf had instituted general procedures to be followed in the Office of Form Control. *Proceed from the general to the specific. Before beginning the detailed work, make an overall sanity check.*

Sondra did a quick count. Twenty tanks. But according to the red tell-tale on each, all were empty. That did not seem right. "You have no children taking the humanity test at the moment?"

"Indeed we do. They are in the next chamber." Maria Amari was moving again, returning through the great sliding door and along a short corridor to enter another room. "Since we have some extra capacity, we judged it better to avoid the tanks in the room where the problem arose. Recent tests have all been given here."

Sondra ran her eye over the array of form-change tanks and made a quick calculation. There were twenty more units here, with twelve in use at the moment. The humanity test was currently being administered to a dozen babies, and it lasted about two days. So say, six a day, which meant roughly two thousand a year. Assuming the same failure rate as the rest of the solar system, of less than one in ten thousand births, that would be consistent with a stable population of a couple of hundred thousand people—and that was the stated size of the Fugate Colony. What Sondra was seeing was adequate to the task of the humanity tests, with plenty of extra capacity to take care of natural peaks and valleys in the birth rate.

"All right. Let's go back to the other room. I'd like you to put me down at the tank which produced the feral form, if you know which one that is."

"We do indeed." The woman's thin voice sounded mildly reproachful. "Naturally, that tank was marked as off-limits as soon as we realized that a problem had occurred in it. We will not use it again until we are sure that there is no danger of another malfunction."

Sondra felt another moment of uneasiness, a touch of cold doubt at the base of her brain. The Fugates were doing everything *right*, behaving exactly as she would have behaved herself in the same situation. Her glib assumption, that this was just a question of using flawed equipment and then lying about it, felt less and less plausible. But if it *wasn't* that . . .

The Fugate woman had placed her down gently by the side of one of the great tanks, next to its controller. Sondra saw, to her relief, that it had the size and shape she was most familiar with from her training back on Earth. She knew exactly how to operate it, how to open it, how to take it apart.

She moved to examine the controller's settings, then realized that the two Fugates showed no signs of leaving. They stood motionless and were watching her attentively.

Maybe it was simple curiosity. Maybe they had been told to stay close to Sondra and watch everything that she did. Maybe they had been told to stay close to her, and make sure that she *didn't* do some particular thing. Maybe . . .

"If I have to take the tank controller apart I'm going to be faced with some very delicate operations. I might be able to do the work in my suit, but it would be much quicker and easier to work without it. Is there any way that this room can be taken to Earth-ambient conditions?"

Part of what Sondra said was simple truth. Things *would* go quicker and easier if she didn't have to keep her suit on. More than that, though, there was at least a little personal insecurity. If she screwed up and had to repeat some step three or four times, did she really like the idea of an audience?

And there was a final reason. The Fugates would surely find Earth conditions hard to take. If they stayed, it would have to be for some compelling cause—such as, they had something to hide from Sondra.

The man and woman were looking at each other. Sondra thought she read uncertainty on those great faces, huge and distorted as the floating balloons of an Earth parade.

"We can certainly make this chamber self-contained," said Mario Amari at last. "We can also change the general environment here to match any conditions that you desire."

"Except that we do not know," the Fugate woman continued, "we do not know *what* changes to make for you. According to everything that we have heard, Earth is not a single environment. We understand that temperature and humidity and atmosphere vary widely from place to place, and from time to time."

Naturally there was uncertainty. Sondra realized that no Fugate had been to Earth—or would ever go there. The gravity of Earth would crush those soft bodies. Even lying down, the weight of the torsos would compress their lungs and make them unable to breathe. The Fugate colonists might survive in water, buoyed like Earth's own largest fishes and sea mammals, but the land surface of Earth was forever closed to them.

"I can specify a set of standard physical parameters in which I can operate most efficiently. However" —time for Sondra to learn where she really stood— "I suspect that you would not find those conditions well suited to your own comfort."

"That is of secondary importance." Mario Amari's reply came without hesitation. "Our presence is in no way essential. We are here only to be of service to you, in any way that we can, and if you do not need us we will leave. Tell us when you would like us to return."

"I don't know. It may take me a long time and I would rather work alone. Is there food and drink close by?"

"Certainly." Maria Amari waved a huge arm. "We passed a supply area two rooms back, small enough for use by someone in your form."

It was more evidence of frequent visitors to the colony.

More possibilities that someone from outside had tampered with form-change hardware or software. Sondra could hardly wait to get her hands on the equipment.

"But we need to know your environmental preference," Maria went on. "We will arrange that it be created within this chamber as soon as possible."

Which would guarantee privacy. No Fugate colonist was likely to relish an Earth-normal environment. Sondra listed the standard operating temperature, pressure, and humidity for the Office of Form Control, and watched Maria and Mario Amari as they drifted out of the room. There was nothing in their actions to suggest that they were reluctant to leave. The woman even seemed rather relieved. Once she had released Sondra from the safe confines of her hand she had never seemed quite at ease. They said they had both volunteered, but it must be a bit hard to serve as tour guide and general factotum for a being small and fragile enough to be destroyed with a single accidental move of hand or foot.

The chamber door sealed with a hiss of hydraulics. Within seconds, Sondra's suit monitors showed that the external temperature and pressure were falling. She waited, spending the next few minutes examining the exteriors of all the form-change tanks in the room. Every one was the same model. Every one was outsized by Earth standards, but it bore the BEC logo. That didn't mean too much. If a pirate manufacturing company was willing to steal the BEC patents, it would not hesitate to steal the company's trademark, too.

The real test came *inside* the controller, in the details of hardware and software. To Sondra's knowledge, no one had ever managed to duplicate those exactly.

Conditions within the chamber were still changing, but they were close enough to their final values for Sondra to dispense with her suit. She eased out of it, picked up her portable test kit, and went across to the tank identified by the Fugates as the one where the feral form had passed its humanity test.

She took a deep breath. This was it. Somewhere within this tank's controller lay the exact evidence as to why humanity had been affirmed where none existed. Either she would understand the problem, and return vindicated to Earth; or she would fail to find an answer, and everyone—Bey Wolf, Denzel Morrone, Trudy Melford, Robert Capman—would be provided with the confirmation of her inadequacy.

Sondra ran the standard diagnostics for the tank's computer. It was no surprise to find that the unit passed every one; the Fugate engineers would certainly have done that test as soon as they realized that something had gone wrong. Sondra went to the next level. She removed the cover of the controller and exposed the hardware.

Again, there was the BEC logo. There, too, was the BEC serial number, indicating that the unit had been fabricated on Earth. The date of BEC final inspection was imprinted, together with the identifier of the machine which had performed the inspection. Sondra checked that ID with her test kit. It was a valid one, still operating in the inner system. Either this was genuine BEC hardware, or some pirate had achieved a level of forgery new to the Office of Form Control.

Sondra moved to the next and more difficult step. If there had been later tampering with the original BEC hardware, traces of that would certainly remain. Subtle traces, but the Office of Form Control had developed a whole suite of delicate tests for just such manipulation.

There were forty-two diagnostics, of steadily increasing complexity and difficulty of associated analysis. Sondra began to work through the tests, patiently recording every result in the test kit log.

The first one showed normal unit operation. Second test: normal; third test . . .

After seven hours of continuous work she was finished. She paused, moved across to her suit, and took a stimulant pill and a drink of water. She sat on the floor, to stare at the tank and its controller.

Nothing. No sign of malfunction, no abnormalities. The BEC hardware appeared to be performing exactly as it had been designed to perform. She had found no sign of tampering. The original seals, applied when the unit left BEC, seemed unbroken. This was genuine BEC equipment, exactly as it had been provided from the BEC factory.

Sondra sighed. All that was left were the software functions. Compared with the tests for those, she knew from experience that the hardware tests she had just completed were child's play. Hardware solutions were standardized. Software, by its nature, was as flexible as thought itself. It admitted an infinite number of valid variations. Just because something was *different* did not at all imply that it was *wrong*.

Give up, go home, and say the assignment was beyond her?

Never. Before she did that, she would stay here until she starved or died of exhaustion.

Sondra's stomach gave a sympathetic grumble. How long since she had eaten? Too long, that was for sure. When she had examined the software routines she would treat herself to the best meal that the Fugate Colony could provide.

Until then? Well, she had heard stories in the Office of Form Control, about Bey Wolf in his younger days. When he got his teeth into a problem he would work forty-eight hour stretches, without stopping for anyone or anything.

Anything that he could do, she could do. Properly

regarded, hunger was nothing more than a driving force for work.

Sondra returned to her seat at the tank's controller and went at it.

The stories told in the Office of Form Control about Bey Wolf were true; they were also incomplete. He did have an ability to immerse himself in a problem, with a concentration that ignored irrelevant internal signals like fatigue or hunger. He also had a habit of emerging from that profound introspection every half hour or so. Then his consciousness would sweep over the external world like a radar beam, examining it for danger signals.

It was a habit—not instinct, but learned from hard experience—that Sondra had not yet acquired.

Sondra's task was both easier and harder than any that she had faced in her time at the Office of Form Control. Easier, because the software that she was working with involved the humanity test, and only the humanity test. The bewildering set of metamorphoses offered by purposive form-control, everything from cosmetics to long-term encystment for free-space survival, was not an issue.

But harder, too, because the property under examination in the humanity test, namely, the ability to interact with purposive form-change equipment, was itself so variable. One could not say that every individual was the same in this respect; one could say, with far more accuracy, that everyone was *different*, carrying a unique form-change profile as characteristic of that person as a chromosomal ID.

The programs that Sondra was now examining contained millions of branch points and options. It was conceivable that some of those branches had never before been exercised during the humanity tests. Logical errors could occur with even the best techniques of structured programing.

Fortunately, finding every error was not her job. She could follow the *specific* path that the form-change programs had employed when they interacted with the feral form and declared it to be human. Since every interaction and every executed instruction was on file, there was no particular skill in tracking that path. It was actually rather easy to do using the special ferret routines that Bey had provided. They would detect and flag any invalid piece of logic.

What was far more tricky was spotting a program patch—a place where someone had, for his or her own purposes, taken the original logic and substituted a modified version. That was her own best bet as to the source of the trouble.

Sondra slaved on, totally absorbed in her work. At first it was exciting, with the prospect of a surprise at any point. That lift slowly faded, as more and more of the program was examined and found to be logically perfect. There came a point when she felt sure that she was more than halfway through.

She had no thought of stopping.

If it's not hardware, it has to be software. There's nothing else. Keep going. Don't lose concentration.

But at last Sondra realized that she was coming to the final section, a mere few thousand instructions. She ground her way on to the bitter end, reluctant to admit that the chance of finding anything wrong in the final tenth of a percent of the code was close to zero.

At last she found herself staring at stark truth, in the form of a simple final message. It read PROGRAM COMPLETE; in Sondra's own mind it spelled FAILURE.

There had been no hardware tampering. The machine was just as BEC had delivered it, with the original seal intact. And it was not software tampering, nor syntax error, nor more complex logic error.

It was *nothing*. There was nothing left to look at.

Sondra stood up and began to meander hopelessly around the room, pausing to stare blindly at each empty form-change tank. She felt sick. She was hyperventilating, her head spun giddily, and she was chilled to the bone.

How long had she been here, slaving away to no purpose? She glanced at her watch. More than eighteen hours—eighteen wasted hours, with nothing to show but exhaustion.

And finally, as though faculties that she had held in suspension were suddenly clicking back into use, a horde of questions raced through her mind.

Was it as cold in here as it felt? Was the air as thin as it seemed when it entered her straining lungs? And *where were the Fugates*?

They had left her to work, but surely they must wonder why she had not asked for food, not called them, not said how she was doing or when she was likely to come out. They did not know of her determination to keep at it non-stop until she was finished.

She went over to her suit and checked its monitors. Temperature in the room, close to freezing. Air pressure, less than half a standard Earth atmosphere. At some time while she was working it had dropped, so slowly that she had not been aware of the change. It was still dropping.

She moved over to the chamber door—cautiously, because any exertion left her dizzy and panting. The great door was sealed, and she could see no way to open it. She realized for the first time that the room had no way of communicating with the outside.

Even if the Fugate colonists who had brought her did not return, surely some others would come here soon.

But why should they? There were no babies in these tanks. The humanity tests were being conducted elsewhere.

She went again to the door and hammered on it as hard as she could. She listened. There was no sound but her own breath, rasping in her throat.

She returned to her suit and eased her way into it. As the seals closed, the internal air pressure began to move back to normal suit ambient, slowly enough so that she did not suffer compression effects. Her head cleared, and she had the welcome feeling of pins and needles in her chilled hands and feet.

Sondra sat down at the control station for a form-change tank and inspected her suit monitors. When she came to the colony she had been advised to remain in her suit as long as she was here. That had seemed easy enough to do—provided that she could replenish her air and power supplies as often as necessary.

Which was no longer a good working assumption.

Power would not be a problem. The suit's heating unit was more than adequate. It would keep her body warm, long after she ran out of air. That would happen in six hours, unless someone came or she could find a way to escape. Maybe she could stretch her time to as much as eight hours if she sat very still. First, though, she would have to stop trembling; and her shivers inside the warm suit had nothing to do with outside cold. She glanced again at the suit monitors.

Air pressure in the room, one tenth of a standard atmosphere—and falling. Temperature, thirty degrees below freezing.

Escape. She could not rely on any Fugate appearing to save her in the next few hours, not when they had been happy to ignore her for the past eighteen. She had to find a way to escape.

How?

Her mind felt drained, empty, sluggish, unable to produce a useful thought of any kind.

Bey Wolf's assessment of her to Robert Capman had been accurate: not much above average intelligence. If he could see her now, he would offer a far harsher opinion.

Sondra leaned forward, put her weary head down on the flat surface of the tank's control station, and closed her eyes.

CHAPTER 14

Sondra, deep within the Fugate Colony in the far-off reaches of the Kuiper Belt, was convinced that Bey Wolf regarded her as an idiot. It might have comforted her a little to know that Bey, standing on the surface of Mars, had at the moment no better opinion of himself.

What he had just done might be natural for someone recently arrived from Cloudland. It was inexcusable in a man who had spent most of his life on the turning globe of Earth.

The deep caverns of Old Mars possessed an oddly timeless quality. Temperature was held constant, air pressure at any particular level did not vary. Lighting levels, generated from internal power sources deep within the planet, remained steady. Any significant report or picture that came to Earth from Mars provided as a background an unchanging interior environment. Bey, wandering within the caverns, had accepted the same mental mindset of an unvarying world.

It was a huge shock to ride the spiral escalator up to the surface, and to discover in the final hundred meters that he was arriving during the Martian night.

Bey stood on the frozen surface and stared about him. This was what happened when you did something without bothering to think. He had no idea of the local surface time. Dawn might be minutes away, or a full twelve hours. He had plenty of power and air in his suit, but he was not prepared to stand like a fool for half a day.

He glanced up. Although the atmosphere of Mars was gradually becoming more dense as a result of the terraforming work, it was still negligible by Earth standards. The stars were brilliant and unwinking. The constellations held their familiar patterns, unchanged from the skies of Earth.

Bey identified the Big Dipper and Polaris. He turned to face them. That was Martian north. Actually, *approximately* north, because the Mars polar axis, like Earth's own polar axis, precessed around an axis normal to the plane of the ecliptic. Bey could not recall the current Martian pole star. Polaris would have to do.

If that was roughly north, then *that* must be east. Bey stared off to his right. He was hoping to catch the first glint of light signaling that dawn was on its way. He was disappointed. The eastern sky was dark; but in it, hovering close to the horizon like a hanging jewel, shone a bright point of blue-white light.

It was Earth, which with Venus formed twin Morning Stars of Mars. In an hour or so day would arrive and Bey could get to work. Meanwhile, he would take the opportunity to understand a little more about the world he was standing on. He might also find it worthwhile to ponder what that implied for the new Martian forms. What would it take to survive, naked on the surface of this planet?

First, the easy fixes. One obvious problem was the temperature. On a midsummer day, the Mars surface might occasionally warm up to within twenty degrees of the freezing point of water. Now, close to the end of the Martian night, the monitor in Bey's suit showed an outside temperature of a hundred and twenty below.

But cold was no big problem for living organisms. All

it took to handle it was a good internal heat source—in the form of high calorie food—and adequate insulation. An elephant seal, with its thick layer of blubber, would bask on Earth's polar ice when the temperature was thirty below. An Emperor penguin would stand for weeks in a raging Antarctic blizzard, stoically protecting the single egg balanced on its feet.

It was excessive *heat* that was the real killer. Hundreds of Earth organisms could thrive in surroundings far colder than the freezing point of water. Only a few, the specialized chemosynthetic bacteria living within Earth's hydrothermal vents, could survive much above its boiling point. So far as temperature was concerned, form modification for survival on Mars was no big deal. Bey could think of a dozen ways to do it.

The real challenge was *air*. Vegetation could and did manage to survive in the ultra-thin atmosphere of Mars, but it did so with very slow growth rates. Humans could be slowed, too. The Timeset variation, developed by Robert Capman more than forty years ago, reduced human metabolic rates and perceived times by factors of more than a thousand. But that form was intended for long interstellar missions with micro-gravity fields. It was no use at all on Mars, where the surface gravity was a substantial fraction of Earth's. A Timeset form would fall over before it was even aware that it was off-balance. In any case, the forms that Bey had seen on his last trip were too fast-moving to be the result of any metabolic slow-down.

Bey emerged from his pondering, lifted his head, and stared off to the east. He could catch a hint of false dawn there, a faint line of pink on the horizon. Daybreak was less than half an hour away. Wouldn't it be easiest for the Mars forms to be active only during the day, and to retreat to warmer interior regions at night?

Maybe that was also the answer to the problem of

air supply. There could be a steady absorption and accumulation of oxygen during a night period of dormancy, followed by expenditure during daytime activity. Could the surface forms be using some new method for body storage under pressure? They would in any case need high tolerance for carbon dioxide.

Bey thought of the great whales, back on Earth. They took in air on the surface and dived cheerfully to a depth of a mile or more. The pressure change on their bodies during that descent and ascent was hundreds of atmospheres. During their half hour in the depths, the oxygen/CO_2 ratio in their bodies steadily decreased. It did not trouble them. Bey could imagine ways that the modified alveolar patterns of whale lungs, together with their pressure change tolerance, might be achieved in humans. Embodying those ideas into a form-change program was tricky, but it did not sound impossible.

In fact, it was clearly not impossible. Someone had done it. All Bey had to do was find that someone, and ask *how*.

He roused himself and stared down at the ground. Its temperature was cold enough to burn bare flesh instantly, but the insulated boots of his suit protected him totally. There was no reason why a changed human form could not do just as well, making use of normal organic materials.

It was still too early to distinguish between the dusty reds and stark blacks of the Mars surface, but Bey could see well enough to pick his way across the broken ground. The hangar for the aircar was already visible as a darker hulk against a purple-black sky. He made his way to it, wondering if his surface quest was totally unrealistic.

How many surface forms were there? And what was the chance of encountering one or more of them today in an almost blind search, as Trudy Melford had done last time?

Bey's natural skepticism kicked in. How much of a blind search had it been? Why should he believe that Trudy had done any such thing? Suppose the whole event had been a set-up, of BEC-funded forms planted at a particular place and time so that he could see them and be lured to work on Mars?

There was only one way to find out. Bey went across to the hangar and climbed into the car. He checked that it was fully powered, then gave the command to take off. There was the same gut-wrenching twenty seconds of rough motion across the torn surface. Finally they became airborne, with the car circling steadily and waiting for Bey's next instruction.

He set the course that he remembered from the last time, cruising slowly north at low altitude. He would not dare to fly too far in that direction at this time of day. With dawn came the diurnal bombardment of comet material, the fragments hurtling in to strike at twenty degrees latitude and beyond. The first fireball had already streaked across the sky ahead of the car.

Would the surface forms remain hidden until the barrage was over? Or did the spectacle exercise for them, as it did for Bey, the awful fascination of world-building by planetary turmoil?

The sun was well above the horizon now. Its clean bright disk of early morning started to streak and blur with plumes of dust and steam rising from the shattered surface. Bey forced himself to ignore the rain of comets and focused his attention on the rock structures ahead of the floating car.

Even that proved disconcerting. Like most Earth-dwellers, Bey's knowledge of Mars geography was rudimentary. He knew that the smaller size and mass of the planet must permit steeper rock structures. He also knew that the horizon was closer, and the atmosphere much thinner. What he had not expected was the way that those variables conspired, to produce the effect of a circle of crisp, jagged mountains that sharply vanished at a certain distance, as though the world came to an end there.

He tried to ignore that illusion of a circular cookie-cutter world with the car at its center, and concentrated only on what lay directly ahead. There was little to reward his attention. He was creeping along above a dry, rusty terrain populated with anonymous cliffs, shallow screes, and black boulders. After an hour's flight he had had his fill of sand, rock, and green-black lichen, and had seen nothing that was significant. He became convinced that he had mistaken the direction of his earlier flight; and then, when he was on the point of giving the command to circle back, the unmistakable and contrasting shapes of the Chalice and the Sword popped suddenly into view over the forward horizon.

Bey instructed the car to set down between them. He could not tell if the terrain was rough or smooth, but there was little risk. If the ground was too broken for a safe landing the car's sensors would determine that. It would balk at the command to descend.

Apparently the car had a high regard for its own durability. Even with a surface gravity less than two-fifths of Earth's, the landing—*touch-down* was surely the wrong word—rattled Bey's teeth. He held on tightly to the arm-rests until they at last shuddered to a halt.

"You have air and power sufficient for twenty-one hours of moderately strenuous activity," said a warning female voice as Bey slid open the aircar door. "It is recommended that you return here for replenishment after no more than fifteen hours."

"Sure. Fifteen hours." It was stupid, offering conventional and polite responses to a machine; but everybody did it.

Bey found himself standing on a surface rather more

rocky and uneven than the one he had started from. There was another and more major difference. The dark-green lichens near the surface exit point from Melford Castle had been no more than a thin varnish, a painted coating on the grains of rock. Here the surface cover comprised recognizable plants, their hair-thin central stems reaching up a few centimeters to try to grab a few photons more than their neighbors.

He oriented himself using the Chalice and the Sword as reference points. The ledge of rock where he and Trudy had seen the surface forms lay about a kilometer to the north-west; the sunlight, striking in at a low angle, marked a faint track in that direction where vegetation did not grow. It could be a natural structure, a fault line in the underlying rock where plant nutrients were missing; or it just might be a trail, worn by the passage of many feet.

Bey turned slowly to his left. There was another marked path heading off to the west, and it was much better defined than the first one. It led to an overhanging scarp face about thirty meters high, maybe half a kilometer away. Later in the day the sun would move to illuminate the side of the rocky mass facing Bey, but at the moment it formed a dark impenetrable shadow.

Should he go to the place where he had seen them before, or pursue what seemed like the stronger trail?

When you got right down to it, every important decision in life was made with inadequate information. The tough times were the ones when the decision was irrevocable. This one didn't seem to be. Bey made the mental toss of the coin, and headed west.

The vegetation scrunched slightly under his boots. Looking behind him, he could see his progress marked by thin broken stems. It made him feel slightly guilty. He tried to walk where the path was already well-defined because plants were not growing as thickly. Vegetation on Mars had enough to cope with from natural conditions, without a blundering human adding to the hardships.

Soon he was at the edge of the shadowed rock. The track he was following went right up to the shadow and vanished into it. Bey could do the same, but he would have to use his suit light. Presumably the car had allowed for such a thing when it quoted him his power and air limits.

He set the light to broad beam and turned it on.

And froze.

Right in front of him, standing no more than ten meters within the shadow, a white form was silently waiting.

"Hello." Bey raised his suited arm in greeting. "Can you speak?"

Even as he said the words they sounded inane.

"Of course I can speak." The voice was faint and distorted, carrying to Bey partly through the thin Martian air and partly as ground vibration. It sounded impatient and irritated. Bey noticed that there was no cloud of frozen vapor emerging from the broad mouth to accompany the words. The form did not waste warmed air with valuable oxygen in it merely to produce speech. A smart design would pass it over the vocal chords and then return it to lung storage. And if this form had anything, it was a smart designer.

"My name is Behrooz Wolf. I am a visitor to Mars. I would like to speak with you. I mean, with the ones of your kind who are most appropriate."

"Sure. *Take me to your leader*. Why don't you just say it? I didn't volunteer for this job anyway. Come on." The form turned. "My name is Dmitri Seychel," it said over its shoulder as it headed deeper into the shadow, "though I'm sure you don't give a damn about that. What took you so long? I've been waiting for you ever since your car landed."

Not *it*. *He*. Bey was sure he would have determined

that for himself after a few more seconds. There were a hundred clues as to the innate sex of a form, and most of them had nothing to do with appearance or dress.

He studied Dmitri Seychel as he walked along behind him. His only previous opportunity to examine the surface forms had come from above and far away. Now he could confirm or deny those first impressions.

The body was a little taller than Earth-human average and far fatter. The bulky torso, arms, and upper legs were covered with a pouched suit of gleaming white. Bey suspected that, like the visible parts of the body itself, the suit changed color depending on its surroundings. It was white now, to minimize loss of heat, but it would change to black when exposed to sunlight. The fat body wobbled with each step that Seychel took. Almost certainly it bore an inches-thick layer of protective blubber as thermal insulation.

The extremities were less clearly human. The feet, encased in snug-fitting boots that came half-way up kangaroo-like legs, had thick well-separated toes. Bey noticed that Seychel had no trouble at all in strolling along in front of him like any other human. But those same limbs, from what Bey had seen on his last visit to Mars, permitted surface travel in great twenty-meter bounds. More evidence of clever form-change design.

The hands were either bare and lacking in nails, or covered in long gloves that followed every fold and wrinkle of the skin beneath. The fingers, like the toes, were thick and splayed.

All interesting enough, yet all offering no real surprises. The first evidence of those came in the head. Dmitri Seychel's cranium was big and thickly-haired. Below it his face pushed far forward into a long broad muzzle. That, together with the brown, thick-lashed eyes, gave Dmitri's head something of the look of an irritated Earth camel.

And still all those elements were trivial, the simple superficial changes to an Earth form that might be performed by any sophisticated cosmetic form-change program. The work that interested Bey lay deep within. There must be massive and complex reconstruction hidden inside the head and torso—*functional* reconstruction. Some body organ—a new one, or perhaps lungs with basic modifications—had to extract oxygen from the super-thin Mars air while the body lay dormant. It must somehow ignore the air's carbon dioxide. And it must store the extracted oxygen for many hours, until needed during the active period.

The long muzzle had seen changes of just as fundamental a nature. A whole extra set of air passages must reside there. For one thing, speech had been separated from exhalation. Vocal chords could be exercised without the loss from the body of precious, warm, moisture-laden air. Bey had no proof of it, but he was also willing to bet that somewhere within that long, bulky nose sat an organ that absorbed every trace of water and oxygen from used air. What was finally released to the atmosphere of Mars would be almost pure, dry carbon dioxide.

If Trudy Melford had any notion of the sophistication of the Mars surface forms, there was no wonder she was excited. A genius of a designer had been at work here. Trudy liked to collect geniuses, and turn them to BEC's exclusive service.

That last thought left Bey more than a little uneasy. He was supposedly independent, supposedly retired, and working if he worked at all only on his own projects—all at the moment sadly neglected. Yet here he was, lured somehow to Mars and doing exactly what Trudy wanted him to do. Had she *deliberately* made herself unavailable when he arrived at Melford Castle, knowing that he would then head at once for the surface, and fly here? The car had been all ready and waiting for him.

Well, duped or not, here he was. And oddly excited. The old curiosity for any strange new form-change development was strong within him. Maybe Trudy Melford knew Bey better than he knew himself.

They were winding their way now down a long ramp, with fixed red lights on the tunnel walls. It looked more and more like the inside of a building, except that there was no air but the ambient Mars atmosphere. Dmitri Seychel had not once looked back to see that Bey was following, or offered one more word of conversation. Bey felt like kicking him in that amply-padded blubber-laden behind. If that was typical, what the Martian form needed in addition to any physical modification was a booster shot of sweetness and light.

"Here you are." Dmitri halted at a rectangular opening in the tunnel. "Home of the big cheese, Georgia Kruskal. Have fun."

He went off along the tunnel without another word, leaving Bey hesitating at the entrance of the room.

"Come on in." The thin voice was cheerful, as though visitors from Earth or Old Mars dropped in every day of the week.

Perhaps they did. Bey walked in, and found himself in a room that could easily have been an office back on Earth. There was a desk, a table and chairs, a data terminal, and even half a dozen potted plants. But the plants were all different, and all strange. Some were warty black cacti, others hugged the red soil or turned thin, sail-like leaves to face always to the light.

"Experiments, of course." The being seated at the desk could at first glance have changed places with Dmitri Seychel, and Bey would not have known the difference. "Sit down and make yourself comfortable. I'm Georgia Kruskal, and I get the blame for this madhouse. Tell me who you are, and why you're here instead of skulking in the Old Mars burrows."

"I'm Behrooz Wolf. I'm not from Old Mars. I'm from Earth, formerly with the Office of Form Control." Bey hesitated. Now for the tricky bit. Might as well lay it on the line. "I'd like to know more about the form you are using, because I think I might be able to help you to improve it."

"Oh-ho." The camel snout turned to face Bey more directly, and the liquid brown eyes stared at him. "It's nice to run into someone with real gall. *Improve* us, eh? Fine. *Quem dea vult perdere, prius dementat.*"

" 'Whom God would destroy, she first makes mad.' " Bey did not even blink. He could play that particular game all day long.

Georgia Kruskal was nodding. "First points to you, *hombre*. Maybe you will improve us after all. Why don't you tell me how?"

"I need to have some questions answered first."

"I'll bet you do. So do I." Kruskal leaned back in her chair, which was contoured to fit her bulky body. "All right, your turn first. Fire away."

"Thank you. First of all, are you pure human?"

"You better believe it. One hundred percent, no artificial additives. You and I could get together and start a *bambino* tonight, Behrooz Wolf."

"Sorry. I'm spoken for."

"I'm not sure I believe that." Georgia studied him for a moment. She had the temporary advantage. She could see and understand his facial expressions, while he had not yet learned to read the body language of the new form.

"Anyway," she went on, "let's stay with your question. Everything here is done with form-change programs and without inorganic components. Dmitri's father is standard form and lives back in the Old Mars burrows. I'm Dmitri's mother. You've met Dmitri, so you probably think I have a lot to answer for."

"I did get the impression that I was more pleased to see him than he was to see me. How many of you are there?"

"Last time I bothered to check, about fourteen thousand. And the number is growing. Does it matter?"

"It might." Bey thought of Rafael Fermiel, and the earnest faces of the Old Mars policy group. "A more important question: Are your forms stable?"

"Not as stable as I would like. We still need weekly sessions with the tanks. But the life-ratio is good, we should live as long as an unmodified form."

Georgia Kruskal sounded pleased with herself; as indeed she should be. Most radically modified forms died in just a few years.

So now Bey had to ask the trickiest questions—the non-technical ones.

"Do you use BEC form-change equipment?"

"BEC hardware and basic routines. The more complex programs and interactions are our own."

"Done with BEC's permission?"

"Let's not split hairs. Anyway, I'm sure you know the answer to that question."

It sounded like an answer, but it wasn't one. The time had come to be more direct.

"Does Trudy Melford know about and fund your program?"

There was a long pause. The eyes with their thick fringe of eyelashes closed. The thick lips pursed. Bey waited impatiently. A *yes* would tell him a great deal. A *no* might mean no more than that Georgia Kruskal was lying.

"You ask two questions in one," Georgia said at last. "Does Trudy Melford *know about* this project? Yes, I feel sure that she does. Although she is a recent immigrant by Mars standards, her agents are sprinkled throughout Old Mars. We are known—and hated—there. As for your second question, whether Trudy Melford *funds* our efforts, I wish I could give you a good answer. On the face of it, she does not. Nor does anyone in BEC. But since her arrival on Mars we have consistently found it easier to obtain lines of credit for our work, and for no reason that I can explain."

Bey found himself impressed again with Georgia Kruskal. Like him, she understood and applied the same basic principle: *Follow the flow of money*. The project to develop surface forms for Mars was no different from any other major project. It needed funds, and those funds had to come from somewhere.

"One more question, then it will be your turn. You say you are known and *hated* in Old Mars. Why?"

"You can answer that for yourself, Behrooz Wolf, if you think for a second."

"I think I know, but I want to confirm it. Old Mars is afraid of you. They see you as interfering with their plans."

"Interfering, and worse." The broad mouth widened. It was a smile, toothless and tongueless. Bey guessed that both those features lay far back, out of sight within the long snout. "Isn't it obvious that Old Mars sees us as a major enemy? The policy council is committed to terraforming Mars, making it into a world in Earth's image. They take the Mars Declaration and they misunderstand it. The first colonists wanted Mars to be a world where humans can live. The policy council read that statement, and think *terraform*. But our existence proves that more change is unnecessary. If the comets ceased to arrive and Mars remained as it is today, humans can be quite at home on its surface. We prove that fact daily. Our version of the Mars Declaration would recognize a simple truth: *It is easier to change a human than to change a planet*."

"If you know what you are doing, it is." Bey had no doubt in his mind. She *did* know what she was doing. Why was it, just when you were convinced that you knew every major player in form-change through the whole solar system, another one would pop up from nowhere? "I could go on asking questions all day, but I promised you that would be the last one."

"I'm not sure I believe that, either. But I'll take my turn since it's offered. First question. Do *you* work for Trudy Melford and BEC?"

"No. She thinks I do, but that's not the same thing."

"Not the same thing at all. Do you work for Old Mars?"

"No. They recently tried to recruit me, but that's as far as it has gone."

"I advise you to keep it that way. If you are bought by Old Mars you will work *against* form-change, not with it. So what are you doing here?"

"Damned good question. Curiosity. Terminal nosiness. Habit. Back on Earth, I was head of the Office of Form Control for a long time—"

"Your name and reputation are not unknown to me. Do you imagine that I would sit here and allow myself to be questioned by any casual visitor? Or give even the time of day to anyone with the arrogance to suggest that he might *improve* on my work, unless I had reason to believe that such a thing was possible? *Remotely* possible, I would add. You are not alone in your arrogance." Again the smile appeared, the stretching of thick camel lips. "But I can tell you why you are here, Behrooz Wolf. You are here to *learn*. So let us begin."

Georgia Kruskal tapped at the terminal in front of her with thick fingers, and a wall screen came alive with a brightly-colored form-change schematic. "First I talk, Behrooz Wolf. You look, listen and learn. Then—if you have anything to say—you talk. And then, who knows? Perhaps I learn, too."

CHAPTER 15

Aybee hummed tunelessly and cheerfully to himself as the little high-gee craft prepared itself for docking. All this way to the ass-end of nowhere, when you had real work to do, and probably all for nothing; but once you said "yes" that was what you let yourself in for. So relax and enjoy it.

Bey was just an old worry-wart. Smart enough, sure; but too much pointless worry, and why bother living? Might as well turn up your toes and get it over with.

Aybee saw it the other way. The Apollo Belvedere Smith philosophy of life, if he had ever bothered to define it, was simple: *If anything can possibly go right, it will.*

After Bey's call, Aybee had sent a hyperbeam query to Sondra on the Fugate Colony. She did not respond. Fair enough. Didn't mean a thing, except she was head-down working. She would ignore any messages, just as Aybee did when was really trying to get something done.

But he had promised Bey. Aybee sighed, commissioned the little ovoidal Rini ship assigned for Kuiper Belt use, and zoomed off for the Fugate Colony.

And now that he was arriving, what was he supposed to do? Tell Sondra that she had to go home with him because Bey Wolf said so? Aybee's exposure to Sondra had been limited, but he could imagine her reaction to that suggestion. She would tell him just where to put his advice.

It was a lose-lose deal. If Sondra was fine, as Aybee felt sure she would be, then his journey was for nothing and he would look like a real idiot. He would have no choice but to turn around and head back to Rini Base. And if she *wasn't* all right? Then presumably he was supposed to dash in and save her. Aybee had no doubts about his own pre-eminent abilities. They did not include rescuing damsels in distress.

He had checked the Fugate Colony's standard parameters on the way. The stated internal temperature and pressure were human tolerable—just. That wasn't enough for Aybee. He wanted something that was human *comfortable*. The Fugates could have their atmosphere soup, and good luck to them. He remained in his suit as the docking was completed, then floated on through the airlock.

His ship had beamed ahead to signal his arrival, but that call had been fielded by the automatic equipment on the colony. His personal ID identified Aybee as a Cloudlander, familiar with a wide variety of free-space living conditions. On the strength of that he had received approval for unaccompanied docking. He had been offered—and declined—assistance upon arrival by Fugate staff.

His first look at the interior of the Fugate Colony made him wonder if he had made a bad decision. Everything he saw was impossibly big, even the communications system. It had been designed for use by twenty-meter, thirty ton people, and even Aybee with his elongated arms could not manage the stretch.

But that could not be the whole story. The Fugates, like most of the colonies, conducted regular commerce with the rest of the Kuiper Belt and made use of imported systems and services. Other people, many of them as small or smaller than Aybee, must be regular visitors. They had to be able to work inside the colony without continuous Fugate assistance. That implied the presence somewhere of standard-sized data terminals and information systems.

Trouble was, this chamber was so cluttered and so foggy inside that you couldn't get a good look at most of it. Aybee went on the prowl, floating along past gigantic desks, doors, and transfer chutes. He finally found the data unit he needed over in the far right corner, hidden behind and dwarfed by a rack of space suits big enough to house Leviathan.

It was an old-fashioned design and it didn't seem to have been used for a while, but it responded promptly enough when Aybee turned it on. And sorts and searches, thank Knuth, were pure logic, not dependent on anything so material as physical size or equipment age. The Fugate general query system was also a little primitive, but five minutes of experiment located the record of Sondra Dearborn's arrival at the colony. Her exact time of entry was shown: three days ago. After that it became a bit trickier. There was no sign that Sondra had left, so presumably she was still somewhere within the planetoid. But the file provided no indication of her present location. Chances were that she was working with form-change equipment, but *which* form-change equipment? The data bank showed thousands of tanks, set in many different parts of the colony.

Aybee sighed. Work went a lot faster when you did it alone, but that no longer seemed an option. The record of Sondra's arrival provided the names of two individuals who had been assigned to help her. He gave in, and asked the terminal to put him in touch with either Mario or Maria Amari.

Patience was not Aybee's strong point. He fidgeted and muttered for what seemed an interminable wait, while the colony communications system placed its calls.

The result, when it finally came, did not seem promising. Sondra in her first meeting with the Fugates had been overwhelmed by flesh, by sheer physical size so great that she could not comprehend expressions on the giant faces. Aybee, seeing Mario Amari on a data screen no bigger than his hand, had an opposite first impression of a tiny, puzzled and slightly annoyed baby. The bulging cranium was far too big for the eyes and pursed mouth.

There seemed no expression at all on that diminished countenance as Mario Amari listened to Aybee's explanation of the reason for his call. At the end of it the puzzled look returned.

"Let me be sure that I understand you correctly." Amari's rumbling voice was converted by the data line to the high-pitched, slightly squeaky delivery of a three-year-old. "You know that Sondra Dearborn is here on the colony, working on form-change equipment. You know that Maria and I met her, and showed her where everything is, and how it works. And you are worried about her?"

"Well not exactly *worried*." Aybee didn't like the way the conversation was going. It was obvious that Mario Amari considered he was dealing with a half-wit. "I'd like to know where she is, and check what she's doing."

"Are you a specialist on form-change methods?"

"No." Make that a quarter-wit. Amari was slowly nodding as Aybee continued, "Look, I don't want to be a nuisance for you or anyone else on the colony, but I would like to see Sondra. So if you could just tell me where she is working, and how to get there . . ."

"Do you know your way around this world?"

"Not really."

"Have you been to the colony before?"

"No. Never."

"Then it is probably quicker and easier if I show you where she is. Stay exactly where you are, and do not leave that chamber. I will be with you shortly."

In other words, you shouldn't be allowed to wander the colony without a keeper. Aybee cursed Bey Wolf while he waited. Bey had dragged him halfway across the Kuiper Belt for nothing. Sondra was certainly all right—there had been annoyance but not a trace of concern in Mario Amari's voice. How could she *not* be all right, safe inside the colony? Amari was casual and unworried when he finally came floating in.

"We did not stay with her, because she did not want it." Mario Amari, without asking Aybee's permission, grabbed him in one great hand and headed at once for the colony interior. "In fact, Sondra Dearborn specifically requested that we permit her to work alone in her first analysis of our form-change equipment."

"How long ago was that?"

"Since early yesterday. But she has access to ample food, and to a sanitation and rest area suitable for her needs. Small-form visitors to the colony regularly use the same facilities. If we had heard nothing from her in another day or so, Maria and I would probably have checked back here."

They had floated through a succession of huge rooms, each scaled to match the size of the Fugates, and were approaching yet another one. The doors between the other rooms had all been wide open. Aybee noted that this one was sealed.

"Again, this was at Sondra Dearborn's request." Mario Amari sounded patient and even a little amused as he replied to Aybee's question. If Aybee was unfortunate enough to be a terminal worrier, his voice said, then maybe he was more to be pitied than blamed. "She wanted to work without a suit, in that setting of lower temperature and pressure where she would feel most comfortable. Naturally, that required that this room be sealed off temporarily from the rest of the colony."

Aybee found himself nodding agreement, even as they

approached the room's great sliding door and he glanced at the monitors showing the chamber's interior conditions. That first look brought him instantly to full attention. What he saw bristled the sparse hair on the back of his head.

Air pressure: 40 millibars. Temperature: -68 Celsius.

No human without a suit could survive more than a couple of minutes inside such a room.

"This has been changed!" Mario Amari was staring at the gauges as though he could not believe what they said. "This is nothing like the control values that we employed—and the door has been sealed from outside. We left it set for internal control. Sondra Dearborn must have come out, and re-set the interior parameters. She cannot be inside."

But his actions suggested that he did not believe his own words. He had released Aybee. Now he grasped the door in one huge hand and began jerking at it wildly.

"No, man! Don't even try that." Aybee decided he was not the only half-wit in the Fugate colony. "You got a two-atmosphere difference between the sides of that door. You have to equalize before you open it, or we get a big implosion."

Fortunately the room's own safeguards agreed with him. It took another half-minute to flood the interior with air—compression effects would be the least of Sondra's problems if she were inside—and equalize pressure enough for the door to slide open.

Aybee floated inside, ahead of Mario Amari. His suit protected him from temperature shock, but he heard Amari gasp. The air pumped into the room was warm enough, but the walls and floor were still cold enough to burn anything that touched them.

But maybe it was only a gasp of relief—because the room was empty. There was no sign of Sondra, dead or alive.

"She's not here. Thank Heaven, she got out." Amari, like Aybee, was scanning the interior, with its array of form-change tanks. "She must have."

"Must have. But didn't." Aybee's instincts had taken over as soon as he saw the tanks. "She's still here, and she's all right. Come on, man. I may need a little bit of local assistance for this."

Every trainee in the Office of Form Control was required to take practical tests. One of them called for form-change program modification with re-calibration of a form-change tank. But no trainee, ever, had been asked to do that in six hours or less, nervous, wearing a suit, and filled with the awful knowledge that you would soon be evaluating the quality of your work using your own body as test subject.

Sondra had to make some working assumptions. The chamber's ambient temperature might drop close to absolute zero, and the air pressure to vacuum. A human, suitably changed, might survive in that situation for a couple of days. It called for total hibernation and a severe alteration to body chemistry. Re-vivication probability was down around ten percent.

But that was the worst case. The tank itself would provide some thermal protection, maybe hold a little air. The chance of survival increased rapidly with every trace of oxygen and every degree of higher temperature.

Sondra did all the calculations that she had time for. She knew they were not enough, but she would have to act based on what she had. She recalled Bey's words: *Intuition is what remains after all the facts have been forgotten*. Fine. But pray that intuition was also something that guided you when there was no more time for calculation.

She reviewed the program changes one more time; entered them into the tank's controller; climbed slowly into the tank; adjusted the sensors, electrodes, and catheters as best she could, to interact with an adult form a fraction of the size of a Fugate newborn; and then faced the final, most difficult judgment call.

She could not make the form-change tank attachments to her own body while she remained inside her suit. When that suit was removed, she would have no more than a few minutes before anoxia robbed her of consciousness. And the longer she waited, and the lower the chamber air pressure became, the quicker anoxia would set in.

Sondra lowered her internal suit pressure and switched to pure oxygen. She hyperventilated for a couple of minutes, until she felt her head swimming.

Now. Before she had a chance to change her mind or think more about the implications of what she was doing. Suit off.

Forty seconds.

Into the tank harness.

One minute twenty seconds.

Connections—fourteen of them. Can't afford to rush. Can't afford to make a mistake.

Two minutes twenty seconds.

Sondra's lungs were empty. She felt them collapsing within her rib cage. Five more connections, just five. Not much to ask. Her head was swimming again.

Three minutes and thirty seconds.

Two more attachments. Tank turning dark, have to work by feel.

Four minutes something.

Last one. Was that right? Can't tell. No more feeling in fingertips. Spears of ice, down throat and into chest.

Five . . .

Total darkness. *Personal* darkness. Strange way to go. But when it came to the final moment, maybe every way seemed like a strange way to go. And go *where*?

No one had ever managed to answer that question. Maybe she would do it, be the first.

Sondra turned to solid ice, wondering if her personal darkness would ever end.

When you plunged into a form-change that was both unplanned and desperately hurried, you gave little thought as to what you were likely to find waiting for you when you emerged. You were far more likely to be wondering *if* you would emerge.

But if you did think about it, there were certain things you would not expect to see as you struggled back to consciousness. One of them was the smug face of Aybee, whom Sondra had left a few days earlier back on Rini Base at the other side of the Kuiper Belt. But there he was. He was lolling before the open form-change tank and chomping on some sort of sugary cake.

He nodded to her in a self-satisfied way as soon as he noticed that her eyes were open. "Right on schedule. How you feeling?"

Only a moron would ask a question like that. Sondra doubled over in agony as a first breath burned into her lungs. She could not speak, but her glare was intended to crisp Aybee's skin.

"The old Wolfman was right, you know." Aybee went on as though he had not noticed her reaction. "I was sure he was talking through his hat when he asked me to fly out here, but he wasn't. 'Course, you might say he was only *half*-right. No real reason to worry. Even if I hadn't come along, the Fugates would have took a look for you eventually. They'd have dragged you out. But you wouldn't feel as good as you do now."

Good? She had to speak, even if it killed her.

"I could have *died* here," she rasped. "If I hadn't known how to—" She ran out of air.

"*If* you hadn't." Aybee finished the cake and licked

his fingers. "But you did. Way I see it, it's pretty straightforward. If you're smart, you figure out you gotta do the form-change bit and crawl into the tank if you want to survive. If you're not smart enough to do that, then you die and no big loss. Plenty of dummies in the system already, one more won't be missed."

Sondra decided she was going to kill Aybee. She didn't know when or how, but it was going to happen. Unfortunately, for the moment there were higher priorities.

"Who did it, Aybee? Who sealed this room and changed the air and temperature settings so it would kill me?"

"Dunno. The Fugates are working on that—they don't like what happened any better than you do. No clues so far."

"And *why* would anybody try to kill me?"

"That's easier. You came here to find out why the Fugate form-change equipment said something was human that wasn't. I'd guess somebody didn't want you passing that information on." Aybee showed real interest for the first time since Sondra had awakened. "Except that don't make logical sense, either. Someone wants to kill you, why do a half-assed job of it? Shoot you, or chop your head off, something final—don't fool around with air and temperature. By the way, what *did* you find out?"

"Nothing." The feeling of failure that swept through Sondra was worse than her physical woes. "That's why none of this makes sense. I have no information to pass on to anybody, because I didn't find one thing wrong with the form-change system here in the Fugate Colony. The hardware is just as it came from the BEC factory, with its seals unbroken. The controller software passed every test I could give it."

"That so? Now you got me a little bit interested. You telling me there was no secret to hide?"

"Nothing that I could discover. When this chamber locked up on me I should have been ready to give up. Except that I wouldn't have. If I hung around, it was only because I couldn't stand the idea of crawling back to Bey Wolf and admitting that whatever was going wrong here, I couldn't find it."

"You telling me you're ready to get out of here?"

"No! I want to know who tried to kill me."

"I'm sure you do. But I'll tell you right now, the chances of finding out *here* are just about zero. You don't know this place. You don't know the Fugates, you don't know the colony's geography, you don't who's been coming and going."

"What are you saying? That we shouldn't even try?"

"No. I'm saying that if someone on the colony had a go at you, the Fugates themselves will try to find out who it was. You already admit they don't seem to have any form-change secrets. So how do you think they feel, when a visitor comes here to their turf and nearly gets knocked off? I'll tell you. They're as pissed as you would be if someone was murdered in your own house. They'll try and find out who done it. It don't matter if you're here or not."

"That's what I said. You're telling me we're useless—that there's nothing we can do." Sondra was beginning to feel better. She was also beginning to feel very peculiar inside, in a way that she found hard to analyze.

"Didn't say that." Aybee scowled horribly at her. "You gotta listen better. I said there's nothing useful to be done *here*. See, chances are whoever tried to do you in isn't a Fugate at all. It's somebody from outside. And if that's true, you an' me got lots to do. We zip outa here, lock into one of the big government data bases for the Kuiper Belt, and see who's been coming and going."

"The Fugates could do that, too, working from here."

"They could. But for this the balance tilts the other

way. They know this colony inside-out, but they don't know the Belt. I do. An' I'm smarter than a hundred Fugates. So let's go do it. All right?"

"I agree. But one other thing first." Sondra had finally identified the odd feeling inside her. It was starvation. The form-change tank had kept her alive and hydrated, but in doing so it had not provided any form of nutrients. After more than two days without food, her body was short about ten thousand calories. She stood up and stepped forward out of the tank. "No arguments on this one, Aybee. Before we go anywhere, or meet with anyone, or talk with anyone, or do *anything*—I get to *eat*."

Way to go!

Sondra watched drowsily as Aybee skipped through the transportation data bases of the Kuiper Belt. He did it effortlessly (and illegally, though that obviously did not worry him), without seeming to think, the way that sea-gulls flew or Bey Wolf evaluated the results of a form-change program. It was a thing of beauty, a joy to watch. At least it was a joy at the moment, for a person who had escaped death just a few hours ago, and who had even more recently stuffed herself with high-calorie food until her stomach rebelled and vetoed another bite.

Maybe when her brain was fully engaged it would be time for feelings of her own inferiority. But for the moment, and for the next half-hour or so until she fell asleep . . .

She jerked upright. She was doing it already. "Are you finding anything?"

Aybee nodded at her question. He didn't seem to mind that he was doing all the work. Actually, Sondra had the feeling he would be annoyed if she tried to help—and at the rate he worked, the most that she would do was slow him down. The Rini ship, through some method that Aybee did not attempt to explain, permitted real-time access to the entire Belt transportation manifest, both cargo and people. Aybee was wandering now through a listing of ships and destinations, grunting to himself in disgust.

"Too much." He tapped a key, and a long list began to race through the display area. "You want to know how many people from BEC traveled to the colonies in the past month? Take a peek. There they are, all seven thousand of 'em. At least a hundred of those could have done a quick skip over to the Fugate Colony on 'official' business."

"I don't think the Fugate trouble had anything to do with BEC."

"Makes things worse. If it's not just BEC you can multiply my number by a thousand. Let me try something else, see who came out here hi-speed from the inner system." Aybee began to enter another query string. "And while I'm doing that, maybe you can tell me something. The Wolfman says you listened in on his chit-chat with Robert Capman, when Capman said to look at the history of elliptic functions. What did you make of it?"

That took thought—far more thought than Sondra was capable of at the moment. She shook her head. "I didn't make anything of it. Not a thing. Did you say Bey talked to you about it?"

"Well, more like he *asked* me about it."

"What did you tell him?"

That question was a mistake. Sondra realized it within twenty seconds, as Aybee started to talk about people and times and concepts that she had never heard of. ". . . Abel, Jacobi, and Gauss . . . invert the problem . . . doubly periodic and analytic . . . theta function . . ." She lolled back in her seat, listened to the babble of words, watched Aybee's agile fingers rippling across the control panel, and knew that she was going under. It was peaceful and pleasant and satisfying, nothing like the black descent into unconsciousness of the previous day, but it was just as certain.

Aybee's sudden exclamation forced her closing eyes to blink open again.

"Hey! Look at that." He froze the display. "There's one to think about, from just a couple of weeks ago. Ultra-high transit, Mars orbit to the Belt. Destination, Samarkand."

"Mmm? S'markan." That meant, don't talk to me any more, I'm too far gone. But Aybee didn't interpret it right.

"Yeah, Samarkand. Old-fashioned Belt colony, one of the originals. But that's not the weird bit. Take a peek at the ship logo. GZM. Know what that stands for? GZM is Gertrude Zenobia Melford—it's the flagship of the whole Melford fleet. So what's old Trudy been doing, zipping out to Samarkand and back? Isn't that the last place in the Belt you'd expect to find her? Isn't it? Hey, you!"

He moved in front of Sondra and pushed his face close to hers. She did not move. Aybee glowered down at her.

"That's really great. Stuff yourself like a pig, then pass out on me. Wait 'til I talk to the Wolfman. For this one he owes me *bigtime*."

He pushed Sondra's seat away from the vertical, and her limp body rolled back with it like a rag doll. Aybee gave her a final glare, then turned back to the console.

He was not really annoyed that Sondra had passed out on him. Rather the opposite. All real work was done solo, everybody knew that, and given his choice he didn't even like to be *watched*.

Cross your fingers. With any luck she would sleep for a *long* time; that way, by the time she woke up he should have a decent mapping of those make-no-sense travel patterns through the Kuiper Belt.

CHAPTER 16

Every inch of space on the desk was occupied. A jumble of diagrams and flow charts and scribbled notes had been produced and discarded, until they covered the desk top and overflowed onto the floor. Around the walls of the room, every display held its own nested set of schematics.

Bey felt totally at home. The setting possessed the totally organized chaos of his own office. It was the shocking intrusive voice in his ear that felt alien: "Six hours remaining air supply at moderate activity level. Replenishment recommended."

He heard the warning of the suit's internal monitor with astonishment. It insisted that he had been on the surface of Mars for fifteen hours. To him, it was no time at all since he had followed that trail of flattened vegetation toward the overhanging rock.

Georgia Kruskal noticed his change of posture. She paused in her explanation of a flow-chart detail and looked up at him questioningly. Bey was learning to read the expressions in those thick-lashed, liquid eyes.

"My suit." He tapped on the helmet with a thin-gloved hand. "Telling me I ought to go. I've been here longer than I thought."

The broad camel's mouth stretched wide into a smile. "Time flies when you're having fun."

Bey nodded. It was more than a joke. There was nothing in the world—in any world—more satisfying than digging into the heart of a new form, grasping it as a whole, turning it around in your mind, and sensing its shape. Not its *physical* shape, which anyone could see; its *logical* shape, with its envelope of possibilities and future potential.

Bey himself had that gift. So did Georgia Kruskal. He knew it, and so did she. Within a quarter of an hour of first meeting they had moved to a shared concentration so deep that Bey had no other memories of their time together. Had he eaten, or drunk anything? Had she?

It was not important. The only important thing was the ideas that had flowed between them.

"You are free to stay here as long as you like," she said. "I do not have to tell you that. We can easily renew your suit supplies." Georgia gestured around her at the sea of notes and drawings. "I will not say that I am *humbled*—that is not within my compass of feelings—but I will admit that I have learned something."

"Me too." Bey stood up and stretched. "But I must go. Other work to do."

"I am sure there is. Projects of your own are awaiting your return." Georgia Kruskal also rose.

It was a comment, not a question. She was merely acknowledging the importance of Bey's own work. The effect was to make him feel guilty and slightly resentful. No one else knew it, but he *had* been doing important work back on Wolf Island—as important as the surface form project here on Mars. Somehow he had been persuaded to put it to one side.

Or rather, for some reason still unclear to him, he had persuaded himself that he should come to Mars. It was his own conviction of something new and profoundly important that had allowed his work on Earth to be interrupted. *No man is demolished save by himself.*

"I will walk with you to your car." Georgia had taken him by the arm and was already leading the way, back through the dim-lit corridor. "It will take a little while to learn how the ideas you have given us work out in practice. I hope you will return here to see for yourself. You will of course be welcome at any time. Even" —she paused, and swept Bey from head to foot with an evaluating stare— "to move here permanently. New Mars is the future. Old Mars, like Earth itself, is the past." The muzzle turned to face him. "I see that you are smiling."

"Probably." They were already at the surface, and Bey saw what he should have realized before they left Georgia's office. Fifteen hours after dawn brought you to the early part of the Martian night. He faced a blind flight to Melford Castle, lit only by stars and the wan inadequate gleam of Phobos and Deimos. "You see," he went on, "what you are saying is something I have heard all around the solar system, everywhere from Cloudland to the Kernel Ring to the Kuiper Belt. And now from Mars: Earth is history, it's over and done with. A new idea from Earth is a contradiction in terms."

"Perhaps you hear it because it is true."

"Perhaps. Or maybe it's just like the bumble-bee."

"Bumble-bee?" They were close enough to the aircar for Bey to see it as a faint shape in front of him. Georgia had paused, her thick-fingered hand tight on his arm. "I have heard that word. But I have never seen one."

"It's an Earth insect. A big, fat-bodied bee with little short wings. From an aerodynamic point of view, a bumble-bee cannot possibly fly."

"So?"

"The bumble-bee is stupid. It does not understand aerodynamics. So it flies anyway." Bey opened the door of the car and stepped up into it. "And the people on Earth are too stupid to realize that they cannot have new ideas. So . . ."

Georgia was invisible on the dark ground. Bey heard her thin chuckle in the darkness. "I hear you. But here on Mars, your bumble-bee truly cannot fly. While a man from Earth, as you have so clearly proved, can have new ideas. Your design of an organic radio for vacuum communication is totally new to our thinking, and may be hugely valuable. More important still are your ideas on form stabilization. You belong here, Behrooz Wolf, here on this new frontier. Think about that. Go and do your Earth work. But as soon as it is finished, return—and stay."

The car door closed on her final words. Bey gave the command to return to the home hangar. Thirty unnerving seconds followed, of lurching, swaying movement in total darkness; then suddenly the car was airborne, lifting steadily and turning in its path.

Presumably it knew what it was doing. If not, Bey was in no position to over-rule its decisions. He crouched low in his seat, peered into blackness, and was aware of a nervously growling stomach.

Hunger? It had to be. That sort of indulgence would have to wait until he was out of his suit and inside Melford Castle. He pushed away thoughts about his insides. Other matters had priority. *Come to Mars, Behrooz Wolf.* It was the third proposition of that kind in just a few weeks. Rafael Fermiel and the policy council had tried to recruit him to their cause, the protection of the interests of Old Mars. Georgia Kruskal wanted him to join her project, the creation of a New Mars on the surface.

And Trudy Melford wanted him on Mars—for what?

In his years with the Office of Form Control Bey had met a fair number of fanatics, individuals whose life revolved around a single issue. Sometimes they were easy to spot. Anyone who had ever looked into the glowing, magnetic eyes of Black Ransome would know at once that this was a man obsessed by power. But Cinnabar Baker, who controlled much of Cloudland, seemed at first meeting a relaxed and easy-going woman. You had to see a lot of her before you felt the formidable will-power and the dedication. Georgia was a fanatic, too, of the second kind. Easy-going on the surface, but she would do anything to further the cause of New Mars. And she had a huge ego—even by Bey's own standards.

Rafael Fermiel did not seem like a fanatic at all. He acted like an ordinary, worried man. Unless he was far more subtle and devious than he appeared, someone or something stood behind him and the Old Mars policy group, driving them on. And, if Bey's instincts meant anything, that same someone was providing the vast funding that supported the Old Mars terraforming efforts. It was a strange contradiction, that *Old Mars* stood for transforming the planet until it was just like Earth, while *New Mars* wanted a world without additional changes.

And Trudy Melford?

As before, Bey's thought came to this point, and stopped dead. If Trudy was fanatical about anything, it was a need beyond Bey's understanding. She owned BEC, and that made her the richest woman in the solar system. It did not prove anything. Sometimes wealth and power merely created the desire for more of the same. But neither money nor power seemed to drive Trudy.

Anger?

Revenge?

Deep insecurity?

Bey sighed. Maybe Georgia Kruskal was right. He ought to be back on Earth, doing what he knew how to do. Instead he was far from home, trying to do what he didn't know how to do. The aircar was feathering down through the quiet night sky of Mars, closing on what he hoped was an invisible runway.

Bey was tired, more than ready for food and sleep. It was just as well that he didn't know what he was going to get.

✧ ✧ ✧

The flight back had not been exactly frightening, but any silent, sightless run above a surface so inhospitable to a standard human form carried with it at least a little tension.

Bey felt easier at once when the car landed and rolled on to place itself in the hangar. The walk in the dark that followed called for the help of a flashlight taken from the car, but it did not take long. The first half of the ride down the escalator was nothing more than boring. By the time he reached the way-station lock and could at last remove his suit, most of his attention was already looking ahead to an early visit to the Melford Castle dining-room.

A little sign stood at the way-station lock exit when Bey emerged from it: MAINTENANCE WORK SCHEDULED FOR ESCALATOR. ALTERNATIVE ROUTE AVAILABLE VIA CARGO CHANNEL, WITH POSSIBLE DELAY.

He moved to the dim-lit escalator and stared down its segmented spiral. It was working, exactly as usual. Either the maintenance work was all finished, or possibly it had not yet begun.

He stepped onto the broad, shelf-like top step, and was carried smoothly downward. Five hundred meters to go, at maybe five meters a second. Almost two minutes of descent, with nothing but blank walls and the spiral above and below to look at.

Bey stared at his feet. Each step was made of some kind of lightweight plastic honeycomb. He could see through the wide-spaced square grille of the white plastic to a similar step ten meters below, and imagine that he could see through *that*, to another and still lower step, until every space in the grille at his feet was filled by some part of a step beneath. *Olbers' Paradox, escalator version: Why is the sky dark at night? Answer: In this case, it isn't*. He could see nothing below but white steps.

What was far more difficult to understand was just how successive plates of the escalator were linked, and it was harder yet to comprehend what happened at the bottom, where the steps must somehow turn around and ascend again to the top of their segment. He tried to visualize a double spiral, simultaneously descending and ascending. An unfolding double helix. *Escalator DNA; continuously unraveling*.

Bey was not so much thinking as drifting, passing the time in idle and random association until this piece of his journey was over and he could get on to the next one. When the unrelieved pattern of white at his feet was broken to become a fine grid of black, it did not alarm him. It did not even particularly interest him. It meant only that the escalator ride was almost over, and would soon discharge him onto the hard black surface of the tunnel to Melford Castle.

But some piece of his mind, far beneath conscious level, must have been keeping an exact count of escalator segments. He suddenly knew they should not yet be at the bottom—certainly not within one turn of the helix.

He stared hard at the step he was standing on. The dark beyond the grille was more prominent, as though some other step beneath it was no longer there. That was impossible. Unless he had miscounted and they were approaching the bottom. Or unless . . .

Bey looked, not down but along the stepped spiral of steps ahead. He could see eight steps, stretching away to form a full hundred and eighty degrees of turning descent. For a moment he was reassured—until, as he watched, the most distant step below him vanished.

In its place stood nothing. Not another and different color of step, not the approaching floor of the tunnel. Nothing. Except that as he looked, he saw a faint, far-off light. *That* had to be the tunnel, its wall lights at least twenty meters below him—the height of a tall building.

As he watched, another step vanished from sight. It must somehow be curving back under the escalator and re-ascending. But who cared where it went, or how? The gulf in front of Bey was closer. The escalator was still moving steadily down. There were only six more steps ahead. After that the one beneath his feet would disappear in its turn. He would drop, fifteen meters to a stone-hard floor. Ten meters were often enough to kill a man.

He turned and began to run back up the turning staircase of the escalator. After ten steps he risked a glance behind. It was still six steps to the edge. He could keep up with the escalator—just, in a true Red Queen's Race, running as fast as he could to stay in the same place.

But for how long? He had seen no halfway point where he could escape from the escalator. The only way he could reach safety was to run all the way back up to the top: half a kilometer, vertically, while the descending escalator steadily nullified his upward progress. Bey knew that was far beyond his physical powers, probably beyond the endurance of the best athlete in the system.

He was already panting for breath. The thinner air of the Mars interior atmosphere offered him less oxygen. Muscle fatigue provided the growing pain of lactic acid build-up in his calves and thighs. His efforts had bought him a couple of minutes of thinking time, but at a price. Even with the reduced Martian gravity, another thirty seconds would put additional exertions beyond him.

Bey spun around again to face the descending steps. When the one he was standing on vanished he would face a fifteen-meter drop. Lie flat until the last moment and then hang at arms-length, and it would become a bit less than thirteen meters. A thirteen meter drop on Mars. What did that equate to on Earth?

Aybee could have told him the answer in a fraction of a second. Unfortunately, Aybee was a few tens of billions of kilometers away. Bey was on his own. Mars surface gravity, about forty percent of Earth's. Terminal velocity for a given distance of fall proportional to the square root of acceleration. So thirteen meters on Mars was like thirteen times the square root of 0.4 on Earth; say, thirteen times—

No time. And no choice, even if he didn't like the answer.

Bey was again facing up the escalator, his feet placed on the step below. When he felt it vanish beneath them he gripped the leading edge of the step above him. The one his knees rested on would be gone soon, in another second or so. He had to hang on until the step he held reached its lowest point before turning to ascend. Then—

It all happened while he was still thinking it through. His hands released as soon as he felt the edge of the step begin to turn. And then he was falling.

The lower Mars gravity offered one other small advantage. The duration of his fall was longer. He could orient his body upright, bend his knees slightly, and hope to land and roll.

Bey did everything perfectly. His reward was a sharp cracking sound as he hit. He felt a horrible shooting pain in his left ankle, followed immediately by the equal agony of a breaking left arm and ribs as his body rolled into the hard floor of the tunnel.

He lay still, the left side of his face flat against the smooth surface. He could feel cold sweat bursting out all over his body. He had the answer now to his question, how far was a thirteen-meter fall on Mars? It was too far, too much for human flesh and bone. He felt as though any form of movement would kill him.

But he knew that no form of movement would also kill him. The tunnel, one kilometer down, was balmy compared with the surface of Mars, but it was still at freezing-point. Heat was seeping out of his body into the cold tunnel floor. A few hours of that and he would be dead, regardless of his injuries.

He lifted his head and stared a worm's-eye view along the cold, black floor. The chance that someone would conveniently wander along the tunnel to save him was flat zero. He would be almost as well off waiting for a savior out on the barren surface. If he didn't do it, no one else would. He had to make his way to the little cars that ran to and from the entrance to Melford Castle. He had to lift himself into one. And somehow, at the other end, he had to lift himself out.

There was just one problem. He couldn't do it. By pushing with his right leg and pulling with his right arm, he could advance a painful few feet along the tunnel before he had to rest. The car he needed was over a hundred meters away.

Think of the alternative. Bey made another great effort and dragged himself a little farther. A hundred meters was nothing but two meters, repeated fifty times. You moved, and you moved again. Or you died. The square root of 0.4 was close to 0.6. And 0.6 times thirteen meters—Bey pushed and pulled and inched forward—that was less than eight meters. Trained acrobats on Earth could take a fall of eight meters and not think twice about it. Which only proved—*pull and push and move*—what you already knew, that you were not a trained acrobat.

Even if you were, climbing into a car with a broken ankle, arm and ribs would be quite a trick. Something new would be needed for that. Better think it through. Bey slithered his way along like a crippled snail. Or maybe better not think it through. One problem at a time was enough. More than enough.

He lifted his head. Good news: The car was noticeably

nearer, and the pain in his ankle was marginally less. Bad news: Before he could reach the level of the car, he would have to hoist himself up a two-foot step on the tunnel floor.

One problem at a time. Bey humped and slithered and scrabbled, until the fingertips on his right hand were bloodied and broken-nailed. At last he was as close to the car as he could get. It was maybe five meters away; and he could no more lift himself up the two-foot barrier than fly across it.

The car was open and waiting. It could respond to his voice command and move freely backward and forward. What it could not do, ever, was move *sideways* toward Bey. It was a rail car, it sat on tracks, and its motion was totally fixed by them.

Bey sympathized with it. Both of them were stuck in grooves, their actions completely decided by outside constraints.

He could order the car to proceed at maximum speed and smash into the courtyard of Melford Castle. That should arouse enough excitement to bring someone here. Only it wouldn't work. The car's own safety system would over-ride any command and slow it down before it approached the castle.

He lifted his head as far as he could and surveyed the walls and ceiling of the tunnel. Nothing there. Both were simple plain surfaces, made of compacted regolith. There would be scheduled maintenance monitoring, looking for fallen rocks from wall or ceiling, and unlike the waiting car the machines that did the work were smart and mobile and general-purpose. But their inspections would be few and far between. He might wait for weeks before the next one was due.

Wrong again. His desiccated corpse would wait for weeks. Bey, the real Bey Wolf, would be long gone.

He stared again at the rail car. It could hear his

commands, but it had no voice circuits to reply to them. That was no problem for a passenger, who could see the internal displays. Bey, lying flat on the floor, enjoyed no such privilege.

Did it have visual sensors, enough to make sure that it did not run into fallen rocks? Probably, and it would surely report what it saw to the maintenance machines. But it probably saw only things in its immediate path.

But it might *accept* other reports.

"Attention. There has been a major rock fall, close to the rail car escalator terminus." Bey spoke as loudly and clearly as he could, aware that his voice was shaking. He was tempted to continue, adding a warning that fallen rock might form a danger to traffic. Except that he would be wasting his time. The car was *simple*. If it accepted a message at all, it would be a simple one.

A loud buzzing click came from the car. Bey prepared to repeat his message, thinking that a communications system might be switching on; then he realized that the car was moving. Before he could move or speak again, it accelerated smoothly away along the tunnel and vanished from view.

Bey lowered his head, until his face was again touching the floor. It was colder than ever, but it no longer felt unpleasant. Wasn't freezing supposed to be one of the best ways to go, with death stealing over you like a gentle sleep?

Maybe it was—if you were ready to go.

Bey lifted his head and deliberately flexed the muscles of his left arm and leg. The pain was quite intolerable and it brought him up to full alertness. He waited a few seconds, then did the same thing again. Isometric exercises with broken bones. A new form of calisthenics, guaranteed to keep the subject awake. Again. And again. Every thirty seconds.

Bey squeezed his eyes shut, gritted his teeth, and

counted out the interval. Thirty seconds. Again. And again.

He was still doing it half an hour later, when a hiss sounded just a few feet away. He opened his eyes. A wheeled, multi-armed machine stood there facing him. The arms were reaching out, reaching down. They were strong enough to move two-ton rocks, but they were not used to dealing with delicate human tissue.

"Hey! You can't just pick me up like that—I have broken bones. I need careful handling. I need—"

What Bey needed was lost in a scream of pain. It made no difference at all to the machine, which could not hear him. It was a simple rock-clearer. What it had just picked up was not what it had been sent to pick up, namely, a fall of rocks. This object was in the way and it certainly had to be moved; however, its final disposition must be referred to a different and more sophisticated machine.

Decisions like that went far beyond rock-clearer grade level.

CHAPTER 17

The full extent of Sondra's failure didn't hit her until she was fed, rested, and back inside Rini Base.

She had traveled all the way from Earth to the Carcon and Fugate Colonies, seen everything there was to see, examined form-change hardware and software in enormous detail—and learned nothing. Nothing about the anomaly of the feral forms, that is. Someone had tried to kill her, but what had she learned from that?

She needed to talk it over with somebody but Aybee was useless. He was retreating again into his own world of physics, unpersuaded that there had really been a murder attempt.

"Be logical." He was frowning over an equation, a single line of squiggles that went right across the screen. "I told you, if somebody wanted to zap you they'd choose a better way. For one thing, it didn't work."

"It would have, if you hadn't come along when you did."

"Nah. You could have survived in that tank for weeks. The Fugates would have found you and hauled you out."

"Whoever did it hadn't realized I could change the tank so it would keep me alive."

"So what? If I want to off somebody, I don't fiddle with air pressure and temperature. I do it more direct.

A nice big explosion, or a hundred thousand volts in a terminal keyboard or toilet seat, or nerve poison in the food."

"Not if you want people to think it might have been an accident."

"Hey, I think it *was* an accident. One of the Fugates screwed up and changed that chamber to open space conditions, but they didn't want to admit it."

This, from someone who had actually been present. How would it sound to Denzel Morrone and the Office of Form Control, tucked away safe back on Earth? They'd all say she was just being paranoid.

"I wish I could talk to Bey Wolf about this, Aybee. I bet he'd know what's going on. He was the one who told me my answer would be out here in the Kuiper Belt."

"Yeah. But your answer to *what*?" Aybee swiveled impatiently around in his chair. "Did he tell you that? See, everybody looks at the world from his own point of view. I call it the ground state of the resting mind. It's like an excited electron, left to itself it drops back to its ground state. And your brain does the same thing, left alone it returns to and thinks about what it's really interested in. With me, the ground state is physics. With the Wolfman, it's form-change methods. Question is, what is it for *you*?" And, when Sondra showed no sign of answering, "Look, if you want to talk to Wolf be my guest."

"I don't just mean sending him a message. I mean *talk* to him on Wolf Island, in real-time."

"I know you do. But this here is Liberty Hall." Aybee gestured around him. "You're on Rini Base, where the fancy stuff is standard. I'll patch you direct to the inner system through the kernels."

"You can really do that?"

"Would I lie to you? It's how I talked to Bey before I

took off for the Fugates. Takes a few minutes to set up the links, but then you only have just a short chat lag when either one of you speaks. I'll fix you up with your own line, too, so you can talk private."

Aybee was already busy, setting up the pathway. Sondra started to thank him, but as he waved her away she realized the truth. He would set her up with her own line to the inner system so that *he* had privacy. He had suffered through the past few days as a favor to Bey Wolf; now he couldn't wait to get back to physics, the "ground state of his resting mind."

The trouble was, the connection was not going to Aybee's liking. He was grunting and muttering, trying different combinations.

"Not on Wolf Island." He glanced up at Sondra. "In fact, not anywhere on Earth, unless he switched his personal code right out of the system. What do you think?"

"Mars?" *I'll bet Trudy Melford has her claws in him again.*

Sondra had a sudden faint memory of something else. Something about Trudy, something that Aybee had mentioned just after they left the Fugate Colony. She had to ask him about that, and all the stuff about the history of elliptic functions that she had not been able to take in at the time.

But not right now. "Try him on Mars."

"Sure. He called me from there last time." Aybee tinkered again with the path settings. After a couple of minutes he shook his head. "No good."

"He's not there?"

"He is. His ID shows a definite location. See that code, *Melford Castle*. Melford Castle! I didn't realize the Wolfman was in so deep with the high and mighty." Aybee was too intent on the displays to notice Sondra's reaction to his phrasing. "But he's not answering. He's busy, or he's in bed."

Or both. "It doesn't matter. I don't want to talk to him any more."

She couldn't leave it at that. Aybee had turned to stare. Her anger—a totally irrational irritation that she could not explain to herself—was showing through. "I really shouldn't be talking to Bey anyway, I ought to be in touch with the people who sent me out here. Can you reach Earth's Office of Form Control?"

"Anything that turns you on. You want me to leave a 'call waiting' for the Wolfman?"

"No. I mean, yes. Tell him I'd like to talk to him. But tell him I wouldn't want it to interfere with his other activities—whatever they are."

God, she was at it again. It was a great relief—probably to both of them—when Aybee finally nodded and said, "We got a call going in to the Office of Form Control. You can pick it up a couple of rooms down."

Sondra fled along the corridor to the room that Aybee had described. In front of the terminal she paused, marvelling at her own stupidity. The link to the Office of Form Control was ready and waiting. In trying to turn aside Aybee's curiosity she had forced herself to communicate with her own office. And she had nothing to offer them but an admission of failure. After pushing for permission to fly all the way out to the Kuiper Belt, she had learned nothing new about the feral forms.

Maybe she could get away with a check of her own answering service, and escape.

She sat down and signaled the interaction to begin. She expected the standard response, which would ask where she wanted the call routed. Instead she found the smooth, well-groomed face of Denzel Morrone staring out at her.

He seemed as surprised as Sondra. As well he should be. He was three levels up from her, head of the whole show. He would normally speak to her only when he decided he wanted to, or she made a special and formal request.

"Excuse me." At the moment Sondra would have made a special request *not* to speak to him. "I didn't expect my call to go—"

"All Rini-transmitted calls from the Kuiper Belt and beyond are screened by my office." Morrone's surprised expression was gone, replaced by the usual bland facade. "I trust that what you have to report is significant enough to justify the use of such a high-priority channel."

I can't blame Aybee. He was just trying to help.

"I believe that an attempt was made to kill me while I was on the Fugate Colony."

"Indeed?" One eyebrow lifted perhaps a millimeter. Sondra immediately regretted her words. She should have thought everything through before she spoke.

"That is an extraordinary accusation," Morrone continued. "I hope you are able to justify it. It is a far cry from the investigation of a couple of humanity test failures, which is the reason that your journey to the Kuiper Belt was approved by this office, to a claim of attempted murder. Tell me, please, exactly what happened on the Fugate Colony, from the moment of your arrival there."

She was in the trap, just as she had feared, and there was no way out. Sondra described everything in detail, from her reception by the two Amaris and on through her painstaking examination of the form-change equipment. She began to talk about her modification of the tank controller, with the tricky and delicate modifications she had been forced to make.

"But what did you *discover*?" Denzel Morrone interrupted her as she was telling how the air pressure and temperature had continued to plummet. "I mean, what do you know now that you did not know when you left Earth? I am referring, of course, to the reason that the feral form passed the humanity test."

Sondra swallowed hard. Here came the worst part.

"Nothing. I could determine no way that the test might have failed. I still see no way."

"Indeed." Denzel Morrone studied his well-buffed fingernails, refusing to meet Sondra's eye. "Maybe we can both agree that *something* certainly failed. Go on."

It was obvious what he was implying. Sondra bit back her anger. She described the sealed chamber, the deadly temperature, the thinning air.

"Certainly, certainly." Morrone flourished a large, fleshy hand to cut her off. "All the form-change tanks in that chamber were empty, you already told me that. There was no reason to keep the place warm and pressurized."

"But I was *inside*—"

"Of the two hundred thousand and more people who live and work on the Fugate Colony, a small handful knew that you were a visitor; and just two of those realized that you were inside that form-change room. No doubt some member of the maintenance staff, engaged in routine duties of cleaning and sterilizing an area—"

"The room was an interior chamber, not near to the outside. It couldn't have happened that way." Except that as she spoke, Sondra realized that it surely could. The very fact that the Fugates had been able to provide the chamber with her preferred working environment implied that it had its own controls for temperature and pressure.

"I would appreciate it if you will refrain from interrupting me when I am speaking." Morrone's tone was as polite and easy as ever. His face told a different story. "As I said, this sounds to me like an accident, and a simple and natural one. It is not attempted murder. It is merely a case where one personnel unit on the colony was unaware of the actions of another. When you attain the management level where a large number of people work for you—assuming that such an unlikely event ever occurs—you will realize that in spite of the best possible safeguards and written regulations, occasional misunderstandings are inevitable."

The unforgiving mouth pursed. "I feel sure that is what happened on the colony. As for the rest of your report, I need to consider it in some detail. It would not be fair to you if I failed to mention, here and now, that I am greatly disappointed by your total failure to achieve progress on the project assigned to you. That, too, I must consider in detail." The carefully groomed head nodded. "In *great* detail."

Sondra opened her mouth to reply, although just what she would say she did not know. And then it became totally irrelevant. Before she could offer a word in her defense the connection was terminated at the other end. Denzel Morrone nodded and vanished from the screen.

The interaction had been a disaster. When two individuals as different as Aybee and Denzel Morrone listened to the evidence and arrived at the same conclusion, what chance was there that *anyone* would think as she did? It would need someone with superhuman intelligence and intuition to define a different answer that took into account all the facts. No matter what Sondra might have thought in her early student days, she did not claim superhuman intelligence. Anyway, too many people had recently told her otherwise.

It was time to run back to the inner system with her tail between her legs, and hope for Denzel Morrone's good will. It was not something for which he was famous. Sondra sat down at the terminal and asked for a preliminary transit ship schedule to Earth.

And then she changed her mind; she would ask for something quite different.

The message was short, but only because she had slaved on it for hours to reduce her original rambling request.

In its final form she was pretty happy with it. If it failed, nothing was lost. And if it were successful . . .

To: Robert Capman

From: Sondra Dearborn

In a recent conversation with Behrooz Wolf, you stated "on some future occasion I would like to meet her." I am the "her" in question, and I would very much like to talk with you. I could do so over a link, although my preference would be to meet with you in person, and as soon as possible.

Aybee wandered in while the message was still on the screen. He whistled and shook his head. "Dream on, girl. Did Capman really say that he wanted to meet you?"

"He did. But I don't know why. Did you ever meet him?"

Aybee shook his head. "Not yet. But I've had messages from him, 'cause he reads a lot of my stuff. Field theory, mostly. You don't *ask* for a meeting with Capman, by the way. He grants you an audience—if he feels like it."

"Bey Wolf has no trouble getting through to him. Capman even tried to recruit Bey, to change to a Logian form and go to work on Saturn."

"That's different. Him and Bey have what you might call a special relationship. Bey was the only one who realized what Capman was, way back when everybody else in the system was convinced that the man was a multiple murderer of small children."

"I know all about that." It was another legend of the Office of Form Control. "Nothing wicked was going on."

"Sure, you know it now, we all do. Pretty easy with hindsight. But it took real insight to sniff out what Capman was doing back then, and Capman himself was the first to realize that. Like I say, the Wolfman's a special case. The chances of you or me or anyone else asking for a meeting with Capman and getting one right off the bat is like a snowball's chance—"

Aybee paused. A message was creeping onto the display, its data points filling in from random noise like a pointillist painting.

"—a snowball's chance on the Ganymede ice cap," Aybee finished. "What do you say to that, then? Guess you're on your way to downtown Saturn. Leave your rings in the hotel safe."

To meet in person. Except that of course you couldn't, not really, when one of you needed an oxygen atmosphere and the other lived in mostly methane. No matter what type of air was provided one of you would choke and die. The best you could manage was a talk with a glass wall between you.

So why had she asked for a face-to-face meeting? Maybe it showed a suspicion that any long-distance link could be tapped. Bey Wolf's paranoia was infectious. There was no such thing as safe conversation unless it was a direct one between two isolated individuals—and perhaps not even then.

Sondra sat waiting, more nervous than she had ever been. The ship she had ridden to Saturn had parked itself in equatorial orbit not far below the innermost ring. Less than two minutes after her arrival she had seen another little ship rising up to meet her from the brown and crimson thunderclouds of the Saturn upper atmosphere. The new ship lacked any sign of the usual tongue of flame or laser boost needed for flight out of a deep gravity well. It simply rose and rose, until it was clearly homing in on the vessel waiting in orbit.

Sondra felt the slight vibration of a smooth docking. She waited, staring expectantly at the transparent wall. Not many people in their whole lifetime got to see a Logian form. Still fewer were privileged to meet with Robert Capman.

The door of the room at the other side of the partition

slid open. A bulky grey form appeared, moving easily on massive triple-jointed legs to stand close to the glass. It raised a hand in greeting.

Sondra had to tell herself that, regardless of appearances, a human being was waving to her. Or rather, he had started his life, like all Logian forms, as a human. Sondra herself, or any man or woman given an injection of Logian DNA and access to a form-change tank, could become as Robert Capman. And if she really wanted to (though few Logian forms ever did) she could then change back to human form.

Capman was studying her, his pearly, luminous eyes drinking in every aspect of face and body. If they ever met again he would recognize her instantly. It was the least of the Logian talents.

"Sondra Dearborn." Capman's voice was soft, its sibilants slightly emphasized. "Sondra *Wolf* Dearborn. Tell me why you are here."

"I have a problem. I am unable to solve it. I seek your help."

"Ah." Capman sounded totally non-committal. "I thought you would know our strict rule: No Logian form will interfere in human affairs."

"I've heard it often enough, but I don't believe it." Sondra had decided even before she left the Rini Base that she had nothing to lose. She might as well stick her neck out and go for broke. "In fact, I can prove to you that your statement is not true."

"I would like to hear that argument."

"Do you admit that you have offered the Logian form to Behrooz Wolf?"

"That is true."

"And he refused."

"That is unfortunately the case. However, I have not abandoned hope."

"And when it comes to form-change, Wolf is one of

the best humans in the solar system. Would you agree with that?"

"No." The head bobbed forward in the Logian laugh, but Capman went on before Sondra could express her surprise. "I would not quite agree. Behrooz Wolf is not 'one of the best humans' in the solar system. When it comes to form change he is *the* best. *Others abide the question*, he is free."

Capman sounded uncomfortably like Bey himself—she was sure that last bit was some sort of quotation—but Sondra could not allow herself to become distracted. "So he's the best. Now suppose that one day you talked him into changing his mind, and coming to Saturn to be a Logian form and live with you. And suppose that later on a problem arose that Bey could have solved, and no one else. But now he's a Logian, so he follows the Logian rule, and says he can't become involved. Isn't *that* interfering in human affairs, by taking Bey out of circulation?"

"Indeed it is." Capman was nodding approvingly. "Please do not think for a moment that such an argument is new to us. *Every* Logian form removes a person from the human pool. In addition, our very existence—particularly the knowledge of our existence—has an inevitable effect on a great deal of human thought and behavior. What would you have us do? Cease to exist?"

"No. I want you to do just the opposite." Sondra leaned forward, wishing she could reach out and grab Capman by the arm. "Become *more* involved in what we do. Give advice."

"That avenue is not open. Not at the moment."

"Then at the very least, *listen* to what I have to say. If after that you choose to offer no comment, that is your option."

White membranes slid down and hooded the luminous eyes. Capman's head sank to his chest. After a few seconds he looked again at Sondra and nodded slowly. "Speak. Tell your story."

The moment of truth. She had one shot, and she had to get it just right. She had rehearsed what she wanted to say over and over on the flight to the inner system. According to Aybee it was a miracle that she was getting even this chance with Robert Capman.

The good news was that one shot with the Logian form was apparently all it ever took. Capman was super-bright even by Aybee's snooty standards, and he would catch on to everything instantly.

Aybee had offered one other piece of advice: "Provide more data and raw facts than you think anyone could possibly need or want or be able to take in. You can't flood a Logian."

Sondra started at the very beginning, when the news had first been given to her that she had a new assignment, and ground on through every event with what she felt to be stupefying detail. She showed all the data she had on the Carcon and Fugate forms. She spoke of her meetings with Bey, and of her unsuccessful attempt to enlist his direct assistance. She mentioned Bey's conversation with Capman, and was ready to skip over its content—after all, Capman had heard it for himself—until her audience interrupted: "Your recollection, please. Exactly as *you* remember it."

Sondra did her best, most uncomfortable when she spoke of Bey's evaluation of her brains—or lack of them. Capman clearly did not care. He sat impassive and focused. She plowed on, and finally came to her trip to the Kuiper Belt, then her close call on the Fugate Colony and her "rescue," though he would not admit it as that, by Aybee.

Capman neither moved nor spoke until the very end, when Sondra was summarizing Aybee's careful but inconclusive analysis of ship movements in and around the Kuiper Belt, with emphasis on trips to and from the colonies. She had been tempted to omit this information as irrelevant, but suddenly Capman was sitting up a little straighter. Did she imagine it, or was there also a gleam of speculation in those hard-to-read eyes?

"The record indicating trips by Gertrude Zenobia Melford's flagship to Samarkand." Capman's thick-fingered paw lifted in the murky, methane-rich air on the other side of the glass panel. "In full detail, if you please."

Sondra backed up, considerably puzzled, and presented the mass of data. With Aybee as a grumpy observer she had run through those records a dozen times. They had both agreed that the trips were odd and apparently meaningless. They seemed just as meaningless now, as she plowed through the thousands of entries for Capman's benefit.

"Curious." Was it imagination, or was Capman truly interested for the first time? One hand was touching his fringed mouth. "Curious, and anomalous."

He was silent for maybe ten seconds; according to what Sondra had heard about Logians, that was a long, long time. Difficult problems a Logian solved at once. Impossible ones took a little longer.

Finally Capman nodded. "I now have a question. Most of the calls made to and by Behrooz Wolf since your first visit to him form part of the general data records for the inner system. Have you reviewed those calls?"

"No. I didn't see how they could have anything to do with this."

"They are data. '*It is a capital mistake to theorize before one has data.*' "

"That's exactly what Bey Wolf said to me!"

"No doubt. We both cite a higher authority. But now, if you will, continue."

"There's nothing to continue *with*. That was the end."

"I thought as much. Very interesting. And in its way quite entertaining." Capman bowed, the thick body tilting forward a fraction. "Perhaps we will meet again. I cannot say that I approve of Behrooz Wolf's interest in you, but I do understand it."

He was turning, moving toward the chamber door.

"Wait. You can't leave." Sondra banged her fist on the glass, realizing too late that could be a dangerous act. "You haven't let me ask you anything."

The broad head turned and bobbed. Capman was *laughing*—laughing at her.

"Did I not inform you at the outset that our rules do not permit Logians to become involved in human affairs? However, Sondra Dearborn, I am going to bend that rule."

"You are? Then do it!"

"I do so when I make this statement: Based upon what you have told me and what I have told you, you have enough information to complete without assistance from anyone the task assigned to you by the Office of Form Control."

He bowed again and turned. The door in the adjoining chamber slid open and the great Logian body drifted out through it. One minute later, Sondra felt the slight jolt as the two ships separated and the Logian vessel headed for Saturn re-entry.

Sondra was alone again in space; not sure what she was supposed to have learned, but convinced, deep inside, that whatever she had learned would not be enough.

CHAPTER 18

The scene was much as Sondra had imagined it in conversation with Aybee: Bey on Mars, lying waiting in the ornate bed. Trudy Melford, scantily-clad and breathless, hovering over him.

But there were certain major differences. Trudy's arms and legs were bare, because that was her standard Martian day outfit. She was panting hard because she had run up eight flights of stairs rather than wait a few seconds for an elevator. And although Bey was waiting, it was not for anything that Trudy might do.

He was trussed and wrapped like a mummy, with swathes of bandages on his left arm, leg, head, and chest; a pair of annoying tubes ran into his nostrils, a line of electrodes nestled along the back of his neck, I/V's dripped into his good arm, and catheters had been inserted into body locations that he preferred not to think about.

It was depressing to feel like this, and be told that he was doing well. He was waiting impatiently for the medical equipment, clucking and chuntering at his bedside, to take a closer look and refute that optimistic assessment.

"I down-loaded from your message center." Trudy sat on the other side of the bed from the robodoc, her breasts still heaving disturbingly. "Nothing important. You should certainly stay at the castle until you are fully recovered. I can bring the best medical services in the solar system to you right here."

Bey reached out his right hand and picked up the little message transfer unit that Trudy had dropped carelessly onto the bed. Her definition of important might not coincide with his.

"Did you find out what happened?"

"We're not sure." Trudy's blue-green eyes met Bey's for a moment, then darted away. "It looks like an accident—the whole bottom section of the escalator had been removed for routine service. There should have been a notice that warned of scheduled maintenance."

"There was. I ought to have been more careful."

"Not really. There's no way that the escalator should ever have been running. The machines always stop it during repairs. Someone had to start it again, deliberately. I said, it *looked* like an accident; but I don't believe it was."

"Then what was it?"

"Sabotage." Trudy's gaze came back to meet Bey's. "A deliberate attempt to kill you."

"I'm not worth killing. In any case, no one knew that I was up there on the surface. Not even you, until the machines hauled me back to the castle."

"That's not true. At least one person did." Trudy gestured to the message unit. "You'll hear it on that. There's a call from Rafael Fermiel, asking you to contact him, in his words, 'as soon as you return from your trip to the surface.' How did he know you were going there?"

"I don't think he did. He *assumed* it, because he and his policy council think that I designed those surface forms myself. You know Fermiel?"

"Everyone on Mars knows him. He is the leader of the Old Mars faction—the Old Mars *fanatics*. If they had their way there would be no form-change in the

Underworld except for necessary medical repairs. They believe that the surest way to make sure that the Mars surface environment will become a close copy of Earth is to forbid radical form-change here. If Fermiel thinks you are the designer of the surface forms, then he has a motive to kill you. We also know that he expected you to visit the surface."

No form-change in the Underworld. Bey's aching head spun with that thought. It had implications. And more fanatics. It occurred to Bey that Mars was full of them, Georgia Kruskal and Trudy Melford and now Rafael Fermiel. Might Bey be one himself, and not even know it?

"Fermiel tried to recruit me. He doesn't have a reason to kill me, at least until I say no to his offer."

As a deliberate attempt to force a strong reaction from Trudy, it was a failure. She smiled. "He tried to recruit you? How strange. What does he have to offer you that I don't?"

"Safety, maybe. You haven't told me how someone could have entered Melford Castle and rigged the escalator."

"I don't know that yet. But I will." The blue-green eyes hardened. "Believe me, I will. You'll be safe here."

She knows who did it. Or at least she suspects. "If Rafael Fermiel is so against what you want to do, why not oppose him and the Underworld openly?"

"I can't do that. Neither I—nor BEC—is in the business of planetary politics."

Wrong answer. With Trudy's interest in the surface forms she ought to be a fervent New Mars supporter and a strong opponent of Old Mars. Why wasn't she? She said the Old Mars group were fanatics, but she did nothing to oppose their efforts. As for the suggestion that BEC did not play politics, when BEC had done it so cleverly and consistently for two centuries . . .

Bey was getting ideas, swimming vaguely around the base of his brain; he had a lot of thinking to do and he could not do it. The pain-inhibitor electrodes running along his neck from the fourth to the sixth cervical vertebrae did not interfere with the thinking process; BEC's best engineers had certified that fact. But how did they know? Who had ever been able to measure the *quality* of thought, to say how the processes that went on in the brain of a Darwin or a Newton was different from the normal?

Bey struggled to sit up. "You tell me you are not in the business of politics. Well, neither am I. And I don't want to *find* myself in the middle, when I choose not to be. I've made up my mind. I want to head back to Earth."

"You can't! You're too sick."

"Let me be the judge of that. What I need is a form-change machine and repair programs tuned to my own body. The best place for those is Wolf Island. That's where I'm going."

Bey had been testing again, and this time it worked. For just a second he saw the other side of the Empress. Trudy's face filled with an iron determination, the fixed stare of a woman who was operating under total compulsion. Then it was just as quickly gone. She was smiling at him, sweetly and sympathetically.

"I know how you must feel. You've had a terrible experience here at the castle, and you don't trust my word that it won't happen again. So go home to where you are comfortable. Go to Wolf Island, use your own form-change machine, and recuperate."

She didn't quite tell Bey there was no place like home, but he would not have been surprised if she had. In spite of that brief moment of a different look, she radiated warmth and concern.

And then he felt vulnerable, more like a sacrificial

lamb than the wolf of his name. Trudy could buy or sell him a thousand times over, he had known that before ever he met her. Now he realized that she could also sweet talk and cajole and beguile him—and he *liked it*. He could resist money, but could he resist the rest? Flattery never failed. If a woman would re-make her whole body into a form attractive to you, that ploy worked even if you saw through it. Even if you were convinced that she was doing it for her own motives, part of you still responded. Trudy was more dangerous than he had realized, smart enough to know when she should hold on and when she should let go.

"But promise me one thing." She leaned closer and ran gentle fingers around Bey's jawline. Her soft, concerned voice was like another physical caress—probably all the excitement that he could stand in his present condition. "As soon as you feel well enough to receive a visitor, let me know. I've been planning a surprise for you for a while, but this certainly isn't the time for it. I want you at your best. Just tell me when."

Bey had been gone from Wolf Island for only five days, but when he returned it felt like an alien place.

Part of that was surely the change in him. He had left in good physical condition, except for the slight natural myopia that a routine form-change session would have fixed. He returned a wreck, wearing a mechanical exoskeleton provided by the Martian robodoc. It allowed him to walk and carry things while keeping his own broken arm and leg completely still, but at the price of turning him into a clanking metal-and-plastic automaton that had Janus and Siegfried growling and snarling until the hounds were close enough to the jetty to catch his scent. And even with the pain-inhibitors still on his neck he ached all over and had trouble thinking. He couldn't wait to get to the basement lab and into a form-change machine.

There were other changes, though, that were not in him and which he could not ignore. Jumping Jack Flash had the run of the island when Bey was away from it, but usually he stayed inside the house. It was clear when Bey got there that the chimp had been feeding himself and the two dogs regularly, but there was no other sign of him.

Bey hobbled out into the fierce afternoon sunlight. He called "Flash! Flash!" as loudly as he could, but it was another five minutes before the pygmy chimp came wandering along, walking almost upright on the paved path from the island's rocky center. Instead of the usual greeting, jumping up to Bey and perching on his shoulder, Jumping Jack Flash stood and surveyed him with brown, sad eyes.

"Is it this?" Bey gestured with his right arm at the exoskeleton. "I don't like it any better than you do. Come on. Let's see how quickly I can get myself back to normal."

The three animals trailed quietly along behind as he went back into the house and descended to the basement level. He went into the lab and inspected the control panel for his preferred form-change tank. He knew what he wanted—the fastest repair program that he could stand. He also knew the risk of that. Once before he had used a form change that went far outside the envelope of accepted programs. It had almost killed him, and would have done so if someone else had not found his unconscious body. This time there was no one around to perform that favor.

He turned, and found the three animals still there, watching closely. He shook his head.

"Not you in the tank this time, my friends. Me."

They understood his body language if not his words. The two dogs flopped to their bellies on the smooth tiled floor, while Jumping Jack Flash approached and lifted his hand to run a rough knuckle under the exoskeleton and along Bey's jawline.

Bey reached up and gripped the chimp's hand. "First Trudy, and now you. But at least I know that you don't have a hidden agenda." Bey studied the glowing brown eyes and serious face. "Or I think you don't. It's a shame you can't speak, Flash. And you're so *close*. Maybe if we humans hadn't come along and taken over, in a few million years . . ."

Bey went back to his programing of the form-change machine. So close, so very close. It was far more than the ninety-nine percent of common DNA. Four hundred years ago, long before DNA had been dreamed of, almost a hundred years before Darwin, the great Swedish biologist Carl Linnaeus had made up his mind. He didn't dare to say that humans and chimps belonged in the same genus, because that would have created a religious fire-storm. Humans were supposed to be special, God-created, unique. But Linnaeus had confided his own true feelings in a letter to a friend:

> "I demand of you and of the whole world that you show me a generic character to distinguish between Man and Ape. I myself most assuredly know of none, and I wish somebody would indicate one to me. But if I had called man an ape or vice versa I would have fallen under the ban of all the ecclesiastics."

You couldn't work with chimps for more than a week or two without sharing Linnaeus's opinion. The line was hard to draw. But somehow, the form-change equipment could do it. No chimp had ever managed a form-change.

Bey began to set up the final parameters for his own program. Maybe it was the *purposive* element that the chimp could not manage. The thoughts of a chimp—there was no doubt that Jumping Jack Flash had thoughts—were probably foggy and imprecise, a more extreme version of Bey's own muddled thinking when the electronic pain-inhibitors were doing their job.

Successful form-change implied a basic capability for precision of thought.

That insight pulled Bey himself to a higher state of alertness. If his brain was operating at half-power, he had to be extra careful in setting up form-change sequences. He went over everything again, slowly and carefully. Only when he had made every check that he could think of did he turn again to the animals.

"Six days, and I'll be out of the tank again. All right? You have plenty of food and plenty of water. Flash, save a few of the papayas for me. I noticed there were lots of almost-ripe ones when I was coming up from the beach, and I know what a glutton you are."

He climbed laboriously into the tank. His exoskeleton had been designed for slow, linear movement, and climbing was not on the list of recommended activities. Getting the skeleton off was even harder work. Bey struggled free and dropped it in a heap outside the tank rather than neatly disassembling it.

The pain-inhibitors at the nape of his neck came off last. Bey almost screamed when their action ceased. With the help of the exoskeleton he had moved as no man with multiple broken bones should ever move, and now he was paying for it. He made the interior connections of the tank one-handed, with trembling fingers. When he was finally done he swung the heavy door to and sealed it. His last sight of the animals showed that they were still outside and silently watching.

He leaned back, waiting for the program to begin. He was proposing to do in six days what normal protocols would do in seventeen. His remedial program was safe enough, not pushing the limits in any area. It would even suppress all traces of conventional pain while it was operating.

Unfortunately, there was such a thing as unconventional pain—pain deep down at the individual cell level; pain as the body's operating parameters took an excursion far from normal to regions of internal temperature and chemical imbalance that meant death without the help of a form-change tank's careful monitoring and adjustment of hormonal and nutrient levels; pain beyond belief or description.

As that pain began, Bey asked himself why he was doing this—why wasn't he taking the standard seventeen day route? What was the rush?

That was when he realized, for the first time, that something would be waiting for him when he emerged. Something of thought, some analysis that would need every scrap of his brain-power undimmed by pain inhibitors. For such thought he needed to be in top physical condition. But thought about *what*?

It was intuition again; intuition in its most maddening form, offering strong opinions and even orders without allowing the logical mind any justification or argument.

Bey lay back in the tank and allowed deep pain to wash him away on its tide. When that tide came back in, maybe he would finally learn the reason for his suffering.

CHAPTER 19

Sondra's first impulse was to call Bey and ask him what calls he had made in the past couple of months about the problem of the feral forms. Two minutes' thought convinced her that was a terrible idea.

First, the ship that she was on had no provision for a high-speed link to Earth or Mars. With a standard radio signal she would sit in Saturn orbit for many hours before any reply could possibly come to her. More than that, Bey didn't know anything about the flight of Trudy Melford's ship to Samarkand, a journey that Robert Capman had pronounced to be "curious and anomalous." That must have something to do with the problem.

And finally there was the simple matter of pride. Capman had told her that she had enough information to solve this for herself, without assistance.

Not enough *brains*—he had carefully avoided any such statement—but enough *information*.

Which meant that if she *didn't* solve it by her own efforts, everything that Bey had said about her would be true.

Sondra ordered the ship to quit Saturn orbit, but not to head for Earth and the inner system. She had decided to head *outward* again, for the Kuiper Belt. She set her destination as the colony worldlet of

Samarkand, but after a few minutes she changed that instruction. First she must head for Rini Base. Capman had told her that she needed to query the inner system's general information bank and learn what calls Bey had made or received since she had first met him. The only efficient way to do that was through a rapid link, and Aybee on Rini Base controlled the only one she knew about.

All the way out to the Kuiper Belt she pummeled her brains. There was a logical explanation to her problem. Knowing that, and knowing that someone else knew what it was while she did not, was worse than if there were no explanation at all—even if the other someone was a Logian form,

She thought and thought; and got nowhere.

By the time the ship reached Rini Base, Sondra had her tail thoroughly between her legs. Aybee did not seem to notice. He was tinkering with a little chain of silver elements, and he did not even look up when she drifted in through the jumble of cables and cabinets that defined what he called his office. But he knew she was there, because after a while he grunted and said, "Wouldn't see you after all?"

"Saw me. Listened to me. Left me."

"Figures. Most people don't get far with Capman. What you want with me? I'm busy."

"What is that thing you're working on?"

"You wouldn't understand if I told you." He glared up at her for a moment. "What you want?"

"If you're as smart as you think you are, how come Capman hasn't recruited *you*? He asked Bey Wolf to go to Saturn long ago, and become a Logian."

As a way to annoy Aybee, it was a total failure.

"Sure he did." Aybee looked smug and poked at the silver chain with a little metal awl. "Know why? 'Cause the Wolfman's gettin' way up there in age, that's why.

The Logians don't take anybody 'til he's well into geeze stage."

"You mean until she's *done* something in the world—instead of only talking about it, like you."

Aybee just grinned and kept his attention on what he was doing. "We're in a mood today, aren't we? Anyway, the Logians don't *say* they wait until you're past it, because if they did no one would want to go. What they say is good high-flown waffle—you know, 'until someone fully knows what it is to be human, and has experienced a full human life with all its joys and sorrows, it is not right for that person to change to Logian form.' That sort of rubbish."

"It sounds reasonable to me."

"Reasonable, but not true. Big difference. You can see why they say it. No one likes the idea they're being taken because it's drool time." Aybee glanced up again. "Anyway, stop changing the subject. What you want?"

"A real-time link to Earth, the way you did it for me last time."

"You think I got nothing to do but fix up message lines and chase you halfway across the solar system?" Aybee laid the silver chain down on his desk top. "Ah, nuts, I might as well give this up anyway. I can't make it work. Experimental physics is for animals, it's no better than plumbing."

"And after the call I want to arrange for a passage to Samarkand."

"A passage for *one*, right? You, not me. No worries. Just don't tell 'em you're from the Office of Form Control."

"Why not?"

"Dunno, quite. But they're dead against form control on Samarkand." Aybee was poking at the control board on his desk, patching a line through to the inner system. "They don't have much time for BEC, either. That's why

I said, it's the last place in the Kuiper Belt that you'd expect to find Trudy Melford. Why you going there?"

"Robert Capman's suggestion."

"Then you better take it seriously." Aybee tapped a key and waited. "There you go. Same message unit as last time, whenever you're ready. How soon you want the ship?"

"Whenever you can have one. I'm going to download selected files from the inner system data bank. Then I'll call the Office of Form Control. And then I'll leave here for Samarkand."

"Sooner the better." Aybee picked up the awl and poked savagely and morosely at the silver chain. "Only this time, don't expect me to come and haul you out of there. Damn thing, hold still there."

No better than plumbing. As Sondra left the room she crossed her fingers and wished that Aybee would encounter a blocked toilet on Rini Base. It was a rare event, but in low gravity it was supposed to be something spectacular.

It was impossible to study file records at the rate that they streamed from the inner system general data base to Sondra's local storage. All she could catch was an overview and an occasional rapid snapshot of the video.

Bey was one of those rare individuals whose incoming calls outnumbered the ones he placed by at least twenty to one. Sondra caught fleeting multiple glimpses of Jarvis Dommer, all gleaming teeth and oozy charm—of Sondra, herself, earnest or determined or worried-looking—of Maria Sun, elegant and exquisite, and one of Bey's few outgoing calls (Sondra resolved to take a closer look at that interaction)—of Trudy Melford, eating you up with her eyes, just like in real life.

Somewhere in the visual and audio messages, racing in at a few hundred times real-time, Sondra was supposed to hunt down a clue. But not at this speed. She would study at leisure during the journey to Samarkand.

As the flow of input from Bey's open file came to an end, Sondra switched the destination to the Office of Form Control. She didn't expect any help from them, but at least she ought to tell them that she was working hard and doing her best.

It was no surprise that her Rini-transmitted call was routed again to Denzel Morrone's office. This time she was ready for him.

"Director Morrone." She spoke at once, as soon as the office pick-up was made. He was apparently not ready for *her*, because the full mouth in his smooth baby face gaped open for a second. "This is Sondra Dearborn. I want to report that I am making great progress on the feral forms. My plan is to remain in the Kuiper Belt for just a few more days, then return to the inner system."

Morrone had caught up with her. His face now wore a scowl and his mouth was turned down in a grim line. "Stop it right there. I don't know what your plan is, and I don't care. After the wild story that you offered to me as your last report, I informed you that I needed time to consider what you have been doing—or failing to do. I have now completed such consideration. You will not remain in the Kuiper Belt. You will return to Earth."

"But I've almost solved it! I have enough information in my possession, right now, to explain what happened." Morrone didn't need to know that the source of that statement was Robert Capman, or that Sondra had no idea *which* information held the key. Sondra hurried on. "A few more days, that's all I need, and I'm sure I'll have the whole picture."

"Ms. Dearborn, you appear to have trouble hearing me and I do not believe that it is the quality of this outrageously expensive connection." Morrone leaned closer, so that his face filled the whole image display area. "Don't you understand, Ms. Dearborn? You have *failed.* I do not expect failures in my department. As of this moment you no longer have anything to do with the feral form problem. I am also relieving you of all other responsibilities within the Office of Form Control. I want you to return at once to the inner system. When you get here we will discuss what your new position—if any—is to be within this department. Now, that is all I have to say. I do not wish to talk to you again until we do so in person."

The connection was suddenly broken. Denzel Morrone's face remained in the image display, slowly fading. Sondra stared at it until the last faint trace was gone. What had ever led her to think that the man had a pleasant face?

Return at once to the inner system. The command had sounded explicit enough. It needed the help of Aybee to see it differently.

"You got to pull it apart." He had come on Sondra when she was still sitting devastated at the communications unit. "What's Morrone mean, *at once*. In zero time? That's impossible. Go on the fastest commercial ship you can charter? Cost a fortune, and the Office of Form Control's too stingy to pay for that. On a Rini ship, which is faster still? The only way to get one of them is by filing a request with me, and you can tell Morrone that you asked me and I told you to shove it. No. What he means is a good, fast, cheap way on a standard commercial carrier that offers an out-and-back through the Kuiper Belt. There's bundles of them, charter mostly, and I can arrange one for you."

"But what use is that?"

"Trust me." Aybee had given Sondra an exaggerated wink. "You didn't mention Samarkand to Morrone, did you?"

"Not a word."

"Good. See, it's going to turn out that the best route for you to the inner system calls for a short stopover in Samarkand. Get it?"

"I do. I don't know why you are doing all this for me."

"Isn't it obvious? To get rid of you, Sondra D., and let me go back to the good life. It's my own fault, I should never have promised the Wolfman *anything*." Aybee was hunched over his data unit. "Will one day at the colony be enough? It's all I can guarantee."

"Then it will have to be."

But now Sondra, waiting for final entry permission to the Samarkand colony, wondered if it would be. On the three-day journey from the Rini Base she had studied the records of Bey's calls over and over. She could describe the pattern on Maria Sun's ear-rings, the inordinate number of teeth that Jarvis Dommer displayed whenever he smiled, the calculated imperfection of Trudy Melford's nose in the form she had chosen especially for Bey Wolf.

Sondra also had Capman's assurance that all of this would be enough. That was what had provided her, at last, a suspicion as to what had been happening. What she could not understand was *why*.

In particular, why had she, Sondra Dearborn, been thrown into the middle of all this mess?

Samarkand was supposed to provide the answer. It was this or nothing. The opening door in front of her was her last chance.

She went on through with the fourteen others of the visiting group. Like them she was officially described as a tourist, a simple working type from the inner system who was spending ten years' savings to come out and gape and marvel at the wonders of the Kuiper Belt. A few were on their way home, but most of them would be going farther out to sample the still-stranger expanse of Cloudland, with its vast open spaces, great Harvesters, and billion-kilometer thinner-than-gossamer Space Farms.

The tour guide was a native of Samarkand. If he was representative of the wonders to come it would be a dull day. He was short and dumpy, with a pale face and fair, straggly hair. He offered comments on what they were seeing in the monotone of one who had said the same thing hundreds or thousands of times.

"Established in 2160 by the League of Brethren, originally from the Central Asian region of Earth. The Brethren took as their guiding doctrine the sacred rights and natural goodness of all things, and that doctrine continues to be applied here in the Colony." He was leading them through a long, spiral room that vanished into the distance. Groups of workers, fat and thin and tall and short but all seemingly cheerful, were standing at thousand after thousand of identical machines. They were chatting to one another, and it was clear that the equipment mostly ran itself.

"We honor the guiding doctrine." The tour leader's nasal drone went on and on. His eyes were half closed. "Because of this we refuse to consume *any* living organism—not even the single-celled ones which form the basis of most food production through Cloudland and the Kuiper Belt. Here you see our food being synthesized from elementary inorganic components, water and minerals and carbon dioxide and nitrogen. Observe the steadily increasing complexity of the molecules at each stage, as higher order synthesis is performed."

The other tourists were already bored. Sondra could see their attention beginning to wander. She sympathized, but she could not allow herself to blank out. Somewhere here was the clue that she needed.

Somewhere?

Where?

She glanced from the guide to the workers that they passed. They were worse than *ordinary* looking. Back on Earth they would have drawn attention by their ugliness. Not just the occasional man or woman, either, but every one of them. And not the standardized ugliness of Cloudlanders, whose elongated stick-thin bodies and arms and short legs were all ugly to Earth eyes in the same generic way. The workers here had *customized* ugliness, all different.

Sondra started, and looked at the people of Samarkand through new eyes. Could that be it?

She had carefully remained at the back of the group, remaining as inconspicuous as possible. She didn't want to draw attention to herself now, by asking their guide a question. As they moved on to another assembly line, she whispered to the bored-looking man next to her: "These people look as though they could really use a form-change session."

"I know." He nodded at a stooped man standing by one of the machines, and grinned. "See him? If I looked like that I'd be in a tank sharpish, before anyone else could have a look at me."

"Me too." Sondra took care to glance in all directions before she spoke again. "I haven't seen any tanks, though. Did you notice where they were when we came in? Suppose one of us was taken sick and needed remedial change. Where would we go?"

A woman on the other side of the man had turned to listen to the muttered conversation. Sondra stayed in through a few more remarks about the unattractive appearance of the people of Samarkand, then allowed herself to drop out of the exchange. She stepped a little closer to the back of the group. She was not missed. A couple of others were now peering about them, examining the workers or looking for evidence of form-change equipment.

It took a few minutes, but finally as they moved through to a smaller chamber one of the more aggressive members of the group piped up.

"Excuse me." It was a big dark-haired woman, wearing one of Earth's popular peasant girl forms. "I have a question."

The guide, in mid-sentence monotone, ground to a halt. He stared uncomprehendingly at the interrupter.

"We've seen a good bit of your colony." The woman waved an arm at their surroundings. "But we've seen no sign of your form-change tanks. Where are they?"

It was like watching someone return from the dead. The guide stood up taller, his eyes popped open, and his pale cheeks turned pink.

"Form-change tanks!" He glared at the woman who had asked the question. "You may search Samarkand from one end to the other, and you will find no such thing. We have no place for decadence in our world."

"But what if you get sick? Hey, what if *I* get sick?"

"Weren't you listening to me? I told you already, the guiding doctrine of the League of Brethren is based on the *natural goodness* of all things. That includes human beings. We have no need of form-change to cure sickness, because sickness is no more than a failure to allow innate goodness to triumph over evil. The rest of the system may choose an unnatural method to combat the evil within, but we prefer our way. *Nature's* way."

The tour guide had left his prepared script far behind. Sondra, drifting away from the back of the group, decided that she liked him rather better this way. He was a kook, but now he was a kook with his own principles and convictions.

The woman who had asked the question did not agree. She had not enjoyed the answer at all. Sondra heard her voice rising in pitch and volume as she slipped through into an adjoining room.

"Are you telling me what I think you're telling me? That if I get sick when I'm here on your dumb colony, you're going to tell me to *argue* with myself, instead of somebody dumping me into the nearest form-change tank? Well, let me tell *you* something, mister . . ."

The chamber that Sondra had entered was empty. She moved through it rapidly. The argument would help, but there was no way of knowing how much time she had before her absence from the tour group was noticed.

She had apparently left behind the main manufacturing region of the colony. The turning corridor along which she was hurrying had many closed doors, one every few meters. At the end lay a larger open door leading to a much bigger room.

Sondra paused a few feet short of the entrance. She could already see what was inside the room. She had realized that many rooms like this must exist within Samarkand as soon as she heard the tour guide speak of decadence and the absence of form-change equipment. But she did not want to go any closer.

The view from a distance was quite bad enough. The people inside the room were slumped in upholstered chairs or moving unsteadily from place to place. Sondra saw faces with sunken, bleary eyes and withered cheeks, topped by white and scanty hair. Limbs were bony and lacking muscle, skin was wrinkled and marked with moles and spots of dark brown.

It might have been a scene from the files of the Office of Form Control, showing the terrible end results of illegal form use. Sondra knew that it was not. It was a picture of the world as it used to be, before purposive form-change had banished the specter of aging. People—

except on Samarkand—employed the machines in biofeedback loops that permitted them to remain in peak physical condition throughout their whole lives, until finally the brain lost its power to follow the biofeedback regime. At that point irreversible physical and mental decline began.

Death had not been banished from the solar system. But now it came quickly, in just a few days.

Except on Samarkand. Here on Samarkand death crept in slowly, stealing life a little at a time. Muscles weakened, senses faded, eyes and ears lost their sensitivity. Hearts and lungs faltered and failed. Life was a long decline, its end a long disease. Sondra had not noticed this on the tour, for a simple reason: very old people could not and did not work.

She paused, leaning against the wall of the corridor.

No form-change machines. None. Not a single one, anywhere on Samarkand. It was not like the situation on some of the poorer worlds of the Belt, where for economic reasons machines were few and far-between and used only for urgent remedial medical work. Here it was a proscription, an outright ban.

But this was the colony, of all worlds in the Kuiper Belt, that Trudy Melford had chosen to visit. The flagship of the BEC fleet, with Trudy as passenger, had been here just a few weeks ago. There had been other and earlier visits.

"Curious and anomalous" indeed. Robert Capman had clearly known how the people of Samarkand felt about form-change equipment.

It didn't make sense.

Except that suddenly it did—all of it. Because if this room was on Samarkand, what else must be here?

Sondra was filled with a sudden huge urgency. She had to get off this world as soon as possible. She must head for the inner system, exactly as Denzel Morrone has directed. She would call Bey on the way, and tell him that they had to meet.

But not this time on Wolf Island, nor at the Office of Form Control.

This time they must meet on Mars.

CHAPTER 20

The absolute certainty that she knew the answer had supported Sondra all the way in on the long return trip from Samarkand to Mars. Even Bey's cryptic reply to her message had not worried her, though she did wonder what he meant by the last part of it: "I have other business on Mars that I must complete in advance," it said. "Start the meeting without me if you have to—but whatever you do, don't *finish* without me. I'll be bringing visitors."

Now, on the last stage of the journey, nervousness came rushing in. What real evidence did she have? Very little, and she was about to take on one of the most formidable forces in the solar system. She had better have her arguments in order.

The autocar was creeping its way into the courtyard of Melford Castle. Didn't the very fact that Trudy Melford had agreed to meet *prove* that Sondra was right? She had offered no reason for wanting a private session with Trudy. The BEC staff member who took the message had seemed astonished that she dared to ask for it on the way from Samarkand—and dumbfounded when he contacted her after her arrival on Mars, to tell her that Trudy had said yes, they could meet in her private chambers.

The knowledge of where she was added to Sondra's

uneasiness as the elevator slid silently up from the courtyard and halted at the fourth floor of Melford Castle. For a century and a half this building had been the power center of the greatest economic force in the solar system. And the woman waiting for her as the elevator door opened formed the absolute hub around which all that power revolved.

Trudy Melford wore a long, severe dress of black, unrelieved by any form of decoration. She nodded once to Sondra and turned to lead the way back through a long hallway to a dark-paneled office. Sondra slowly followed. There would be no formal niceties or offers of bogus hospitality at this meeting.

Trudy gestured to Sondra to sit in a brocaded upright chair at a polished cherrywood table and placed herself in another one on the opposite side. "You think you have something to say of interest to me?" Dark eyebrows raised. "Very well. My time is valuable, so I would appreciate it if you will be as concise as possible."

"Your time is valuable. But you can spare enough time to make trips all the way out to Samarkand, in the Kuiper Belt." Sondra saw the frown on the other woman's face. "I'm sorry, if I am to be concise that is not the place to begin. Let me start where I started: with a problem assigned to me by my superiors in the Office of Form Control.

"At certain colonies in the Kuiper Belt, babies were born which after a couple of months took the humanity test. The humanity test in the Belt is no different from anywhere else in the solar system. A baby passes and is pronounced human if and only if it is able to interact with purposive form-change equipment.

"In this case, however, there was something wrong. Three babies passed the test, but it quickly became clear that they should have failed. What I have been calling the 'feral forms' were not human. The humanity test, after a hundred and fifty years of successful use, was failing. I was told to find out why.

"Do you have any questions about this?"

Trudy Melford was listening intently, elbows on the table, her chin resting on her closed fists and her face impassive. She shook her head. "I am here only to hear what you have to say."

"We'll see. Anyway, I discovered nothing useful in my examination of the forms, or of the data concerning them, when I was on Earth. So after I had consulted Bey Wolf I headed out to the Kuiper Belt to see things at first hand. Did you know, by the way, that I tried to persuade him to work with me on this problem? And he refused, because you had lured him here to work for you."

"I have an important form-change project on Mars, one well-suited to Behrooz Wolf's unique abilities." Trudy's face gave away nothing.

"An inconveniently timed project, from my point of view." Sondra realized that the two of them were still fencing, although the flashing rapiers remained out of sight. "So I went to the colonies alone. I learned even before I arrived that the colony mutation rates are naturally higher because of increased radioactivity. That would give more humanity test failures than usual, but it doesn't explain at all why things that should have been failing were passing.

"I had no answers. So I dug into the actual form-change equipment, both hardware and software. Know what I found?" Sondra studied Trudy's impassive face. "I think you do know. I found *nothing*. The hardware was genuine BEC equipment with the original seals unbroken. The software showed no signs of tampering, and it checked out down to the last binary branch."

Sondra paused and turned as she heard footsteps behind her. It was Bey Wolf. And in spite of his message, he was alone.

On the other side of the table Trudy was standing up, her face pink. "Bey!" She looked right through Sondra. "I didn't expect you. I'm sorry, but at the moment I can't—"

"It's all right. I'm part of the same meeting." Bey nodded to Sondra and sat down next to her. "Don't let me interrupt. Just carry on."

Carry on—if she could. Sondra stared at Trudy. Could anyone blush on demand? Maybe Bey Wolf produced strange effects on both of them.

"I was just saying that both the software and the hardware out in the colonies was perfect on the form-change equipment that produced the humanity test anomalies. So where did that leave me? I had run out of all the reasonable explanations."

"*When you have eliminated the impossible, whatever remains, however improbable, must be the truth.*" Bey waved his hand. "Sorry, sorry, it's a bad habit that I don't seem able to kick. Keep going. This time I promise I'll keep quiet."

Sondra was beginning to wish he had not shown up. Her job was hard enough, without random interruptions. Where was she?

"I had to take what I had found to its logical conclusion. The hardware was exactly as it had been delivered from BEC. The software was error-free. There was only one other possibility: the hardware had a hidden flaw *when BEC delivered it*. It had been produced that way in the BEC factory. And knowing the BEC quality control procedures, that told me the change must have been *deliberate*."

Sondra paused and waited. This was the point where Trudy should stand up and object. BEC's reputation for two centuries of reliable delivery was on the line. The other woman remained silent. Trudy was certainly tense, but it was the tension of someone who was also waiting. Sondra had to continue.

"But of course, a deduction that makes no sense and explains nothing is just as bad as no deduction at all. *Why* would BEC—or anyone—want creatures to pass the humanity test that should have failed it? I didn't have an answer. There didn't seem to be an answer.

"Then I wondered if maybe the target was not the colonies, as it seemed to be at first sight. Maybe the target was the *humanity test*. It has to be infallible, or it is useless. If it can fail three times, people would argue, who knows how many more times it might fail?

"That seemed to lead to a bigger mystery than the one that I started with. Why would anyone possibly want the humanity test to be called into question?

"And there I stuck, until it was suggested that I *invert* the problem." Sondra glanced at Bey. He looked as though he was about to speak, but he placed a hand over his mouth and waved at her to continue.

"Thanks, Bey." Sondra turned again to Trudy Melford. "Invert the problem, and what do you get? Not that *non-humans* are taking the humanity test and passing it, but maybe that *humans* are taking the humanity test and *failing*. It's an awful thought, some poor human baby, taken and disposed of in the organ banks. But that is what would happen.

"Or that is what would *usually* happen. There might be very special circumstances, under which someone with great money and influence could take a baby who had failed the humanity test and destroy all evidence that the test had ever been given. Of course, there would still be a problem. What would the parent do with the baby? The child could officially no longer exist. He would be unable to interact with form-change equipment, otherwise he would have passed the humanity test. And it would not be enough simply to establish a false identity for him. He would still be discovered, because form-change is used routinely through the whole solar system.

"But it is not used *everywhere*. There are a few places, like the Samarkand colony, where form-change equipment is not only not used, it is *banned* from use. Naturally, such a colony also rejects any suggestion that humanity depends on form-change equipment. A child could grow up there, without fear of discovery. That child's parent could visit." Sondra met Trudy's eye. "If she had sufficient wealth, she could visit as often as she chose. Suppose that Errol Ergan Melford, the infant son of Gertrude Zenobia Melford, did not drown four years ago in the Aegean Sea before he had the chance to take the humanity test. Suppose that he had taken it—and he had *failed*. Suppose that he is alive today, and living in the Samarkand colony. And suppose that his mother has a long-term goal, of doing something that only the Empress of BEC *could* do: changing form-change equipment, to cast doubt on the humanity test itself—so that one day her son might return and lead a normal life in the inner system."

This was the crucial moment, the place where Sondra was afraid that Trudy would dig in her heels. All she had to do was scoff, deny everything, and ask for hard evidence. Sondra had none, and she knew she was not likely to get any. Errol Ergan Melford's tracks were four years old and surely thoroughly covered, while Trudy was free to travel anywhere in the solar system that she chose to go. She was under no obligation to explain her visits to Samarkand to anyone.

Sondra waited, suddenly sure that her trip to Mars had been for nothing. But Trudy did not act either annoyed or defensive. She seemed pleased, and she was actually *smiling*.

"Suppose that I agree with you, Sondra, and tell you privately that everything you have said is correct? You are not recording this—I am sure of that, because you were scanned on your way into Melford Castle. So what do you propose to do now?"

It was the last answer in the world that Sondra had expected. She glanced helplessly at Bey. Trudy seemed to be admitting everything. But she was also telling them: *So what if I did what you say? You can't do a thing to me.*

And she was right. As soon as Sondra returned to Earth she was going to be fired or assigned to a basement-level job with nothing to do with feral forms. And even if Bey became involved, the Samarkand colonists would never cooperate with Earth's Office of Form Control for anything.

"I don't know what I will do." Sondra felt she might as well be honest. No matter what happened, she had been given the satisfaction of solving the problem.

"That's a good, honest answer." Trudy's attitude to Sondra seemed to have changed completely since the accusations were put out on the table. There was no sign of resentment as she went on, "Look, I know that if you don't produce an answer accepted by the Office of Form Control, your career will suffer. But I have influence there, and I'll make sure that it doesn't happen. All right? Is that all right with you, too, Bey?"

"That part of it is fine." Bey's eyes were hard to see, his gaze directed down to the table-top. "And Sondra, you did a great job sorting out what has been going on in the Kuiper Belt. But some of us know that it's not quite the whole story."

Trudy's smile froze. "What do you mean?"

"Let's start with easy things." Bey turned to Sondra. "I have to say this with you present, even though I know you won't like to hear it. Trudy is right. She can certainly make sure that your career won't suffer at the Office of Form Control; because Trudy happens to have Denzel Morrone thoroughly in her pocket. Right, Trudy?"

"You have no reason to say that."

"Which is not quite the same as a denial. Morrone is on the take from BEC, and he has been for years. He has to go, Trudy, and quickly. You have to help me make that happen. The head of the Office of Form Control can have faults—God knows, I proved that often enough—but being for sale isn't one of them."

"Lots of things go on in BEC at the detail level that I don't know about. Why do you think I had anything to do with Morrone? I've never even met the man."

"Maybe; but he had to do something specific for you. You knew that there were going to be problems with the humanity test, because you had arranged them. So you passed the word to Morrone, probably through Jarvis Dommer—a hint from you goes a long way in BEC—that someone junior and inexperienced was to be assigned to the feral form problem.

"Morrone picked you, Sondra. Just a couple of years out of graduate school, not much practical experience of form-change and little knowledge of the Kuiper Belt."

Bey lifted his head and stared at Trudy. "And you, Empress, you agreed with his choice. He didn't pick Sondra for what she might *do*, you see, he picked her out for what he didn't think she could possibly do. Morrone doesn't have the whole picture, I feel sure of that, but he knew that Sondra was supposed to see so far and no farther. You *do* have the whole picture. You thought that Sondra would probably find nothing, in which case the humanity test would become increasingly suspect. At the very worst, if she was extra smart or became extra lucky, she might realize that you had been making visits to Samarkand, and draw some conclusions from that. You were prepared for it.

"But there was one piece of information that neither you nor Morrone had at first. You didn't realize when she was selected that Sondra Dearborn was related to

Behrooz Wolf, and she might try to drag me in to help her.

"And now here's the funny thing: I wouldn't have helped Sondra at all—I had already told her to go away and solve her own problems—if you hadn't heard that she had been to see me, and become nervous. You decided to be double safe and tuck me safely out of the way here on Mars. But you tried a little bit too hard. I began to ask myself, why am I being recruited? What can I do that a BEC employee can't do? And if I'm valuable, why now and not three years ago when I first retired from the Office of Form Control? It seemed like too much of a coincidence, Sondra and you appearing on the scene at just the same time. So I became a little bit more interested in what Sondra was doing."

Trudy was not smiling at all. Her blue-green gaze was fixed on Bey's face with a total and fixed intensity. Sondra, watching both of them, suddenly understood Trudy's expression. The Empress of BEC, a senior force of the solar system, was *frightened*.

"And then your BEC people got into the act." Bey sighed and shook his head. "It's an old, old story, one I suffered with myself for half a century. Your employees try to do what they think you want done, but they only know half the facts. So they do things you later wish they hadn't done. Jarvis Dommer—I feel sure it was his work—somehow guessed that you were worried about Sondra. He arranged for her to have an 'accident' out on the Fugate colony. Since it was supposed to be an accident it couldn't be made foolproof, and Sondra was smart enough to survive. But it was more evidence, proof to me that we were close to learning something that you really didn't want learned."

"I didn't intend for anything bad to happen to Sondra. I didn't even know anything was going to happen." Trudy Melford stared at them across the table. "Believe that,

Sondra, if you believe nothing else. As for your accident, Bey, I had nothing to do with that, either."

"You don't surprise me. There's a problem with people like Dommer, who only really work for money. So long as you are paying them top rate, they are good, loyal employees. But the moment some other group offers them *more*, they automatically work for them and not for you."

"I pay Jarvis Dommer very well—ridiculously well."

"But someone was willing to outbid you. My bet is that the Old Mars team got to Dommer. They thought—wrongly—that I was behind the surface forms, and they decided it would be cheaper to put me out of circulation than buy me."

"Rafael Fermiel?"

"No. I'm not sure I can even suggest the name. By the way, Fermiel should be arriving here in just a few minutes. He was doing something for me, then he'll be along. Georgia Kruskal, too, the designer and leader of the Mars surface forms. So I'd better press on.

"I was out of the picture for a while, sitting in a form-change tank recovering from my own 'accident.' I didn't know anything about Samarkand until Aybee Smith told me that Sondra was going there, and why. Then I dumped the transport records. I found that sure enough, you had been making trips out there, yourself. But you know what, Trudy? You were a little bit careless. You didn't fix the *old* transport records. They show that you visited Samarkand only during the past year. That's not long enough if Errol Ergan Melford had been out there for four years. I added that to my own set of puzzles.

"The list was starting to grow. Let me give you another item or two on it: If you are really interested in the surface forms, and I believe you are, why weren't you all for them and deadly opposed to the Underworld? Yet when we talked about it you came across as neutral, telling me that you didn't play politics—when it's BEC's main stock in trade and everybody knows it. And here's another puzzle for you: Why did you move BEC Headquarters to Mars? I know what you told me, that it was simple economics. But I did a little of my own digging. I found that the Planetary Coordinators on Earth were willing to give BEC a deal every bit as good as the one that Mars offered. You didn't *need* to move—didn't need to, at least, for the reason that you gave. What other possible reason could there be, for such a major undertaking? You had to move all the records, the business, the castle itself. Is there any single explanation that could cover the whole list?"

"Get it over with, Bey." Trudy Melford was nothing like an Empress now. Her lips were trembling and her face was set and bloodless. "I know that you know. Just tell me what you want."

"I can't do that yet." Every few seconds Bey was glancing impatiently toward the door.

"You mean *won't*. Don't play with me, Bey Wolf. I'm not a mouse."

"And I'm not a cat, Trudy. I don't enjoy hurting people."

"You don't even have to tell me what you want. I'll give you *everything*. Everything I possess if you'll keep what you know to yourself."

"I can't do that, either. Damnation, where are they? Trudy, if I'm right it may not be as bad as you think—"

"It couldn't be." Trudy leaned forward until her head rested on the smooth table top. "You have no idea what I think—how I feel."

Sondra had watched in total amazement. She had little idea what Bey was talking about, but in a few minutes she had seen Trudy Melford change from the Empress of BEC, a regal woman in full control of herself, to a pathetic lump of misery. In spite of herself, the sympathy swelled inside Sondra. She went around to Trudy's side of the table, sat down next to her, and took her hand. And then, at what should have been a very private moment, in came a chubby red-bearded stranger, bounding along on the balls of his feet.

"Done," he said to Bey. "Took a bit longer than I expected, but you were exactly right."

"Where is he?"

"Outside."

"What the devil's the point of having him out there before we've seen him? Bring him in, Fermiel."

"Sure." Red-beard bounced away again, leaving Sondra wondering what could possibly come next.

"Come on, Trudy." Bey was speaking again, almost chiding. "You can't let him see you like this. It would upset him."

"He's here?" Trudy Melford straightened up at once, staring wild-eyed about her. "But how—how did you find out what he looks like and where he was? *Nobody* should know that, except me and a few people in the Underworld."

"There is far more to a person than external appearance." Bey paused. Rafael Fermiel had entered again leading a small blond child. The boy took one look around the room and ran to Trudy Melford's arms.

"Mummy!"

Bey gazed at Trudy and the little boy with curiosity and huge satisfaction as they hugged each other. "Sondra, I don't think the two of you have met. I feel sure that there is an official Mars name, which Trudy can tell us, but let me use his Earth name. Allow me to introduce you to Errol Ergan Melford."

CHAPTER 21

Trudy had the child clutched in a great bear hug. "It's all right, sweetie. Everything's going to be all right." She glared defiantly at Bey over the boy's head. "You can do anything you like to me, I don't care. But can't you leave him alone?"

"I could, but I don't think I ought to." Bey came around to stand by Trudy and placed one hand on the top of Errol Melford's shoulder. "He deserves something better in life than skulking in the deep Underworld." The fair head turned up to look at him with clear, trusting eyes. "Errol, my name is Behrooz Wolf. I work with your mother."

"Are you her friend?"

"I hope I am. I hope she will think so, too. Will you do something for me?"

"I'll try."

"Will you wait outside again with Mr. Fermiel for a little bit longer? I need to talk to your mother again."

"Business?"

"Business."

The blond head nodded. Bey waited until Fermiel had led the boy out of the room, then he sat down on Trudy's other side. He stared thoughtfully at Trudy and Sondra.

He did not speak, until Sondra said tartly, "Are you going to sit there forever? Or are you sometime going to explain what's happening here?"

"Sorry." Bey sighed. "*I summon up remembrance of things past*. Sorry, I'm at it again. I'm not supposed to do that. But all this carries me back a long way." He roused himself and reached into a shirt pocket. He took out a single sheet of paper and placed it on the table. "Some of this you already know, Trudy better than anyone. But let me summarize.

"A baby, apparently normal physically and psychologically, who failed the humanity test. A mother who couldn't bear the idea of losing him, of seeing her child dumped into the organ banks. So she used her money and her influence to erase the evidence that the test had ever been taken, and then faked her infant son's death. But that couldn't be the end of the story. What was Trudy Melford going to do with Errol Melford?

"There was more than one possible answer to that question. She could send him to a place like Samarkand, far off in the Kuiper Belt, where humanity tests and purposive form-change had no place. But if she did that, she would see her son only rarely, maybe a couple of times a year.

"Was there somewhere closer, and almost as good? Well, there was the Mars Underworld. It was not as safe as Samarkand, but the struggle between Old Mars and the developing surface forms was having an effect. Although form-change was not banned outright in the Underworld, it was increasingly unpopular. Errol could hide there, with a new identity. And his mother could see him as often as she chose—particularly if she moved to Mars herself, along with BEC Headquarters and Melford Castle. Then she might see him every day. Relocation would be a major step, but who was going to argue with her? She was the Empress, she made the rules.

"You did all that, Trudy, and still you were worried. It was hard to see how it could happen, but suppose someone learned that Errol had not died in the Aegean Sea. Suppose they suspected that he was still alive?

"There was an answer to that, too. Make a false trail that showed Errol had been shipped off to live on Samarkand—a trail, by the way, that we never found, but I feel sure it's there. Go to Samarkand yourself, a place that the head of BEC would never normally choose to visit. That would 'prove' that Errol was living there.

"And do one other thing, too. Trudy Melford is the absolute ruler of BEC, and she controls BEC's production line. So make slight changes to machines intended for certain high-mutation-rate colonies, changes that would allow a few cases to pass the humanity test when they should have failed it. That became a real concern of mine, when I first suspected what was happening." Bey paused. "Trudy, it could have gone both ways. Did the changes ever *fail* an individual who would otherwise have passed?"

"Never!" Trudy glared back at him. "Do you think I would put some other mother through the hell that I went through? A few feral forms passed. That was all."

"But as a result the humanity test itself came under suspicion and increased criticism. When its results were questioned, Errol would become a little bit safer. The Office of Form Control would 'investigate' the problem, but Denzel Morrone would make sure that the right person was assigned to it."

"Uhhh! The *right* person." Sondra banged her hand on the table. "You mean the *dumb* person. You mean me!"

"Sorry, Sondra. Morrone did it, I didn't. I told you there were things I had to say that you would not like to hear. Anyway, Morrone assigned you. But he remained close to what was happening—too close. I sensed that very early. He was the director of the whole office, and this was a relatively small and apparently unimportant project. Normally a junior staff member would have no direct contact with him. But he had to stay close, because he intended to remove the investigator if she did too well. He would track her activities. At worst, Sondra might be allowed as far as the false trail to Samarkand. But no farther.

"It seemed that nothing could possibly go wrong. And in a sense, it didn't. The fact that Sondra was related to me, and came to see me, was really irrelevant. I had my own work to do. I wasn't about to become involved. But you and I had met before, Trudy, and it seems I have a reputation at the Office of Form Control. Even though I had retired, you were afraid."

"With justice." Trudy gestured to the door through which Rafael Fermiel had taken Errol Melford. "I was afraid, and I had every right to be afraid. You were Bey Wolf, the legendary Bey Wolf. I was afraid of what you might be able to do. I was afraid of something exactly like *this*. And I'm still afraid. Even if you found out that Errol was alive and on Mars, you ought not to have been able to find him. There are five separate links between him and me, and no one should be able to follow the whole chain. How did you do it?"

"I didn't." Bey tapped the sheet of paper sitting on the table in front of him. "Tracking people is not my game. Form-change, theory and practice, is. The humanity test is based on the ability to perform purposive form-change. I have been thinking about that test for more than fifty years, and I have a first-rate reason to do so. Because although I passed the test—obviously, since I am here—I came perilously close to failing. I discussed the problem long ago with Robert Capman, who is known to you by reputation if not in person. We concluded that there is a certain psychological profile which differs a little from the human norm, in specific ways. Individuals with it have real trouble with the humanity test. I have such a quirky profile. So does Capman. And so, I suspected, might Errol Melford."

Bey picked up the sheet of paper and smoothed its creases. "This is not Errol's psychological profile. I did not have his to use. This is my own, as it was when I was four years old. I gave it to Rafael Fermiel, and I asked him to screen the juvenile population records of Old Mars. Not for the usual things, name and parents and residence and personal history, but in terms of psychological profile parameters. I gave Fermiel tolerance ranges for each parameter, and said I wanted to determine any individuals whose profile matched the one that I gave to him within those tolerances. You might say, I was looking for myself at the age of four, or the closest thing to it. I squeaked through, Errol failed. Fermiel came up with five reasonable fits—I want to know more about them—and just one excellent match. I asked him to locate that individual, and bring the person here. He had no idea who he was bringing. I did."

"But now Fermiel knows." It was Sondra, not Trudy, who spoke. "He heard you say the name. You can't ask him to keep quiet, Bey. It's all in the open and everyone is going to find out."

"They are. But can't you see—both of you—that it doesn't *matter* any more? I'm telling you, Errol is going to be all right. He doesn't need to hide."

"But the humanity test. He failed the test. Anyone who fails the test . . ." Trudy spoke softly, her voice trailing away as it came to the unspeakable thought.

"He did. But I have seen Errol, and I am prepared to testify, as former head of the Office of Form Control, that he is a normal human. I am tempted to say, super-normal. Anyway, before people bother Errol Melford they will have to fight their way past me." Bey sat up straighter, unconsciously squaring his shoulders. "Me, and if I have to involve him, Robert Capman. He's in the Logian form, and I'm retired, so maybe some people think *we are not now that strength which in old days moved earth and heaven*—sorry, I seem to be quoting again—but what we have to say still counts in anything involving form-change. The decision-makers will listen to us. They won't touch Errol."

"Are you saying it's over?" Trudy spoke in the uncertain tones of someone unsure that she could believe her own words. "That he can come out of hiding? Errol can live with me all the time, instead of just when the castle is quiet?"

"That's exactly what I'm saying."

"Then . . ." Trudy leaned over and took Bey's hands in hers. "Then I'll say again what I said before. If I have Errol, you have me and everything I possess. No exclusions. Tell me what you want and when you want it."

Bey leaned back a little from the intense stare of those blue-green eyes. He read in them hero worship and unconditional surrender. Even if they were temporary offerings, he was uncomfortable with both. And behind Trudy he could see Sondra, scowling most horribly.

He was saved from an awkward answer by the sound of loud argument outside the room.

"That must be Georgia." Bey stood up in relief. "I didn't intend for her and Rafael to meet without my being present. Wait a minute."

He hurried out. When he returned he was accompanied by Errol Melford, Rafael Fermiel, and a third being that Sondra stared at in disbelief. It was like an obscenely fat kangaroo with the long muzzle of a camel, and it was dressed in snug boots and a form-fitting white suit with pockets all the way down the sides.

Errol at once ran to his mother and sat on Trudy's

lap. She hugged him fiercely. Fermiel came to sit at the table opposite Trudy. Oddest of all, the fat kangaroo moved to the end of the table and crouched comfortably on its haunches.

"Introductions," said Bey. He waved his hand. "Sondra Dearborn. Trudy and Errol Melford. Rafael Fermiel. And" —to Sondra's surprise he pointed to the kangaroo— "Georgia Kruskal. Georgia, you've amazed me yet again. You're not wearing a suit."

"I know." Georgia grunted, in a tone an octave lower than usual. "We can operate at these temperatures and pressures for a few hours, but now I'm here I've decided that I don't want to, ever again. Like sitting in a kettle and breathing hot onion soup. Are you going to say why you asked me to come here, or is it all still a big mystery?"

"I'll tell you." Bey sat down at the table between Rafael Fermiel and Georgia Kruskal. "At least, I'll tell you part of it. There are things I still have to sort out, and I can't do most of them until I'm back on Earth.

"I have some bad news for you, Georgia. Some for you, too, Rafael, before you start to gloat. But also some good news for both of you.

"Let me begin where I began: ignorant. Before I came to Mars a couple of months ago I had no idea that there was a war going on here. I only learned it when both sides tried to sign me up as a new recruit. It's not a shooting war, but it's still a real battle. Old Mars versus New Mars, the Underworld against the new forms. The territory at stake is the surface of the whole planet. You, Georgia, like it pretty much the way it is. You, Rafael, conceive it as your sacred duty to make it look just like Earth.

"Now, don't hassle me yet" —the other two were starting to protest— "you'll get your turn later. First, let me tell you who each of you has as your allies. Maybe you'll get a surprise or two. You, Georgia. BEC hasn't been funding you, but they'd do it like a shot if you needed money. Right, Trudy?"

"Right." Trudy nodded at Georgia. "I've been fascinated since I first flew over the surface and learned of your existence. I asked Bey Wolf to learn all he could about you." She turned to him. "That was genuine, you know, nothing to do with—the *other*."

"You can talk about that if you want to—no need to hide any more." Bey turned back to Georgia. "But I doubt if Trudy is as interested as I am. You are the most intriguing new form I've seen in twenty years, even if you are technically illegal. I don't have BEC's money, but you can add me to your list of allies."

"Some things are more important than money." Georgia's broad camel's mouth smirked triumphantly at Rafael Fermiel before she again faced Bey. "You gave me a dozen new ideas in a few hours, things I would never have dreamed of trying. We already have a form-change program for an organic radio transmitter and receiver. We'll try a tank experiment in the next few days."

"I'd like to see it. But now, before you get too uppity, let's talk about the Fermiel camp. First, he has everyone who believes that the Mars Declaration must be honored. You think they are kooks, Georgia, but there are lots of them. They won't go away. Second, Trudy Melford has been sympathetic to Old Mars and the Underworld. And before *you* start looking smug, Rafael, let me tell you that the practical motive for that sympathy went away a few minutes ago. If you want Trudy's support from this point on, you will have to earn it.

"Third, I suspect that you will have my support; but I can't confirm that until I have a conversation with someone who isn't here at the moment. Now here's your bad news, Rafael: even if you have my support, I suspect that you are going to lose part of your funding. You won't have enough in the future to do anything that you like.

I'm thinking especially about the terraforming. It may have to slow down."

"But the Mars Declaration—"

"Is a piece of paper, like any other. It needs to be interpreted in today's terms, not those of a century or two centuries ago."

Rafael Fermiel's red beard jutted pugnaciously at Bey. "You'll never persuade the Old Mars policy council of that."

"Quite right, I won't. *You* will. And Georgia Kruskal will help you."

"Wait a minute." Georgia rose up from her haunches. "If you think I'm going to work with a bunch of wombats like the Old Mars flapheads—"

"I do. I expect you and Rafael to sit down and work out a way of doing things together. This is one planet, with one future. You can't both win. You have to cooperate."

"And if we don't?"

"Then I'll make a prediction. No, I'll make a *promise*." Bey stared from one to the other in frustration. "If you two don't find a way to work together, I'll pull my own support from both sides, including my technical input on the surface forms. Trudy will take all BEC support away. I'll do my best to make sure that every cent of outside funding that goes to Old Mars dries up at once. And I'll set the Office of Form Control going on an investigation of Mars illegal forms."

Fermiel frowned at Georgia Kruskal. "He's threatening us—both of us."

"He can't do that!"

They turned in unison to glare at Bey.

"I can, you know." Bey stared right back at them. "I just did. God, if you only knew how I hate laying down the law like this to anybody. I'm *retired*, for God's sake—and I couldn't stand this sort of stuff when I wasn't. *The expense of spirit in a waste of shame*. There I go again. Sorry, but I've had it. Trudy, you're the Empress. Take over. Bang their heads together, make them compromise. You asked me what I wanted from you, and I'm telling you. Make these two see reason. Me, I'm heading for Earth."

"You can't do that!" This time it seemed that everyone in the room spoke in unison. The only exception was Errol Melford, who was still staring in fascination at Georgia Kruskal's animated snout and wobbling layers of body fat.

"I can." Bey stood up and started for the door. "It's my home, I have unfinished business there, and I'm going. Sondra, if you want to see this thing through to the finish you should come with me."

"What are you going to do?" Sondra hurried after him.

"We're done with the easy stuff." Bey turned at the threshold. It was a strange tableau. Everyone was frozen and silent at the table, watching his departure. He nodded to them. The nod said, *Don't waste your time gaping at me, you have work to do. Get to it*!

He spun around with Sondra at his side.

"Now we have to tackle the hard part."

CHAPTER 22

"What you are telling me," said Sondra, "is that the humanity tests are no damned good."

"Not quite that." The fast-moving skimmer was approaching Wolf Island, and Bey was squinting ahead in the late afternoon sun for a first sight of home. "It's fine in almost every case; but occasionally, maybe one time in a billion, it misses. The trouble is, when it does fail it's in the worst possible way."

"Humans are judged non-human?"

"Right. I mean, it's no big deal if an occasional feral form is passed as human, like the ones in the colonies. That's a pretty trivial problem."

Bey ignored Sondra's outraged gasp of protest. A lopsided pyramid of rock had come into view, jutting above the swelling ocean surface, and he was staring at it with satisfaction.

"It's the other way round that's intolerable," he continued. "Babies, genuine humans with unusual talents and mental powers, dumped into the organ banks. They have odd psych profiles, and when they're different enough to exceed program tolerances the test judges them non-human."

"But if that's true how come no one has ever noticed?" The idea of babies slaughtered and dissected for the organ banks sent chills up Sondra's spine. "I mean, you're saying these are unusually smart people."

"They are. But they're *babies*. They never have a chance to prove themselves. And if they were the smartest people in the world, how would we recognize their *absence*? It's hard to notice what isn't there." Bey's manner had become unusually grim. As the skimmer docked the two hounds stood at the jetty, wagging their tails madly. But Bey fondled their heads absently and led the way straight toward the house.

"Lop the top-end tail off the distribution of human intelligence and creativity," he went on, "and it would make no measurable difference to the population. Only one person in a billion is out beyond the six-sigma level. That's what we're talking about here. But eventually those one-in-a-billion make a huge difference. Ninety-five percent of all human progress comes from less than one thousandth of one percent of the population."

To Sondra, he was suddenly nervous as she had never seen him before. On the journey back from Melford Castle he had become increasingly serious and preoccupied. He had refused to tell her what came next, answering her questions only with a terse, "Wait and see."

Could it be his vow to have Denzel Morrone fired as head of the Office of Form Control? Sondra had been dreading her own next meeting with Morrone—she had disobeyed his direct orders—but it was hard to believe that Bey had any such worries. Trudy Melford had promised Bey anything he asked, and she had such political clout that the dismissal of a medium-level official from a government department ought to be child's play to her.

But if it wasn't that, then what was it?

Bey was heading downstairs and straight for his communications center. He nodded to Jumping Jack Flash, who peered up at him with perplexed brown eyes as Bey at once sat down and entered a call sequence unfamiliar to Sondra.

"I'm afraid we have to wait a while," he said. "Maybe three hours or more. Why don't you help yourself to some food, or have—"

Bey paused. The terminal was already flashing a response. While Sondra was still wondering who—or what—could be three hours' signal time away and yet provide an instant reply, the image display area came alive. She found herself staring at a familiar figure. There was no mistaking the massive head with its ropy strands of hair and luminous eyes.

Bey seemed even more surprised than she was. "How the devil can you—"

Capman's head bobbed forward, in the Logian smile. "No magic today, Behrooz Wolf. Not even unfamiliar science. I have been expecting and waiting for your call."

"But where are you?"

"Very close by—look up to your north, and you could in principle see my ship. I am parked in Earth geostationary orbit."

"You couldn't possibly know that I wanted to speak to you!"

"I made no such statement. Perhaps it was I who wished to speak with you." The Logian's face was quite unreadable, at least to Sondra. "However, your last remark suggests that you in fact *do* wish to talk with me. I am curious to learn the subject."

"I don't believe that. I believe you already know very well why I placed my call."

"If that is the case, then there can be no possible reason for delaying discussion." The great head bowed forward to Bey and Sondra. "I await your remarks with interest."

Bey bowed in return and stayed with head bent for a long time. At last he sighed and straightened.

"This will be more questions than comments. But first

let me tell you what I know. You are familiar with the Mars terraforming operation, to make the planet more like Earth?"

"The whole solar system is aware of it."

"Right. But I said *familiar* with it. Most people know about the project the way I did before I went to the Mars Underworld. Superficially. In other words, they don't really *think* about it at all."

"Assume that I am, as you put it, *familiar* with the project."

"Then let's get right to the central question: Who is paying for the terraforming effort? Someone pays for everything, no matter what the project is."

"The terraforming project is funded by the Old Mars policy group, seeking to fulfill the intent of the Mars Declaration."

"That's what everyone believes. But that's not really an answer, is it? The cost of a full-scale terraforming project is prodigious—everything from purchase of Cloudland comet fragments, to the flying of the volatiles to Mars impact, to the creation and use of bespoke organisms for the absorption of atmospheric carbon dioxide and release of bound oxygen. The Old Mars contingent is wealthy by Mars standards, but nowhere near rich enough to pay for everything that's going on.

"As soon as I had been out on the surface of Mars and seen the scale of the operation for myself, I had my doubts. I wondered if maybe BEC had a hand in it somewhere. The company could afford such a thing if it decided it was important enough to BEC operations.

"But I couldn't make sense of that, either. First of all, Trudy Melford went to Mars only recently, three years ago, and for reasons nothing to do with terraforming."

"Reasons which I presume that you now understand." The Logian stared curiously at Sondra, standing by Bey's side. "May I ask, did you make that deduction, Miss Dearborn?"

"Not really." Sondra stared back, and wondered to what extent that hulking form in its methane-rich atmosphere was still the human Robert Capman. "I got part of it right—a little bit."

"You got *most* of it," Bey corrected. "And Sondra would have deduced the rest if she had been able to look at Errol Melford's picture, as I did, in Trudy's private quarters at Melford Castle. But don't let me get side-tracked. Trudy went to Mars long after the terraforming effort was started. Also, she has a real interest in the surface forms, and BEC's commercial gain would be maximized if the terraforming *stopped*, because if Mars becomes like Earth anyone can live on the surface without needing form-change. The modification developed by Georgia Kruskal is able to colonize the surface as it is today, but only with extensive and continuing use of form-change equipment.

"So I had a mystery. But I still didn't rule out BEC funding for the Old Mars efforts, because Trudy seemed so oddly sympathetic to them. We found out why when we learned about Errol Melford. And that was when Trudy, with no more reason to lie about it, flatly denied that she was funding the Old Mars terraforming project.

"Dead end. But *somebody* was pouring resources into changing Mars to be like Earth. Who was it? Who had the resources? An even better question, who had the *motive*?

"You can count the candidate groups on one hand. First, Earth could do it. They have the money, and they would quite like Mars to become another Earth. New land, new living space, a new sphere of influence. But I'm in the heart of Earth's information networks, and there's no way that anything this size could be happening without my learning of it. So I had to cross Earth off the list.

"The Cloudlanders have the economic clout, too, and they also have access to free comet fragments. But they look down their noses at anything going on in the inner system, Mars or Earth or any place else. The same is true of the Kernel Ring and the Kuiper Belt. To all of them, everything inside the orbit of Pluto is old, dull, and decadent. Nothing would be less interesting than the conversion of one inner planet to be like another one.

"I seemed to have run out of answers. No one had both means and motive. But then I thought again. There is one group in the solar system whose powers sometimes seem just about limitless, and whose motives I have never been able to fathom. I wondered, what about the Logian forms, hidden beneath the shroud of Saturn's atmosphere? Weren't they a candidate, too?"

Capman was shaking his head. "You know Logian stated policy: we do not interfere in the affairs of humans."

"I do know your stated policy. And I know that you have always been very careful to phrase it just that way when we have spoken together. 'Logian *stated* policy'—but not necessarily Logian *actual* policy. As for your opportunities to influence human actions, I can suggest three or four ways you might funnel resources into any solar system activity that you choose—and still have the final recipient unaware of the source.

"So it seemed to me that the means were there. The thing missing was *motive*. Logians can't survive on either Mars or Earth. *Why* would they choose to help Old Mars in its efforts to terraform the planet?

"I couldn't answer that question. But it suggested another idea: If the Logians were favoring the Mars terraforming efforts, that action opposed Georgia Kruskal's desire to keep the surface just the way that it is. She can live there without a suit, in today's conditions—*provided* that she has continuing access to form-change equipment. And that led me to one more thought: the people of every inhabited world in the system make use of form-change, but usually they do not *depend* on it. Everywhere, on every major body from Europa to Cloudland, the natural environment of each world is being changed so that humans can live there in their original form, without dependence on form-change. People in Cloudland choose to adopt a different shape, but that's for convenience, not necessity. I have been to Cloudland, just as I am, and managed very well. But I couldn't survive on the surface of Mars for five minutes. Unless it is terraformed, any human living there will depend on the use of form-change every day, just to remain alive."

Bey paused, as though he had arrived at some profound and significant conclusion. Sondra, listening closely, could not begin to guess what it might be. And yet watching the body language of Bey Wolf and Robert Capman, it was clear to her that a crucial moment had been reached. The style of their interaction had changed. Bey was leaning forward expectantly, while Capman was nodding slowly in a gesture not at all like the bobbing motion of the Logian smile.

And when he finally spoke, it sounded like a total change of subject. "Behrooz Wolf." The deep voice was slow and sad. "You have known me for many, many years. How would you describe my work, and its relationship to the science of purposive form-change?"

If the question surprised Bey, he did not show it. He replied at once. "You have contributed more than anyone in the whole field since the original work of Ergan Melford, two hundred and fifty years ago. Until you adopted the Logian form and moved to Saturn, your whole life's work revolved around the theory and practice of purposive form-change."

"Very well. And your work?"

"I won't try to estimate the value of what I've done. Someone else should make that assessment. But I can honestly say that for more than half a century I have worked constantly on form-change problems; and nothing else in my life has been as important to me as that effort."

"We seem to be in total agreement. We have each devoted most of our lives to the same single end: the advancement of purposive form-change techniques. We have each—despite your modesty—made deep and far-reaching contributions to the subject, more than any other living persons." Capman's massive head lifted, and he stared straight at Bey. "So you, Behrooz Wolf, will find it as disturbing as I did, when I realized that purposive form-change, in widespread, necessary, and universal use, poses a great and terrible threat to the future of humanity. Does that answer your question?"

The gasp came from Sondra, not from Bey. He sat totally silent and still as Capman continued: "I should add that my interest in form-change work and its effects did not cease when I assumed the Logian form. We Logians are not human in appearance, and we sometimes appear to have superhuman powers; but in our concerns we remain all human. And we operate with a very long time-frame."

"You say it's a threat." Bey spoke in a low voice and his face had become paler than usual. "I don't see why. Form-change has done more good for more people than any other discovery in history. I'm not talking about trivial nonsense like cosmetic change, I mean the important things like birth defect correction and medical treatment and healthy old age."

"All hugely important, and all hugely valuable. But not the whole story." Capman swung to face Sondra. "Miss Dearborn, you visited the Fugate Colony. Do you think you could mate with a Fugate?"

"Never." Sondra recalled the lumbering seventy-foot-tall figures. "I mean, I didn't actually *see* their sex organs, but if they're anything like in proportion . . . Anyway, they were repulsive. I wouldn't *want* to mate with one of them, even if I could."

"Which is perhaps of far greater practical importance." Capman turned back to Bey. "You have heard the modern dictum, echoed throughout the solar system: *Easier to change people than planets*. With today's form-change methods that is certainly true. As Georgia Kruskal is demonstrating, forms can be created that thrive in extreme natural environments. But the idea of matching people to settings neglects a profound problem. The celestial bodies of the solar system display an amazing diversity, in atmosphere, gravity, composition, temperature, and size. If humans seek to adapt to each situation, the inhabitants of each world will *diverge* from every other.

"The long-term effect of such a divergence has been known since the time of Darwin and Wallace. It is termed *speciation*. Today, humans constitute a single species. At some time in the far future there could be many; different in size and form and function, fragmented in purpose, unable and unwilling to inter-breed. And all thanks to the use of purposive form-change. If such a future is to be avoided, currently accepted thinking must change. It must become: *Better to change planets than people*. Terraform Mars and Europa, as is happening today. Terraform Venus, terraform Titan, terraform Oberon, terraform Triton, terraform the worldlets of the Kuiper Belt and Cloudland. Modify environments. And by doing so, allow humanity to continue as a single species."

"While you do your best to *prevent* further advances in form-change?" Bey stood up. "I know exactly what you're saying, and I understand its importance. But it has other implications. You are telling me to abandon everything I have worked for all my life. You are suggesting that instead of helping Georgia Kruskal, I should try to destroy the sort of progress that she is making on Mars."

"No, I do not suggest that." Capman's voice was gentle. "I am here to suggest something quite different; something I have urged before, but never so strongly. Come with me, Behrooz Wolf. Change to a Logian form. Be blessed with the augmented Logian faculties. And comprehend, as you will never comprehend in human form, the whole canvas of the problem I describe. There will have to be, as you say, great changes in purposive form-change. Some of them, from the standard human perspective, may appear to be regressive. They are not, but while you remain in human form they will seem so. I do not ask you to undo or fight against your and my life's work. Rather, I ask you to view that work in a broader context, to elevate it to a new and higher level. I ask you to join me on Saturn, and work with me there. Will you do it?"

"No. Maybe. God, I don't know." Bey stared sightlessly around the room, looking right through Sondra. "I have to think through all this. Changing form-change. Maybe *abandoning* form-change. I have to *think*. And I have to get some fresh air."

He headed for the stairs. Jumping Jack Flash, who had been sitting all the time at Sondra's feet, stood up and scuttled after him. The house's outer door slammed shut.

Sondra turned to glare accusingly at Robert Capman. "I've never seen Bey like this before. He's unbelievably upset."

"Inevitably, and naturally. As I suspected when I flew to Earth, Behrooz Wolf had come so far in his own deductions that there was no alternative to telling him the truth. And there was also no way to make that truth palatable to someone so intimately involved in form-change development." Capman's luminous eyes burned into Sondra's. "I have a question for you, Miss Dearborn. Why were you present when Behrooz Wolf initiated this conversation with me?"

Again it seemed like a total change of subject. Sondra stared at the Logian in perplexity.

"Why was I here? I don't know. I guess Bey wanted me here. He invited me, told me to come back from Mars with him, but I had no idea why. Is it relevant?"

"It is more than relevant. It is crucial. He wanted you to know of his own deductions, and also he wanted you to learn whatever he might find out from me about the reasons for Logian involvement on Mars."

"So he wanted me to know. I still don't see what that has to do with anything." Sondra stood up abruptly. "And at the moment I don't have time to share your worry about the long-term future of humanity. I'm worried about *now*. I'm worried about Bey. I'm going to see what's happening to him."

She ran for the stairs. The Logian, stolid and apparently unruffled, remained at his ship's communications console. "Take your time," he called after her. "There is no need to rush back."

Outside it was almost dark, a warm, soft twilight in which the first stars were appearing. Sondra paused close to the front of the house and stared around her. The island was not all that big but Bey could have gone anywhere for solitude, to the top of the rocky central upthrust or down along the seashore. She would never find him by sight as it grew darker. She could shout and holler, but she was sure he would not like that. It also did not fit her own uneasy mood. The weather was flat calm, but her nerves were jangling as though a big thunderstorm was on the way.

She stood still and listened. The night sounds of the

island were beginning. Faint rustles of small lizards and large insects, the former pursuing the latter through the undergrowth. The murmur of small waves ascending the sandy beach. A rush of night wings, as bats and small birds flitted above her head in their hunt for moths and gnats; and, far-off to the left, a muted whine of protest.

Sondra at once headed that way. She had heard that sound before—Janus and Siegfried, waiting impatiently and voicing their complaint until Bey threw the stick or ball out into the shallow water.

He was sitting down when she came up to him, perched on a jagged rock that had to be less than comfortable. She sat down cross-legged on the sand at his side.

"You don't have to do it, you know," she said quietly. "You don't have to take any notice of him at all."

He did not look round, but stared out across the quiet water. It had the oil-black gleam that Sondra remembered from her first visit to Wolf Island. The slow ripples that crept up the beach were tiny. She counted them—one, two, three, up and back. About five seconds between successive waves.

"He traveled all the way from Saturn just to talk to me," Bey replied at last. "A Logian, coming to see a human. It's unheard of. I owe him an answer."

"Then give him one. Tell him no. Tell him you are retired." Sondra placed her hand gently on Bey's thigh. "You've had experience with that particular line, haven't you? Or tell him that you believe he is wrong."

"Sure. Except that I don't. He's right." The dogs ran up from the water to shake themselves and shower the two humans with salt spray. Bey did not even flinch.

"Do you know," he went on, "what Capman said to me wasn't even a surprise. I'd had the thought myself, but I always suppressed it as personal heresy: *Purposive form-change runs contrary to evolution*. We change to match a different environment, but it isn't a *genetic* change. We don't become any better suited to living in a place, generation by generation, the way that all of Nature adapts to its surroundings. In the far future, humans might evolve by natural selection until they could live on Mars as it is today. But they won't do it as long as we have form-change."

"So make that point to people, Bey. *Tell them*. Use the insight to change the way we think of and apply form-change. You can do it, if anyone can. But don't run away to Saturn, not when you are needed here on Earth. You think Denzel Morrone has to be kicked out of the Office of Form Control, and I agree. But who will take over from him?"

"Not me. I worked my shift."

"Other people won't want to hear that. You'd be my first choice, the absolute best person." Sondra listened to her own words, and was surprised by the passion in them. "Not that anyone is going to ask my opinion, I know that. I'm a peon. But you're not. Even if it's only for a little while, you ought to help out when Morrone goes."

"Capman thinks that I should help, too—on Saturn."

"Yes. And you know why?" Sondra felt a faint itch inside her, a mixture of anger and impatience. "It's because he wants you there for *himself*. He likes you. You have a lot of common interests and he loves to talk to you. You are the only person in the solar system who reaches Capman whenever you like. He wants you there on Saturn for *his* sake, not yours or mine. Aybee says that Capman doesn't normally ask people to become a Logian until they're mentally past it, and you're nowhere near that."

"Aybee is wrong, Sondra. I love him like a son, and on the right subjects he's the smartest being in the solar system; but sometimes he's an idiot. You've heard Capman—did you think for one second that he is past it?"

"He's old. Well over a century."

"And he hasn't lost a stroke. I'm not in Capman's league, Sondra, but I'm getting old too."

"Now that's nonsense!" Bey was facing her, but in the dark she could make out his face only as a pale oval. She wished that she could see his eyes. "You're getting old*er*," she went on, "but so am I. We're all doing that, every day. You *pretend* to be old, but it's all a big put-on, part of your act. Anyone who spends time with you soon realizes that you have more curiosity and energy than a teenager. Mary Walton and Sylvia Fernald certainly didn't think you were old where it mattered."

"Now where the devil did you hear *those* names?" Bey was silent for a moment, then he laughed into the darkness. "Aybee."

"Who else? 'The Wolfman and his bimboes.' "

"I'll kill him. Anyway, that was a long time ago."

"Four years, if you call that a long time. I don't. But Trudy Melford wasn't a long time ago, she was *yesterday*. And she made her views clear enough: you can have her and everything she possesses. You'll never convince me she was talking about money. She doesn't think you're old and ready to be put out to pasture. Out to stud, maybe."

Sondra felt the muscles of Bey's thigh tighten under her hand. It was a long time—three waves to the shore—before he said: "She was just trying to tell me how grateful she is for what I did for her son."

"Sure. You think that if you choose to, but I know better. Trudy meant exactly what she said." Sondra felt the level of emotion flare inside her. "Listen, give her half a chance and she'd just love to jump your bones. Try telling *her* that you are too old, once she gets her hot little hands on you. See how much it slows her down."

She had told Robert Capman that she was coming outside to learn what was happening to Bey Wolf. Now

Sondra was beginning to wonder what was happening to *her*. The internal pressure was rising.

And worst of all, Bey was laughing again. This time he was making no sound, but she could feel it in his thigh muscles.

She snatched her hand away from his leg. "What did I say now that's so funny? I'm being *serious* here."

"Sorry. It's just the alien idea of Bey Wolf as a sex object. I'm not used to that. I guess it really is time I went to Saturn, before women start to swarm all over me."

"I don't want you to go." Sondra suddenly realized what she did want. "I want you to stay on Earth, and it has nothing to do with form-change or who runs the Office of Form Control. You keep saying you're getting old, but you'll be around for at least another fifty years. Half a century is enough time for a lot of excitement and a lot of fun. I'm going to quote one of your fusty old dead poets at you—and don't dare ask me how many hours I've wasted reading the stuff since we first met, because I'm not going to tell you. Remember this?: *Grow old along with me, the best is yet to be; the last of life, for which the first was made*. In case you don't recognize what you're hearing, I'll spell it out. Bey, this is a proposition."

He sat rigid. He did not move, he did not speak. Sondra waited, breathless. Her own words had surprised her, uttered before she knew they were present in her brain.

Finally he shook his head. "You're my relative, remember?"

"Your *remote* relative. You taught me how remote."

"It would never work."

"It might not. But it might. How do you know, if you don't even try?"

"*Crabbed age and youth—*"

"Bullshit! You said that to me before, to point out why

you and I couldn't possibly work together. And we've worked together just fine, better than I've ever worked with anybody. I don't want to hear another word of stupid old poetry from you—unless you can make it romantic poetry."

He was standing up, brushing off sand, turning away. She had offended him.

"Bey, wait! Don't go."

He reached out and took her hands in his, lifting Sondra easily to her feet. "I have to. You can come to the house with me if you like, or stay right here if you'd rather. I'll be right back."

"Why do you have to—"

"I've got to tell Robert Capman that I'm not going with him. Don't you think we owe him at least that much?"

The communications center was still active, the display screen still turned on. But there was no sign of a Logian form within the imaging area.

"He's gone." Sondra stared at the control console as though expecting Capman to pop up out of the middle of it. "I can't believe it. He said to take my time, there was no need to rush."

"Because when he spoke to you he already knew he would be gone by the time that we got back." Bey flipped to display the storage stack. "I thought so. New recorded message—and addressed to *both* of us. Here we go."

Capman's head and bulky upper torso were again filling the image area. If he was annoyed by the disappearance, first of Bey and then of Sondra, he showed no sign of it.

"The Logian reputation for perception is quite unwarranted, you know," he said cheerfully, as soon as the display region had stabilized. "If I were really astute, Bey, I would have known your answer as soon as I saw that Sondra was with you for our conversation. That, and your and my shared tendency to masochism, should have sufficed. I can assure you that Saturn is great and the Logian form wonderful, and both statements are quite true. But you would rather remain on Earth and Mars, and *bear those ills you have, than fly to others that you know not of.*"

"I *told* you he just wanted you for chit-chat with him," Sondra hissed. "Bey, he's as bad with quotations as you are."

"Shhh!"

Capman was continuing. "Remain there for the moment, that is. Next year, or the year after, who knows? The Logian form encourages a long perspective. I can wait. And if I am realistic, your presence on Earth and Mars will help to re-shape thinking about form-change better than you could do it on Saturn.

"As for you, Sondra Dearborn." The great head turned toward her, as though even in a recording Capman knew just where Sondra would be standing. "You are young and perhaps incorrigible. But you have fire and courage and conviction. You do not allow yourself to be diverted or intimidated. The two of you will make an excellent team. And who knows? Perhaps Behrooz Wolf will yet bring you to enlightenment, and an appreciation of great literature." The grey head bobbed in laughter. "But I won't bet on it. And now I have work to do. I look forward to talking with you again in the near future. *Both* of you."

A massive arm lifted. Luminous eyes flickered and danced with humor. And Robert Capman was gone.

CHAPTER 23

EPILOGUE

It was long past time to go, and still he had not gone.

Bey, who claimed procrastination as a virtue, was taking it to extremes. Normally he dignified delay by saying that it was a way of keeping his options open. This time he had no real excuse. It was not that he was putting off joining Sondra on the mainland. He was keen to be with her again. After only a week together she was already a familiar presence in his life, and he had been sorry when she left two days earlier.

She had gone to find a place for them to live. She said she did not want him to be forced to share her cramped apartment with Dill and Gipsy. Actually, Bey knew she had a secret suspicion that he would take far too much interest in the progress of the Dill/Gipsy two-woman multiform. He was beginning to understand Sondra's obsessions—and she his.

She had called just that morning to tell him she had found a perfect house, ready to move into. He could fly to join her as soon as he was ready.

And he was ready. He was also oddly eager to see the Form Control office again, the place he had thought himself happy to leave forever. He was quite ready to leave, except for one or two last details; those, and a strange, nagging feeling that somehow he was missing something significant on Wolf Island . . .

"You know how the food dispensers work, the same as usual. Push these two at once, see?"

Jumping Jack Flash, watching as Bey operated the solid food delivery system, grunted his agreement. He reached past Bey and pushed the two buttons. The two hounds moved forward expectantly as a handful of solid pellets rolled down the chute and into the dishes.

"And don't let Janus and Siegfried push them with their noses, you know how greedy they are. They'll eat until they're sick. Just look at them."

The dogs had gobbled the food and were waiting for more.

"You can have all the fruit while I'm gone, Flash. The mangoes and papayas are nearly ready but let them get properly ripe, or you'll have the runs same as last time." Bey looked down at the chimp. "But I bet you don't, you dumb ape. You'll get as sick as you always do."

Jumping Jack Flash stared back at him reproachfully.

"I know, I know, you learned your lesson last time. Anyway, I'll be keeping an eye on all of you through the house remotes. And Sondra and I will come back in a couple of weeks. When we do, I'll fix you up for another session in the tanks. We've been neglecting that, and just when I thought we might be making real progress. Meanwhile, you're in charge. You've been on your own a lot recently, you know how everything works. Anything else you can think of that needs doing? If not . . ."

Bey prowled slowly around the whole house one last time, with the chimp and the two hounds trailing along behind.

"I guess that's it, then." Everything was clean, everything was in order. He had run out of every last thing that might need doing. "Come down to the beach and see me off."

Even the weather was obliging. It was perfect for the journey, blue skies overhead and the faintest breeze from the south. Bey crossed the sand and walked out onto the jetty.

"Stay there, all of you, unless you want to get wet. I'll miss you guys, but don't worry. I'll be back soon."

Bey waved as he stepped into the skimmer. Jumping Jack Flash waved back, one hound standing on each side of the chimpanzee. They all watched as the skimmer made a leisurely semi-circle in the little harbor. Then it accelerated rapidly in a great surge of spray, became airborne in seconds, and arrowed away to the northwest.

The little party on the beach stood silent and motionless until the skimmer was quite out of sight, even to the keen eyes of the hounds. Then Janus whined, pushing at the left hand of Jumping Jack Flash with her muzzle. When the chimp did not respond at once she did it again, more urgently.

He looked down at her with knowing brown eyes. After a few more seconds of waiting to make sure that the skimmer was far away, he led the hounds back across the sand, around the curving stone path and into the house.

They entered the main level, where the food and water dispensers were found; but they did not remain there. Jumping Jack Flash descended, until he was in the basement lab far below the surface.

Janus stepped forward at once into one of the specially constructed form-change tanks. She lay down there. Siegfried moved into another one next to her. Carefully and patiently, like someone who had done it many times before, Jumping Jack Flash made the connections for each of them. Both the dogs were quivering with eagerness when he at last closed the openings of both tanks.

The chimp grunted his criticism of their impatience. If he had to wait, so should they.

Finally they were ready and it was his turn. Jumping Jack Flash climbed into his own tank, carefully made all the necessary attachments and tank inter-connections, and slid the door closed.

There was a brief hum of drawn power. The dials and control panels on the outside of the form-change tanks came to life, then settled into stable readings. The lab became still and silent.

A visitor, walking in, would have judged it dark and empty. Three floors above, night was falling on Wolf Island.

In the basement lab it was close to dawn.